hand-me-downs

To Ronda—
Let's keep separating good
hand-me-downs from
bad.
Best wishes and love,
and many good memories
of working together
Liz
10-31-85

hand-me-downs

a novel by
liz barnes

 SPINSTERS INK
SAN FRANCISCO

First Edition
10-9-8-7-6-5-4-3-2-1

SPINSTERS INK
803 De Haro Street
San Francisco, CA 94107

Cover Art: Judith A. Brown
Cover & Text Design: Pamela Wilson Design Studio
Typesetting: L.A. Hyder and ComText Typography, Inc.,
    San Francisco
Production: Bridget Boylan, Debra DeBondt, Jennifer Hoff,
    Kathi Jaramillo, Robyn Raymer, Sukey Wilder

Publication of this book was made possible by the continuing generosity and crucial support of Angels Ink; and also through the generosity of Marjorie Hilsenrad, in memory of her father Philip Hilsenrad, and of Diane Spaugh, dedicated to her niece, Elizabeth Ashley Spaugh.

Printed in the U.S.A.

ISBN: 0-933216-18-1
Library of Congress Catalog Card Number: 85-61371

Special thanks to Stephens College, Columbia, Missouri, for two summer grants which freed me to pursue Appalachian colloquialisms, the seed from which the story grew. Thanks, too, to the Helene Wurlitzer Foundation of New Mexico for giving me the time and place in which to put *hand-me-downs* together.

To Meredith and Sheldon and all of the other little girls in the world.

ONE

I was only five-going-on-six, but I knew lots of things and thought about them all the time. The most important thing I knew was the difference between me and Til. It was his peejabber. He reminded me of the difference every night when he exercised it, churning it with his hand. Then he would ask me to do it a while. He said if we kept on exercising it, it would reach to his knee some day. He had also told me of my calling. It was to get married to the likes of him and carry babies in my stomach until they got big enough to breathe outside. He said that as long as a peejabber didn't get inside me, I wouldn't have a baby. He said that was the only way baby seeds get planted. He said that men have all the seeds and women are the dirt. I decided then and there that no peejabber would ever get inside me, because I didn't want any baby. I didn't even want a doll, but I got one. Uncle Jay brought me one from out West. A dumb Didy doll that peed when you stuck a little bottle of water in her mouth. The water came out one end as fast as it went in the other.

And I knew that Uncle Jay's face got all covered with mustard when he was defending our homeland during the war, but I didn't know why he didn't wash it off before his eyes got all red. Uncle Jay had helped to blast the Germans right off the map years before I was born when we had a leader named Wilson and they had a leader named Kaiser. Wilson was dead, but Kaiser chopped wood somewhere in Holland every day from sunup to sundown, even on Sundays and Christmas. Daddy showed me a picture of him chopping wood in the snow. And another thing I knew was that during the war Daddy worked six days a week, fourteen hours a day at the old dye plant, but, even by listening hard, I never did find out what colors he made.

And I knew that a long time before that war some of our ancestors fought against each other not very far away in a war they called the Civil War. Mother said she preferred to call it the War Between the States because there wasn't anything "civil" about it. Men from East Tennessee where we lived fought their own neighbors. Mother's grandfather wore the gray uniform of one side and made shoes for the soldiers, and Daddy's grandfather wore the blue uniform of the other side and made shoes for the soldiers' horses, and they had grown up in the same county. The War Between the States didn't make any sense. I'd just have to wait until I got to first grade in the fall to understand it.

I knew, too, that the water that ran in the kitchen sink every day and in the bathtub on Saturday night came in a pipe from the top of the mountain on the other side of the cow pasture. Daddy told me that. I knew that *down* the street in front of our house meant toward the B&B Grocery Store and town, and *up* the street meant toward Leeper's Grocery Store and the cotton-mill village. The B&B Grocery Store belonged to Daddy. Just to him. He had gone without everything to buy out Uncle Ben. We had all helped by going without everything, too. Mother reminded him of that every little bit.

And I knew that Felix was about the smartest dog in town, even if he was only a little feist. We didn't need a telephone, because Mother would just tie a grocery list to his collar and tell him to go to the store. His ears stood straight up, and his tail curled over his back as he ran down the sidewalk. He stopped just once, to lift a leg at the fireplug near the end of the block. He even looked both ways before crossing the highway to the B&B.

Sometimes at dusk, if the jarflies weren't scraping their legs together, I could hear the machinery making cotton in the village two blocks away. The cotton-mill village had row after row of square, dingy-brown houses. Our house was blue and the Diggs' was yellow and the Simpsons' was white. I didn't really know any people in the village, because me and Til weren't supposed to go out of our block without Mother's permission, but I heard Mother and the neighbor ladies whisper about the Reverend Brown, the preacher at Maple Street Methodist over there. They said he knew the hours of every man in his congregation that worked at the mill. Said that he never called on members of Maple Street except when the menfolks were at work and the children were at school. Til helped me to figure that out.

I knew who lived in every unpainted board shack in the alley behind our house. Crazy Pete lived closest to us. His wife had run away before they had any children. Til said he was as black as an African shoveling coal in a basement at midnight. Daddy said he was so thin that if he stood sideways nobody would see him. He was all bent over and walked with his hands clasped over his chest like he was already in the casket. I felt sorry for him even if he did scare me. He lived all alone. Maybe that's why he reached out to me one day and laughed as loud as he could. I ran through the barnyard gate to the house without stopping. Til teased me about being a scaredy-cat. That night I dreamed that Crazy Pete was at our back door and threw a light bulb at me and when it hit me, it busted. I couldn't scream and I couldn't run. Til didn't even wake up.

But Crazy Pete was the only person in the alley I was scared of. The house next door to him had what Mother called "a passel of kids," three not old enough for school and three in school. From the oldest boy, about ten, to the baby, not yet walking, they were beautiful, with strong-looking, chocolate-brown hands and long, lean bodies that glistened where they showed. Their mother had long fingers and kept her nails polished, even with all of that washing she did by hand. They wore a clean outfit every day, summer and winter. Their daddy worked at the Gulf service station across from the B&B. He gave me and Til a dinosaur comic book about every week. It had colored pictures of monsters that could be cut out for jigsaw puzzles, and stories that Til read me about where gas and oil come from.

My nearly-best friends, Sadie and Joe, lived up at the end of the block beside the path that went down the hill to the cow bottom. Til and me visited them every few days when we went to milk, but we never said a thing about it at home. I don't know why, because they traded at the B&B and were about the only niggers Daddy would speak to. He didn't speak to them just because they traded with him, because others that he called "no account" bought groceries from him, and he wouldn't even say howdy to them. Sadie and Joe were nearly a hundred years old.

Another important thing I knew was that just one summer separated me from what Til called jail. He reminded me of that every day with, "Just wait till Old Lady Byers gets ahold of you," and he said it would be even worse when Spit-Ball Kellar got hold of me in the fourth. He imitated Mrs. Kellar, who had a habit of rolling a little ball of spit between her lips with her tongue. Til was eleven years old, going on twelve, and was little for his age, because Mother hadn't had enough milk for him. She said it was no wonder since Maude stopped nursing just weeks before he was born.

I knew that everybody stops breathing some day, like little Charles Lindbergh. He didn't even get to have a funeral. Mother said some heathen threw his little body on a trash heap somewhere in another state a long way from East Tennessee. He was so mangled that at first they didn't recognize him, but they finally knew it was him because his little undershirt had embroidery on it. The day the news came out that he had been kidnapped Mother checked to be sure that all our windows were locked, because somebody had crawled through the Lindberghs' nursery window after dark and carried little Charles off.

Thinking about little Charles made me think about Mrs. Diggs. I heard Mother say at supper one night that she had a 50-50 chance. She lived next door to us and had a strawberry patch on the other side of the fence between her house and ours. She had been sick a long time. Mother said it started with one of those old summer colds you can't shake off. Daddy said she forgot to take the cough syrup he made for her. Til said the cough syrup was nothing but whiskey with rock candy in it. Mother said she doubted that Mrs. Diggs "forgot" to take it, that Daddy's cure was worse than the cold. Mrs. Diggs' husband, Guy, was a policeman and worked lots of nights. He slept lots of days, and me and Til couldn't play between our house and theirs, because we might wake him up.

Mrs. Simpson, who lived on the other side of Mrs. Diggs, ran to our back door early one morning, before me and Til went to the bottom to milk.

"Mrs. Blevins, Mrs. Blevins," her whiney voice floated through our bedroom into the kitchen. I looked out the window when I heard her call for Mother. Her steel-rimmed glasses framed her watery blue eyes, and her face was so fat that her eyes stayed closed when she laughed. She never left the house, even that early in the day, without putting on powder and a clean apron.

We heard her call again through the screen door. We never closed the back door in summertime, just hooked the screen door at the end of the hall between the two little bedrooms that had once been the back porch. Daddy had built the rooms when Emmy was born and Granny came to live with us nearly four years ago. Til and I had the room next to the kitchen, and Granny had the room next to the bathroom and the hall where the icebox was.

Mother finally answered. Then we heard Mrs. Simpson again. "Mrs. Diggs passed in the night." I knew that she meant Mrs. Diggs had quit breathing.

Mother poked the fire in the cookstove. She sounded like she was crying when she opened the screen door. "Poor Guy! What will ever become of him? Come on in."

"Prone with grief," Mrs. Simpson said. "Like a child. I known they should of got a doctor a week before they did. Thought she had a summer cold and her with pneumonie all along. Thought you'd ought to know before Mr. Blevins leaves for the store. Funeral sometime tomorrow afternoon. I got to go see if I can help Guy any."

Daddy yelled like we were in the next county. "You kids get up and help your mother. Maudie, get up and scald them jars. Your mother broke green beans way into the night. Tilghman, go milk. Cassandry, help Emmy dress."

He felt it was his duty to start every day like that. He was not much taller than Til, but you'd never know it from hearing him call us. His voice came from the bottom of him somewhere, slipping past his broad hands and shoulders to his thin lips, but his blue eyes twinkled whether he was ordering us to get up or to go to bed. Besides Granny he was the only one in the world to call me Cassandra. Everybody else called me Cass. He called me Cassandra because that was Granny's name. Emmy was just three days old when he brought Granny from the little log house in the country where she had lived as long as I could remember. He said she could take care of us and help out at the house when Mother was at the B&B. But Mother said that Granny hadn't lifted a finger in the four years she had lived with us, except to spoil Emmy, who slept with her and followed her through the house begging to sit in her lap. Like all of us but Maude, Emmy was little for her age, and Granny had taught her to be afraid of thunder and the dark and to talk baby-talk. She wandered through the house asking for a "be-nan" when she wanted a banana. Sometimes nobody could understand her but Granny.

Daddy yelled again. "That dog in there? He's not in his box. You're going to miss him for good one day. He does well to sleep in the kitchen. Had a dog all my life, but he wasn't never allowed in the house."

For a minute, he stood in the doorway between the kitchen and Til's bedroom, his arms folded across his chest. We knew he meant business. Felix was safe against Til's feet, under the sheet with the flashlight and the Monopoly board.

"I want you up and dressed in two minutes," Daddy said, walking back to the kitchen.

I pulled the sheet over my head, thinking, "He acts like nothing is different. Acts like Mrs. Diggs ain't dead." I felt like crying. Everything had been happy in our sheet tent last night. I owned all the railroads and Boardwalk. And now Mrs. Diggs was dead.

I pulled Felix up to the head of the bed. "We'd better get up before he comes in here and skins us alive."

Til didn't move. "Never skinned nobody alive yet. Just talks about it a lot."

We heard Mother take up for us. "Let them sleep a little while, Albert. School's out. Why do you want the children up at the crack of dawn? Maudie's in her bad time of month and fourteen's a tender age. And Til and Cass are both too little for their age, and Emmy's just a baby."

We could hear him blowing his coffee. "They got me up at the crack of dawn all of my life, and I lived to tell it."

Mother blew her nose. "We need to talk to them a little about Lora. Cass, especially, will miss her. Cass spent a lot of time on her kitchen stool. She was the best neighbor we've got." We heard Mother crying.

Til slid out of bed and put on his shirt and faded overalls. His shirt sleeves hit him above his wrists, and his overalls above the ankles. He never wore shoes in the summer except on Sunday. He shot a stream of spit into the palm of his hand and ran it through his sandy hair, giving the front an extra dose. Mother said he was "shooting up like a bad weed," but he didn't think so. He couldn't forget that the chart said he was too little for his age, and if there was one thing he didn't want to be, it was a runt. She kept reminding him that his grandfather on her side of the house was over six feet tall. Daddy said that Til's small, strong frame seemed made for speed. He ran most of the time. I did, too, to keep up with him.

I pulled Maude's old dress over my head and stuffed it down into my overalls and checked to be sure my little gold locket was there. I never took it off, even to sleep or take a bath. It had pictures of Mother and Daddy, made the summer after they were married. Mother was twenty-one and blonde and beautiful, and Daddy was twenty-seven and curly-haired and laughing.

Barefooted too, I followed Til into the kitchen. I wanted to say something about Mrs. Diggs, but I didn't know what to say.

Mother finally said, "You heard Mrs. Simpson say that Mrs. Diggs passed in the night? She's been bad sick, you know."

Maude was setting the table for breakfast. She always wore a dress now that she was filling out. Til almost had to say "uncle" a few weeks ago when he teased her about the new "lady's undergarment" he saw on the clothesline. "Could've saved some money by buying a roll of adhesive tape," he told Mother.

Mother wiped her eyes with her apron. "Maude, you and Til can go over there with me for a few minutes after they bring the body back from the undertaker. Cass, you can stay here with Em and Granny."

I felt like crying. "Why can't I go? I want to see her, too. She gave me strawberries through the fence."

"Aw, quit your bellyachin," Til said. "You're too young. You'd just bite your fingernails and wet the bed after seeing her in the casket."

Mother narrowed her eyes at Til. "Don't you talk to her that way, Tilghman Blevins. I'll box your ears. All of us but Em and Granny will go for a few minutes. Cass, wear your little blue dress and don't cloud up and cry when we get there."

Til grabbed the milk bucket and headed out, Felix at his heels. "You'd better shake a leg if you're comin with me, Satch." That's what he called me sometimes; it was short for Satchel Britches. I liked it better than Forty Gallons. That's what he called me when I wet the bed.

Mother poured a little coffee into two glasses of milk on the table. "Here, you need a little something warm in your stomach before you go out. When you get back, I'll have hot biscuits and sausage and gravy ready."

"They're too young for that coffee, Clary," Daddy said. "Stunt their growth. You said yourself they're both too little for their age. Cassandry's got to grow some before school. I wish you'd tell me why she has to foller him ever'where he goes. Looks to me like he'd get tired of her."

Me and Til gulped the warm milk.

"Cassie, you will get your killing hanging around after him," Mother warned. "Why do you want to go with him to that old cow bottom? Worries me half to death. Mrs. Simpson said she saw you riding in that old tire again the other day. Said it jumped the curb and hit the fireplug and you got out all addled. Til, I don't see why you can't roll a tire down the street without putting your little sister in it." She cut the biscuit dough with a jar lid. "Enough to scramble her brains, even if she didn't hit a thing. What if she'd roll out in the street and get killed by a car? You'd never get over it." She pushed my hair back. "You are not to get in that old tire again. Do you hear me?"

Maude chimed in. "You might as well talk to a fence post. Anybody would think they were Siamese twins." A ninth grader, she was too grown up to pay much attention to us, and she had a lot to do besides her school work, like cleaning the house and clerking at the B&B.

Me and Til sauntered along the path on our side of the chicken-wire fence that separated our garden from Mrs. Diggs' strawberry patch, past the woodpile toward the barnyard. Who would pick Mrs. Diggs' strawberries? Some more had already got ripe in the night since Mother picked yesterday. We had a big bowl for supper last night, all sugared-down. Daddy said he could eat them four times a day.

Til kicked at the chickens in the barnyard. They all squawked and flapped their wings except the rooster, and when Til drew a bead on him with a cinder, he paraded off, unruffled, as the cinder bounced against the garage. Til shoved the handle of the milk bucket to his elbow and stuffed his hands into his overalls pockets. We went out the gate into the alley, lined on one side with big oil drums full of garbage, and on the other, with cardboard boxes and bushel baskets full of garbage. I pinched my nose.

"You might as well give up," Til said. "You were born with that flat nose and all the pinchin in the world won't make it any longer. Don't know why Mother keeps lyin to you about that."

"Maude says it might help, too, but I know it won't ever be as pretty as hers," I said, holding my nose. Everybody talked about how pretty Maude was getting. She got all new dresses, and I got them second, and when I outgrew them, Mother put them in a drawer for Emmy even though they were so faded you couldn't even tell what kind of flowers was on the material. Til got all new overalls, too, and I got them second; by the time we both outgrew them, the seats and knees were all used up. But they felt better on me than anything else, even a new dress. You didn't have to keep you legs together when you sat down, and they had lots of pockets for hop-scotch rocks and things and a button-down bib pocket for important things like money. I would be glad when I could sew gallus buttons on, cause they were always coming off, and Mother would hand me a safety pin and say that for the life of her, she couldn't keep buttons sewed on for seven. Emmy didn't like overalls much, so they didn't have to last after me. She wouldn't wear overalls except in the dead of winter when Mother made her.

Summer had always been my favorite time of year. Til didn't have to go to school, and we could be together all day long. I always helped him with his chores, and that way we could play more. We didn't have to wear shoes or half as many clothes. The only bad thing was that once in a while Mother looked at our feet to see if we washed them before we put them between her clean sheets. When she fussed and scrubbed them, they smarted all night.

Winter was lonesome and cold. It was hard to "hit the deck," as Daddy called getting up, because the linoleum was cold, and we didn't have any bedroom shoes. Him and Mother had some, but he said children didn't need them, that he never had any until he was grown. He said heat in our bedrooms would keep us from breathing right and give us T.B. Him and Mother had the heatrola in their bedroom, so the only warm rooms in the house were theirs and the kitchen.

Lots of things made me like summer better than winter. The winter world was too little. The summer world was twice as big. It had six dogs in it besides Felix. In the winter the neighbors' dogs stayed in their own house like Felix did. The summer world had butterflies that almost let me catch them and birds that sang before daybreak, and the winter world had clouds and snow that was too dirty to make ice cream and too wet to make snowmen. Once in a while when the snow first fell, Mother would give us an aluminum pan with a few drops of vanilla extract in it for ice cream. But that was the only good thing I could think of about the winter world, except for the warm nights in front of the cook-stove when we were all together. We didn't talk much, but we were together. I didn't talk any if Daddy was reading the newspaper. Mother usually ironed or cooked. Granny held Em in her lap and played patty-cake. Maude read. She kept three books checked out of the library all of the time. Til made darts out of kitchen matches with pin bottoms in one end and paper rudders in the other and threw them at the door frame. I pretended to be looking at a picture book, but usually I just listened, trying to put two and two together to get four, as Mother said when she was trying to figure something out.

But everything happy had to happen inside the house in the winter and outside the house in the summer. In the winter we couldn't even hear the machinery make cotton over in the village, but in the summer we could hear a bee make honey in the back yard. And sometimes we could watch her. Daddy knew all about bees. He even knew that the workers flew as far as fifty miles a day to make honey and still got back home before dark. He wished for the time when he could have some hives of Italian bees. They were the best, he said, and he told us how the girl workers chew the legs off the boy drones and kick them out of the hive before winter comes, because they eat too much honey.

The sun drove the fog out of the cow bottom as we started down the crooked path to milk Polly. Sadie and Joe hadn't stirred yet. I wondered if they even knew Mrs. Diggs. We never had talked about her.

Polly was up to her knees in the cattail swamp. I rolled up my overalls and waded toward her while Til sat on the upside-down milk bucket.

He yelled, "How many times do I have to tell you to grab the halter, not the chain? You'll make her mad and she won't give no milk."

I was still afraid of Polly. I tugged on her halter with both hands and fell down in the knee-deep water. The slime rose between my toes, but Polly didn't budge.

"Watch out for that snake," Til yelled. I had heard it a hundred times. Finally, Polly ambled toward Til. He slapped her hip bone and yelled, "Move your leg, you old heifer," and aimed hard squirts of milk at the bucket. While the white foam rose, I walked the railroad tracks, putting one muddy foot in front of the other and waving a bunch of buttercups in the air to keep my balance.

I rolled my overalls legs down so they would be dry by the time Til got through milking.

"Wanta learn to milk?" he called.

I laid the buttercups down and clenched my fist around a tit and pulled hard. Nothing came. He grabbed the tit up high between his thumb and finger. "It's not hard. Just watch." And when his fingers slid down the tit, a stream of milk hit the bucket.

He could carry the bucket home with one hand, but I had to use both hands and carry it between my legs. He always carried it into the house, because he could swing it up onto the kitchen table.

Mother scolded, "Tilghman, how many times do I have to tell you not to put that bucket on my clean oil cloth? Leaves a dirty ring every time." She got the biscuits out of the oven and put the gravy on the table. "Maude, take Granny her butter bread, and dress Emmy. Cass, what in the world are your overalls doing wet? Don't see for the life of me why you would go wading before the sun warms the earth. You'll catch your death of cold."

Right after breakfast, I was looking out the window as the men took the casket with Mrs. Diggs in it up their front steps. I ran to Til's room and closed the door. I hoped we wouldn't be gone long, because putting on that dress for Sunday School once a week was enough. And I had to wear shoes to go next door in the middle of the morning.

Mother put a dish of fried chicken in a paper poke, and we went in the front way. I couldn't remember ever being on their front porch before. I always went in the back way, and Mrs. Diggs and me just sat in the kitchen.

Three neighbor ladies sat in the front porch swing. Mrs. McCormick shifted her snuff stick from one side of her mouth to the other. In the summer she sat near the edge of the porch when she went visiting, so she could spit in the yard, and in the winter she carried a little baking powder can. Mrs. Simpson sat in the middle. She looked whiter than usual. Granny Feathers' humpback made her sit on the edge of the swing. Her feet didn't reach to the floor, so she held onto the chain. After "Howdy" and "Ain't it a shame?" and "Her so young," we followed Mother into the kitchen to leave the chicken. Then we went into the parlor where Mrs. Diggs lay a corpse. I had been in the parlor once before, when Mrs. Diggs showed me the Star of Bethlehem in bloom.

Mother held me up so I could see her. "Doesn't she look natural, Cassie?" she asked softly. "The undertaker did such a good job on her hair."

Her short brown hair curled around her ears. She had on a new dress and held an artificial lily in her hand. She looked like she was asleep, soft and warm, but I knew nobody could wake her. I turned my head so I couldn't see her. Mother pulled the veil back.

"Cassie, I don't want you to be afraid of death. Touch her and then you won't be afraid of death."

I squirmed to get down, but Mother put my hand on Mrs. Diggs' cheek. It was cold and hard. I stared at the flowers and wished I had thanked her for all those strawberries I had stolen through the fence. I never even thanked her for saving me from being kidnapped back in the spring when a man was crouched outside Maude's bedroom window. I was sleeping with Maude that night, but she was still at a birthday party. Mrs. Diggs watched him from her kitchen stool, since they didn't have a telephone. Mr. Diggs said it was because every Tom, Dick and Harry would be calling to ask him why their kinfolks had been put in jail. Anyhow, we didn't have a telephone either, because Daddy said there was no way we could afford two, and he had to have one at the B&B.

When Maude came home, Mrs. Diggs tiptoed to her front porch and whispered to her about the man. Maude fell up our stairs screaming for Daddy. He jumped up and grabbed his sawed-off shotgun out of the chiffonier drawer and ran outside in his BVD's.

Mother yelled after him, "Don't shoot to kill! Shoot him in the legs!"

Daddy yelled back, "If I shoot, I'll shoot to kill!"

The shot rang out. Daddy said the man jumped the back fence and ran down the alley.

Mother talked for weeks about how nothing but that window screen separated me from a fate worse than death and how much harder it is to raise girls than boys.

Daddy stopped by to see Mrs. Diggs' corpse when he came home from the B&B that night. "Picture of health," he said at the supper table. "Prime of life."

Mother turned the cornbread onto a plate. "Thirty-six in April. Too bad she and Guy didn't have any children."

"He told me she couldn't have no younguns," Daddy said. "He'll be married again afore the first snow falls."

"Don't know why you talk like that in front of the children," Mother said. "Maude, go call Granny, and you all come and eat."

"You know it's the truth," Daddy said. "Guy's a young man."

"There's one thing for sure. If anything ever happened to me, you'd find yourself another one before the sun set twice on my grave."

"Sure, I would," Daddy teased. "And she'd be the pertiest thing comin down the pike. You wouldn't want me to raise these four younguns by my lonesome, would you?"

He laughed and hiked up her dress tail with his foot when she poured our milk. That was his favorite way of teasing her, but she pouted every time he did it and reminded him that he had some vulgar habits.

The next day, Daddy said that he would skin us alive if we didn't stay in until him and Mother and Maude got back from the funeral.

Til sat on the floor putting a new string on his six-shooter rubber gun, the thing of his I envied most next to his half-gallon fruit jar of marbles. My single-shooter, his old gun, lay on the kitchen table, the clothespin trigger on the handle biting the ammunition, a ring of inner tube that stretched around the barrel.

I was sorry that it was raining on Mrs. Diggs' funeral day. I sat on my knees on the high stool and made pictures on the window panes fogged by the teakettle that stayed on the cookstove summer and winter. I pulled my stool closer to the window and drew a stick horse and wondered who Mr. Diggs would marry. I asked Til if we prayed hard enough to God would He stop the rain. Til was making more bullets, cutting the rings of black rubber with Mother's sewing scissors.

"If you're half as smart as Old Lady Gladston lets on like in Sunday School, you could figure that out by yourself. Let me ast you, what's more important, makin the tomatoes grow or playin outside?" He threw the inner-tube valve in the garbage can. "Good thing God can answer that even if you can't. I can't wait till they start gradin you in readin and writin in September."

"Why don't they give grades in Sunday School?" I asked. "I know a lot of Bible verses and I can pray pretty good."

"Prayin ain't half as hard as rithmetic."

"Then, if you're so good at praying, why didn't you get at least a B in arithmetic?"

"Makin A's and B's ain't half as important as Mother lets on like." He aimed at the alarm clock. "Thomas A. Edison failed the first grade. Anyhow, I made it to the fifth." The rubber bullet turned the alarm clock over.

"By the skin of your teeth," I said. "Praying must be a waste of time. I've been praying to go to Aunt Flossie's and Unc's and it ain't even been mentioned. Looky here." I pointed to my horse on the window pane. "This is Lady and I'm gonna ride him next time we go."

"That?" Til smirked. "You ain't got him no bigger than Felix. Lady's taller than Unc, and besides, she's a girl."

"Let's both pray tonight to go. Maybe He'll listen if He hears both of us at once."

"You don't know the first thing about prayin for anything," Til said. "If you was to kneel down there by the window and pray hard enough and long enough for God to end the world, you might convince Him it would be a good idea." He rested his gun on the table edge and squeezed the trigger. The rubber ring hit the window and wiped Lady out. "That's how it would happen," he said.

I shuddered and thought of Mrs. Diggs in the graveyard. And little Charles Lindbergh.

We could smell Granny's asafetida before she came hobbling into the kitchen on her cane. She wore a little ball of asafetida in a dirty muslin bag around her neck to keep her from having dizzy spells. She wasn't any taller than Til and didn't weigh much more, but we all knew she was in charge when Mother and Daddy were gone. Her horn-rimmed glasses were the color of the big hairpins that held the knot of white hair on top of her head. Her black shawl swung from her shoulders.

"Get this mess cleaned up right now," she said.

I put my fingers in my ears. She always yelled. She thought everybody was as hard of hearing as she was. "Your mother and daddy will be home any minute, and your mother will have supper to get."

Til stuffed the bullets into his overalls pockets. Granny tapped my stool with her cane. "Put that back unner the table yonder where you got it, young lady. You're old enough to set the table. Don't see why you can't play quiet like Emmy does. She's been settin in my room all afternoon cuttin paper dolls out of a old Sears-Roebuck catalog."

I shoved the stool under the table so hard it hit the wall on the other side.

"Cassandry, get that stool and put it back where it belongs. Why are you allus in a fit of temper? For the life of me, I don't see why they ever named you after me." She wanted Emmy to be the one named after her.

After I had crawled under the table to move the stool, I stuck out my tongue at her. "Water off a duck's back," I mumbled, scooting across the linoleum where the flowers were still bright. Maude had mopped them right off the floor in the rest of the kitchen.

"What's that, Cassandry Blevins?" Granny squeaked. I froze, crouched under the table. "Don't you sass me none, young lady, or your daddy will take care of you when he gets home." Granny hobbled back to her bedroom just as Mother and Daddy came in the back door.

Two

*M*other changed from her Sunday black to an old faded cotton dress to fix supper. She was always the last one to sit down at the table. "Tilghman, did you wash your hands?" she asked, with a sigh.

Granny answered. "That boy wouldn't never wash his hands if he could get away with it. And I'll tell you another thing. Cassandry wouldn't neither." She peered at Daddy over her glasses. "How much would it cost to swap them younguns' names in court? That thin cotton hair didn't come from our side of the house at all. Not a cotton head in the whole Blevins bunch. And besides, Emmy's brown eyes is pure Hawk. Come from my side of the house. I've heerd tell of changin a name by law and I'm aimin to foot the bill."

Daddy didn't answer.

Mother frowned at me. "Cass, quit biting your nails and eat your supper. Some day you'll be sorry for that nasty habit."

"You ought to know, Clary," Daddy said, laughing. "Sometimes I think you was both born with your fist in your mouth."

I choked on my beans and cornbread. Daddy looked at Til. "You heard your mother, Tilghman. Answer her."

"I always do wash, but I'm not sure it's worth it." He banked his beans and cornbread with slices of onion and tomato. "Same thing to eat ever night," he mumbled.

Daddy shook his head. "Son, there are six others. It's too early to eat your fill of tomatoes. Early beans did extra good this year, but it's still a little early for tomatoes. They won't be in for at least two more weeks."

Til put a slice of tomato on my plate. "Whole grocery store full of food and what do we get to eat? Green beans and cornbread for dinner and cornbread and green beans for supper. And if we don't have green beans, it's dried beans and cornbread."

I shoved the beans to one side of my mouth, because I couldn't get them ready to swallow. "We had fried chicken on Sunday."

"And you can bet we'll have fried chicken next Sunday," Til said. "What do you think we keep the barnyard full of chickens for?"

Mother put another slice of tomato on Til's plate. "You kids will come to want if you don't learn to be thankful. Lots of children going to bed hungry tonight. You don't know what it is to want."

"Was Muddy Creek Church full?" I asked.

Mother answered, "Mrs. Diggs wasn't very outgoing, but she was a good neighbor. We were all there." She turned to Daddy. "Don't you think they did a good rendition of 'When the Roll Is Called up Yonder'? I just love that old sacred-harp singing."

Daddy nodded and got up from the table to turn on the radio. He never missed Lowell Thomas and the news.

Mother stacked the dirty dishes for Maude. "Albert, let's take the children to hear the Reverend Carmack. Mrs. Simpson tells me he is mighty good. Been preaching to a full house every evening."

Me and Til had seen the sign in front of the tent in the cow bottom:

TENT REVIVAL, THE REV. MORDECAI F. CARMACK
Nightly at 7:30, June 8-22.
Swap an hour of your time for salvation.

Daddy pulled his chair up closer to the radio. It was election year, and he said almost every day that old Hoover had shot his wad and got this country in the biggest mess ever. When the man came on to advertise gasoline, Daddy answered her. "Thought I'd go over and keep Guy company a little while. You and the kids can go."

"Guy will need your company a lot more next week when Lora's kinfolks go back to Georgia."

Daddy put on his shoes, and except for Granny, we all walked to the cow bottom. I was surprised when they made Til and me wear shoes. Even tennis shoes didn't feel good, particularly after they got wet when we crossed the bottom. Mother said she had half-a-mind to get herself a pair of tennis shoes to wear around the house, but she was sure they gave people that old athlete's foot. I ran ahead to walk with Til. I wanted to be with him even if he was always ordering me around, telling me to hold this for him or get that out of Daddy's tool box. And even if sometimes when he watched me undress at night, he laughed and said I wasn't all there. Just like my nose.

Slapping at mosquitoes, we joined the little group outside the tent. When the Reverend Carmack walked up in his black suit, swinging the Bible by his side, the group moved inside quietly. Us Blevinses took up a whole bench.

The Reverend Carmack paced slowly back and forth in the front as the pianist's fingers lolled up and down the keyboard, playing soft chords. After everybody got settled and the women began fanning, the Reverend Carmack announced, "We'll open our worship tonight by singing all three verses of 'Love Lifted Me.'" He held the hymn book up. "They's one in the back of the bench right in front of you. Ever'body join in, young and old alike, and know the victorious feelin of being saved when you're sinkin deep in sin, when you're far from the peaceful shore, and they's not a one of you here tonight that don't know what that means." He walked over to the Bible on the table. "St. Matthew said, 'Whosoever looketh on a woman to lust after her hath committed adultery with her already in his heart.'" He motioned for the pianist to begin the hymn. Daddy said she was his wife, but you'd never know it from the way he just motioned her to start and stop.

I knew my ABC's but couldn't read the words that fast, so I sang fa, sol and la just like Maude had taught me. The shape notes made the tune easy to read. Daddy didn't open his mouth, but he helped me hold the book.

The Reverend Carmack wiped his forehead with a big white handkerchief. "Now, if the Lord will help us, we're going to render a little song with a big message." The pianist began playing "On Top of Old Smoky." I heard it every Saturday night on the Grand Ole Opry. But the preacher twanged out words I had never heard.

God depended on Adam;
He depended on Cain;
He depended on Jonah

To tell of His name.
He depended on Judas,
But he proved untrue,
An now, my dear brethren,
He's dependin on you.

A lot more verses followed, about Paul being struck blind on a road. It must have been over in Virginia a few miles away, because the Reverend Carmack mentioned Damascus. After the song, he wiped his forehead again and announced that the Holy Scripture came from the Fiftieth Psalm. "I was shapen in iniquity and in sin did my mother conceive me." His voice quivered. "It's a psalm of grief."

He started out in a low, slow voice. "Some of you women think you can't do nothin wrong in the name of love. You think that just because in the Song of Solomon it says that my beloved put in his hand by the hole in the door and my bowels were moved for him, that you can't sin no more with man. Some of you blame all of this type of sin on man. Well, I have got news for you." His hair fell down across his eyes. His voice rose. "Yes ma'am, I've got big news for you tonight. He don't have to put in his hand by the hole in the door. *You* unlatch the door *for* him."

He kept on talking about things I didn't understand. Once I pulled Daddy's sleeve and whispered, "What does he mean, lying in dust in the fields?"

Daddy whispered, "Lust." I still didn't know what he was talking about. The Reverend Carmack kept talking.

"Some of you even argue that a soldier entered Mary to give us our sweet Savior Jesus Christ, and that makes ever thing all right. If you believe that, brothers and sisters, you can't hope for no more than a one-way ticket to hell."

He was growing hoarse. He reached for the aluminum pitcher. The ice tinkled as he poured a glass of water. He gulped it down and gasped for breath. His words came slower.

"I know this ain't the proper time for a Christmas sermon, but I'm deeply troubled about this story going round that says Mary laid with a soldier. You should be deeply troubled, too, if you love your sweet Savior as you ought to." His voice rose again. "Some varmint wrote that book to make a pile of money, and he's makin it, cause a lot of you has already bought it. You have got it on that table by your bed, that table that ought to hold only the holy Word of God. Yes sir, he's makin a pile of money poisonin the minds of young and old alike. I have a copy of that book on the shelf in my study, and I have wrote acrost it in big letters, POISON." He spoke slowly. "I have read it. So I know whereof I speak."

His voice fell to a loud whisper. "Now, it says right here in Chapter One, Verse Twenty-seven of St. Luke's Gospel that Mary was a virgin. It don't say she was a girl, or a young lady, or a maiden. Them words can mean any number of things. It says she was a *virgin*, and that can mean only *one* thing." He held the open book up in the air and slowly waved it from side to side. "And it says right here a little further on that the Holy Ghost would come upon Mary and overshadder her, and, by the love of Sweet Jesus, that's exactly what happened. You don't want to argue with that, do you?"

He yelled louder and louder. "It wasn't no soldier at all that overshaddered Mary. It was the Holy Ghost, the one and only. You oughtn't to waste your precious time on that book. Remember, your days are numbered as surely as the hairs on your head."

Sweat trickled down his neck. He pulled his coat back and stuck his thumbs in his vest pockets. His voice got low again. "Lots of you women here tonight can't get your mind off another woman's husband, and you men ain't had but one thing on your mind since you was old enough to blow your nose. Take my word for it, it will turn on you. Take my word for it." He pounded his fist on the table. "What you think is *love* will turn to bitter gall in your mouth, and some day when she's undressin quiet in the dark and puttin on her lacy nightgown while her husband is at work, bitterness will creep into your heart and you will know hate first-hand. And when she puts her arms round your neck, you'll know *hate*."

He took another sip of water. Sweat rings made the arm pits of his coat even blacker.

"Some of you already know what I'm talkin about. And you will back off from that bed tonight, that bed that don't belong to you, and you will go walkin in the garden alone with your sweet Savior. And you will hear that sweet voice in your ear, and you will *know* what it means to be *saved*."

He crossed his arms on his chest and lowered his voice. "But ever one of you knows some man or woman that ain't saved. I'm goin to ast you to bring them with you tomorrow night to worship with us."

The pianist had already begun to play "Whiter Than Snow," and when we were through singing it, the Reverend Carmack spoke in a whisper. "And now we've got a lot of work to do. It's summertime and lots of folks are goin on vacation, traipsin round, and they fergit to take the Lord with em. Our work don't take no vacation. It goes on summer and winter. I'm goin to ast you to take God with you when you go on vacation. Take Him with you by rememberin us with your pocketbook and your prayers."

Daddy gave us a penny apiece to drop in the collection plate. He gave Mother a nickel. And then the preacher invited all sinners to the front when we sang, "Stand Up, stand up for Jesus." The pianist's fingers rolled up and down the keyboard. As soon as she struck the first chord of the hymn, the Reverend Carmack stretched out both hands, and the first ones down the aisle were Mrs. Simpson and Mrs. McCormick. They took salvation every time it was offered.

A few other women straggled to the front as the preacher shouted, "This may be your last chance. You may not wake up on this earth in the mornin. You may wake up in the arms of Jesus," and he shouted even louder and slower, "or in the clutches of the devil."

I wondered if Mrs. Diggs had time to choose. I knew little Charles Lindbergh didn't. We were about the same age, and I hadn't been saved. As far as I knew, Mother and Daddy were the only ones in our family who had. Maude hadn't even been saved, but she didn't seem to worry about it. Anyhow, she never did mention it.

The preacher's voice fell to a whisper. "Let me tell you somethin. This ole world is goin to burn to a cinder. It says so right here," and he slammed the Bible down on the table.

Then, suddenly, Til got up and started down the aisle. I started to get up and follow him, but Daddy put his hand on my knee. Mother looked around and whispered about it being too bad that Til hadn't taken time to buckle the legs of his knickers. He looked little standing there with all those grown-ups. Then he knelt in the sawdust.

The Reverend Carmack put both hands on his head and prayed, "Sweet Jesus, take this sinner into your heart and keep him from lust and strong drink. Give him a early start on stren'th to fight the wicked desires of the flesh. Don't let him commit adult'ry in his heart or in his body. Take and hold him in your lovin arms until he learns the real meanin of leanin on the everlastin arms and You call him home. Amen."

I hoped nobody was looking at me. My face got hot, and I couldn't find a fan. The little group that had been saved sang "I Am Thine, O Lord."

On the way home, we didn't talk much. Til dug his hands into his pockets and walked up the path in front of us. I was right behind him, but I didn't ask him how it felt to get saved. I wanted to, but decided to wait until we played Monopoly. I never had wondered about Jesus' daddy before. It could have been that soldier. How else would the Baby Jesus seed get inside Mary? At least, I was still a virgin just like Mary. What did the Holy Ghost look like? I didn't remember ever seeing a picture of him. And how come Til got saved and I didn't?

That night Til got as close to the edge of the bed as he could. I wanted to talk to him, but I was afraid that he was awake and would want me to exercise his peejabber, and afraid that he was asleep and wouldn't answer my questions.

I heard Mother from their bedroom. "Shh, Albert. You'll wake the children." I wondered if Daddy was asking her to help him stretch his peejabber.

Til rolled against me and laughed. "Wasn't nothin to it. You should have gone up there with me and got yourself saved."

He put my hand on his peejabber. Sure enough, it was getting bigger. I asked him if we couldn't make mine bigger, and he laughed.

"You could exercise that little thing till the cows come home, but it wouldn't grow no longer. Can't even call it a peejabber. Not good for nothin but peein."

I heard Daddy give a loud groan and Mother say, "Shh," again. Til laughed. "Boy, he came in a hurry!"

"What do you mean, *came*? He's in bed."

"Dummy! That means he's had his peejabber inside Mother, and it exploded in there. Planted seeds when he groaned. Makes a man feel good all over."

I hoped he hadn't planted another seed in Mother. She said every little bit that she didn't want any more children, that they would do well to get *us* raised. I knew that he had planted four seeds already, Maude and Til and me and Emmy.

THREE

Getting religion made a big differ-
ence in Til. He was smart before, but now he was making money.
I mean really *making* money. He bought him a bottle of green ink
and two sheets of white drawing paper to make dollar bills. But
the printing on the pattern that he got out of Daddy's billfold was
too little, and he couldn't get George Washington's nose to come
out right. The last straw was that they creased forever when he
folded them. So he decided to make half dollars in a cheese box
in the garage.

The problem was doing both sides at once so the grooves
matched. First he made a top and bottom pattern out of plaster-
of-Paris. After he heated the lead in Mother's little frying pan, he
poured it into the bottom, then clamped the top on and let it cool.
Then he picked up the half dollar with Maude's eyebrow tweezers
and laid it in the window sill. In two hours he made $2.50.

"Boy, if we had us a silver dollar, we could get rich twice as
fast," he said. He threw a half dollar against the concrete. It landed
with a thud. He pitched it to me. "Wanta make yourself a dime?
Take this up to Leeper's and get Mother a spool of white thread.
That'll cost a nickel and you'll get a quarter and two dimes back.
You can have one of the dimes."

I stared at the half dollar and decided to hand it to Mr. Leeper
with the eagle up. That side was shinier.

A boy up the street had got two years in reform school for robbing the service station on the corner. How long would a five-year-old girl get for spending home-made money? Would they let you leave reform school to go to first grade? Til was melting more lead, so he couldn't go with me. He never did tell me where he got that lead, and I was afraid to ask him, because I was afraid he had swiped it from the service station or somewhere. Mother was right about him being smart for his age. He was the only one I knew that could make counterfeit money look real. He'd be rich one day, for sure. I wondered if he'd let me help him then.

"Got some of this lead in your drawers?" he asked. "Or are you gettin cold feet about makin a honest dime?"

I put the half dollar in my overalls pocket. He yelled when I got to the end of the driveway. "If Mr. Leeper bites it or bounces it on the floor, run like crazy."

I skipped up the street with Felix behind me. Granny Feathers was out hoeing her garden, but I didn't stop to speak to her. Her poke bonnet hid her face. I slowed to a walk when I got to Leeper's. The brown-sugar smell reminded me of the B&B.

"How's little Blevins today?" Mr. Leeper asked. "They still won't let you cross that highway by yourself? Good thing. That Baxter boy's brains was all over the highway when that truck hit him back in the spring. What can I do for you?"

I stared at the thread box on the counter. "A spool of number 50 white thread. Mother's making me a playsuit," I lied.

"Them overalls *is* a little hot for June, I reckon. She's probably makin you some garments for school. You do start in with your schoolin this fall, don't you?"

"Yessir," I answered, staring at the dark spot on the board floor where the pot-bellied stove stood in the winter. Then I stared at Mr. Leeper's belt buckle and handed him the half dollar. He handed me a quarter and two dimes out of the cash register just like Til said he would. I didn't breathe again until I got outside and broke into a gallop.

Til was on the sidewalk talking to Granny Feathers' goofy son, Si, when I got home. Si held an empty milk bottle to his ear, and was trying to get President Hoover on the line. His eyes always looked in both directions at once. He was at least 30 years old and carried that milk bottle with him everywhere he went. He yelled into it, "White House, Warshin'ton?...Let me speak to Mr. Hoover

...He ain't in?...Tell him Si called and said for him to get out of that house in a hurry...They just left here comin after him...They are blamin the whole dadburned Depression on him."

Til interrupted him. "Si, you blamed idiot, that's a milk bottle, and it don't connect with nothin. It's worth two cents in any store and that's all."

I backed off. Si always smelled like dirty feet. Mother said like as not he never got in a bathtub. He ambled down the street, clutching the bottle to his chest. I handed Til the thirty-five cents and we walked into the garage where six more half dollars were cooling on the window sill. Til jumped up and down.

"Didn't I tell you we'd be rich? Tomorrow you can take these to that store down on Sullivan and those two over on Maple Street. They won't know the difference for sure if Mr. Leeper didn't, and you can have a dime out of ever half dollar."

I never had gone that far from home without Til. "You got to go, too," I told him. "Daddy would whip me."

He poured more hot lead into the mold. I'd never had more than a nickel at a time before. Now I had me a dime and a spool of thread. This time tomorrow I might have a quarter. I clutched the dime in my pocket.

Til laughed. "What's the matter? Burnin a hole in your pocket?"

"How many dimes would it take to buy a music box like Mother's?" I asked.

"What do you want with one of them things? I'm gonna get me a pair of boxin gloves and a bicycle."

That night when Daddy drove into the garage, he found the cheese box and the half dollars on the window sill. "Cass-an-dra" rang across the back yard. "Tilgh-man" followed. We didn't answer. We were feeding the chickens.

"What's been goin on here?" He motioned for us to follow him into the garage. He stomped the cheese box and smashed the half dollars with a hammer and threw them into the oil drum. "I'll skin you alive if I ever catch you up to another trick like this, Tilghman Blevins. Where'd you get that lead? Don't you know that half dollars is made out of silver? Don't you know that counterfeitin money is a federal offense?"

We walked in front of him to the back door. "Quit draggin your tail between your legs and get a move on. Get warshed up for supper. You'd really have somethin to worry about if you had tried to pass one of them. Police wouldn't put you *in* jail. They'd put you *under* it!"

Daddy didn't even have to look at me to know I was biting my nails at the table. "Cassandry, I'm goin to tell you one more time to quit that. Goin to take you to the barnyard and put chicken doo on them fingers or get out the red pepper. Take your pick."

I had heard it a hundred times. I crumbled the hot cornbread into my cold milk and was hungry after all.

Daddy was tireder than usual. "Goin to have to get me some help at the B&B right away. Can't tell they's a Depression on the way people is orderin groceries. Sellin is easy, but collectin is a horse of another color nowadays. I hope undertakers don't have as hard a time collectin after the body is buried as I have after the groceries is et."

Mother blurted out, "Groceries *are eaten*, Albert. There is no such word as *et*. And the first thing you know, you'll hear at least two of these children talk like that. I want you to tell me what Til will do if we don't get him through high school."

Daddy pushed his chair back and looked out the window. "But who'll I get? I'd a heap rather do a job of work myself as to depend on most of the help you can find nowadays. Too dumb to pour pee out of a boot with directions on the heel."

Mother used her worried voice. "I wish you wouldn't talk like that in front of these children, Albert. Til will be big enough to help you before long. He's already big enough to copy everything you do and say."

"Can't depend on him. He gets on that telephone ever chance he gets."

"Let me help," I begged. "I can stack cans on the bottom shelves."

Daddy tousled my hair with his hand. "What I need is a man to make deliveries on Saturday," he said. "You can help some, Cassie, but you got to get your mind on other things right away."

Mother got up and went to Granny's room to see why she hadn't stirred. In a minute she was back. "Albert, go see about your mother. She's either acting contrary or not feeling good."

Daddy took some cornbread and milk to Granny's room. Emmy followed him.

Me and Til got the kindling and coal in for the cookstove while Mother and Maude washed the dishes. Mother sang, "Tell Me the Old, Old Story." I knew exactly what she was about to say. About once a month she got her mother and daddy on her mind and told us that they were getting old up there in the country all by themselves. She finally got up the nerve to ask Daddy about going on Sunday. When she said, "They won't be there forever," he just went into the bedroom to listen to Lowell Thomas tell the news on the radio.

On Sunday morning when we got into the big Dodge touring car that Daddy delivered groceries in, he called to Granny, "Hold down the fort! We'll be back by sundown."

"To my opinion," Granny answered, "I won't have to hold it down that long. You'll get your bellyful of that Methodist stuff by the middle of the day."

They made Maude go with us, but she didn't want to. Her and Maxine Simpson wanted to walk across town to visit a friend. Daddy said like as not they were going to meet up with that good-for-nothin Fred Gaylor. He said the girl that married Fred sure would be driving her ducks to muddy water.

We drove off. Mother pulled her handkerchief out. "What makes your mother talk like that? You don't have a sister that would put up with her overnight." She sniffled. "I'll have you know folks offered condolences to my mother when they found out I had married into the Blevins family."

"That concrete will never hold up," Daddy said when we crossed the new river bridge. "Should have built it out of steel. We'll have to pay for it again in ten year."

Til sounded confident. "By the time it falls down, I'll be ready to build the new one. Gonna build bridges when I grow up."

"With your grades in arithmetic, you'll do well to be a dog catcher," Maude chimed in. Nobody ever talked to her about what she was going to be when she grew up. All they talked about was when she would get married.

Til read the concrete-cross sign out loud. " 'Jesus Is Soon Coming.' Shoot, I heard He had done come and gone."

Mother shook her finger at him. "Don't you make light of that, Tilghman Blevins. It's Sunday."

Spooley Paine was working his corn. "Never did know what Sunday is for," Mother muttered. "Not raised. Jerked up by the hair of the head. Do you reckon that boy has ever seen the inside of a church?"

Til got out and opened the barnyard gate. Granma was standing by the seven sisters rose bush at the front-yard gate in her Sunday black and bonnet.

"'Pon my honor," she squealed with delight. "Look who's here, Jim." They had no way of knowing which Sunday the six of us would show up.

She grabbed Emmy up in one arm and me in the other, but put me down fast and said I had grown too much to be carried. She always looked the same. Never took off her tiny gold hoop earrings. They went all the way through the holes in her ears. Her dark skin made Granpa's folks disown him when he married her, because they thought she had some nigger blood in her. Mother said her high cheek bones made it plain that if it was anything out of the way, it was Indian.

She didn't look a bit like the picture of Pocahontas in Til's history book, but her skin was darker than any other white woman's I had ever seen. Her eyes were so dark that they looked black, even around the rims, and Daddy said she was light enough on her feet to be Cherokee. In the picture that hung over the organ in the parlor she was beautiful. She wore a black satin dress with rows of black string, braided just like Emmy's hair, stretching across her chest between big, shiny, black buttons. Her ruffled white collar stood up against her neck and almost touched her earrings. That picture was made before she had ten boys and two girls. After she had all those children, she still wore her hair the same, brushed back in a bun, but her eyes looked littler and paler and her forehead was lined with wrinkles. I wanted to tell her it didn't matter at all to me if some of her blood did come from niggers or Indians, but I knew we weren't supposed to hear a lot that we heard. She reminded me of Sadie and I loved Sadie. I didn't know any Indians. Mother said the white man had mistreated them from the beginning and had even killed some who had been good friends to the first settlers. Mother said she didn't understand how in the world we could call them heathens when her favorite author, Gene Stratton Porter, had written that without a doubt most North American Indians believe in God and life after death more than a lot of us do. Mother said she wouldn't mind at all being kin to Sequoyah, because he invented ABC's in the Cherokee language so they could write things down.

Granpa had just come home from teaching Sunday School, something he did rain or shine. He had answered the call to be a preacher when he was a young man, but gave up religion in Kansas where they went to start a new life after they were married. They had come back because he got bad sick, and their first baby was born dead, and their garden wouldn't grow in that old dust. Slowly, he got his religion back, but not enough to preach, just enough to teach Sunday School.

Before dinner, me and Til went to drive the Model-T. Granpa never had learned to drive it. Just kept it polished, sitting in the hallway of the barn. But we couldn't get it started. Til got kicked four times by the crank before he gave up and began taking the motor apart.

When Mother called, we went out back of the house to the washstand and washed up for dinner. After we sat down at the big table, Granpa folded his hands in his lap and yelled the grace to God as if He were as hard of hearing as Granny. We ate chicken and tenderloin and two kinds of potatoes and wilted lettuce out of the garden and spiced peaches that Granma had canned last year.

After dinner we had to sit a while and listen to Granpa and Daddy talk about who the next President would be.

"Hoover'll never go in again," Daddy said. "They tell me they's upwards of thirteen million out of work and folks in the coal fields up in Virginny shiverin from October to April. Another term of him and the whole country'll wind up in the porehouse."

Granpa combed his white mustache with his fingers and belched. "Farm prices down fifty per cent. It doesn't pay to keep chickens for eggs or meat, and the bottom has dropped clean out of the pork market." He swung one long leg across the other. "What do you think of that young whippersnapper Roosevelt?"

They wondered how to pronounce his name. Daddy said a woman who traded with him at the B&B wrote the governor's mansion in New York where Mr. Roosevelt lived and asked how to say his name. Two weeks later the mailman brought a box with one red rose in it.

"You can't tell much about his politics yet," Daddy said, "but they tell me he's rich, was born with a silver spoon in his mouth.

Those that never had to work from can to can't won't do nothin for you and me."

They agreed that they didn't want some man in Rome telling the American people what to do. Al Smith was a good Democrat, but a Catholic.

Daddy whittled on a little stick of kindling. "This country will never elect a Catholic to run the ship of state. Irregardless, I'm goin to cast my vote for the Democrat, whether it's Al Smith or Franklin D."

Granpa nodded. "But they tell me if Roosevelt's elected the next thing will be a nigger in the White House."

"Would they change its name?" I asked. Nobody answered.

Daddy said, "Always has been some there. Maids and chauffeurs."

Mother gave Granma her worried look. "Little pitchers have big ears, don't they?" Then she excused us all but Maude. Maude had to help with the dishes.

Granma poured everybody another cup of coffee. I got my glass, still half full of milk. "Please, can I have a little in my milk?"

Granma filled the glass. "I reckon, now that you're old enough to start school. Hard to believe you were born nearly six years ago. You sure don't seem big enough for your age. Run all your fat off, I reckon, trying to keep up with Tilghman. Don't you know that boys like girls with a little meat on their bones?"

My face got hot. Granma kept on talking about my tomboyish ways and bad manners. "You'd do better to be more like Maudie," she said. "She'll make some man a good wife, quiet and neat as she is. And I hope you make marks as good as your mother did."

Mother answered her. "I think she'll learn all right if we can keep her indoors long enough. She already knows her ABC's and can write her name."

Daddy bragged on me. "And she can tie her own shoes and polish mine. I can see my face in em ever Sunday mornin." He didn't put nearly as much stock in book learning as Mother did.

He looked at his pocket watch. "You know what time it's gettin to be, Clary? Half past two. If you want some of them apples, you'd better send the kids to the orchard. Can't leave Granny alone too long and her so puny."

Mother cleared the table and spread a cloth over the leftovers. "Til, get that paper poke out of the car and pick me up some of those June apples. Don't take any off the tree; they aren't ripe yet, and don't get in a hurry and pick up any rotten ones."

The orchard hummed with sweat bees and yellow jackets, so Til climbed the tree and peppered the ground with apples for me to pick up. We put them in our car and went back to the Model-T to pick up the parts Til had taken out. He said it wouldn't run anyway and nobody there could drive it even if it would. So it didn't make any difference that he had taken out a lot of the motor. We wiped our hands and took off our shoes and socks and threw them in the car and ran down to the springhouse, always chock-full of crocks with the tops barely out of the cold water. Covered with thick little square boards, they were filled with buttermilk and sweet milk and thick, yellow cream and curds. Granma kept rocks on top of the boards. She was the only one who knew what was in each crock without taking the top off.

Til threw a rock into the water, below the springhouse, and watched it disappear. "If you fell in there, like as not, you'd never hit the bottom, never even be found." He took hold of my shoulders and shoved me to the edge.

"Can you swim?" he whispered in my ear. I started to cry. He said, "Aw, dry up, cry baby. I'm gonna quit takin you with me anywhere." He started to run toward the house.

"Wait for me," I cried. "Please wait for me. I got a briar in my foot."

He knelt beside me. "Move your head over so I can see to pull it out, dummy. Little old thistle briar. Anybody woulda thought you stepped on a ten-penny nail. You're gettin more like a girl ever day."

We rested a minute, sitting against the trunk of the big cherry tree by the springhouse. "Looky here," he called. "That's him on top, holdin her down. Great God A'mighty, he's got his whole back end in her!"

I got down on my elbows and knees to look at the grasshoppers. "She's not even lying down. She's standing up. Could walk right out from under him if she wanted to."

"Could not. Not the way he's got her pinned to the ground. He's plantin baby seeds by the hunderds."

"How can she hold that many in her stomach?"

"They hatch out, dummy. Some things, like chickens and grasshoppers, lay eggs. Some things, like people and dogs, don't."

Til was already lying in the soft grass with his knickers shoved below his knees. "Just look at that bugger," he whispered. His pee-jabber was standing straight up, all by itself. "It's really growin. You'll have to hurry. They'll be lookin for us."

I knelt down beside him. I felt the soft grass under my knees and could see the crocks under the cold water. We had forgotten to close the springhouse door. The reflection of the cherry tree swayed on the surface of the water that ran out from under the springhouse. Til rose and fell under my hand.

"Faster, faster!" he whispered, but I had to rest. When I got up on my knees, he pushed my head toward his peejabber, and I felt it fill my mouth.

I jerked back and cried, "I don't want a baby!"

"Dummy! I can't plant a seed in your mouth. You don't spit babies out. Gotta fuck you to do that."

I didn't ask him what he meant, but he told me anyway. "Means stickin my peejabber in yours until mine explodes and blows seeds all over your insides, like when you blow a old dandelion. Babies come out of your peejabber."

He pushed my head back between his legs. His peejabber separated my lips. In a minute his whole body got stiff and he groaned and rolled away from me. I felt sick. My mouth was full and slick. I leaned over and got a mouthful of spring water and spit it out.

He pulled up his knickers and closed the springhouse door. Then he grabbed my hand. "Hurry up. They'll be wonderin what happened to us."

Sure enough, Daddy was looking for us in the barn. "Where in the world have you been this time?" he asked. "Ready to leave here a half hour ago, but couldn't find hide nor hair of you. Didn't you hear me callin?"

Til looked at me and started to whistle softly. I whistled, too. I had just learned how.

Granma pushed my hair back. "That whistling doesn't become a young lady, Cassie, especially one that's old enough to go to school. Remember, a cackling rooster and a crowing hen will never come to any good end."

I crawled into the back seat of the car. The sun was still high when we left. Even a sour apple didn't take the taste out of my mouth. I looked out the window, right into the hole of the sun, but couldn't stop the tears. Mother heard me sniffle.

"Sounds like you picked up a little cold," she said. "Running around barefoot again. That ground is damp, not like in town. I'll rub you down with a little Vicks as soon as we get home."

Til asked me to play cow poker with him, but I didn't feel like it. He knew Maude wouldn't play, because she said long ago that it was just too dumb to count cows on your side of the road and look for graveyards on the other side so you could bury all of the other person's cows.

Til showed off, talking about history. "Where do you reckon we'd be if old man Clark hadn't built that port a hunderd years ago to ship sausage and salt down the Holston? That's what ole Spit-Ball said he built it for."

Maude answered, "It was not a hundred years ago, smart aleck. More like sixty. And what makes you think we'd be anywhere else? Only thing different would be the name of the town."

Emmy didn't even wake up. She was sound asleep in Mother's lap. Til talked all the way home. He read the billboards out loud, all about tourist homes and gasoline and roadhouses until Daddy got to the top of the ridge where the rich people lived. They didn't have any billboards in their front yards. Just lots of trees and swing sets and sliding boards. One had a swimming pool in the front yard. Our front yard had two wormy umbrella trees that filled the narrow strip of grass on each side of the walk down to the street. Houses on the ridge were away back from the street; our house was about eighteen giant steps from the street.

Til read the city-limits sign every time we went by it. "Clarksport, Population 24,541." He pushed his feet into Mother through the back of the front seat. Maude pushed his feet to the floor. He kept talking. "Bet they put that sign up in 1917 when this burg was incorporated. Who do you reckon that last baby was?"

The sun set as we pulled into the driveway. Daddy sang, "To market, to market to buy a fat hog. Home again, home again, jiggety-jog."

Granny was already in bed. Mother rubbed Vicks on my chest and made me swallow a little wad of it. That was the first time I ever had liked the taste of Vicks. I knew one thing. I didn't want to taste Til's peejabber ever again. And if I told Mother, she would tell Daddy and Til wouldn't be able to sit down for a week. But what if Mother didn't believe me? And Til would be sure to tell Daddy something that would clear him. They understood each other in a way that Mother and me didn't. I decided to think about it and maybe talk to Til tomorrow and tell him I didn't mind churning his peejabber, but I didn't *ever* want to taste it again. I pretended to be asleep when he came to bed. If he didn't stay on his side, I would go and get in bed with Maude. He stayed on his side and was asleep in no time. I stayed awake until after I knew he was asleep.

FOUR

Granny didn't feel like getting up for breakfast, so Daddy said he'd call Dr. Shaw from the B&B and ask him to stop by the house at dinner time.

By ten o'clock it was so hot it felt like noon. Til and I sat on the bottom step of the front porch and worked on the generator he had taken from Granpa's Model-T.

He unscrewed the top with a kitchen knife and showed me the insides. "These here are both condensers, and they are made of conductors and can store electricity. That's why a generator is called a generator. It generates electricity that's used to start the engine. When I crank, it generates electricity just like it does when I crank the car. When it gets full of electricity, some spills over into this wire that goes to the motor and that's what starts the car. See how it works?"

I nodded, but he didn't even look up. He put the top back on and showed me a wire to hold. "Don't let go of this until you feel something, like you might feel your fingers get numb a little bit. When you feel something, yell, 'Charge!' and I'll quit crankin."

He started cranking, and before long I felt a tingle. Nothing much. Just a tingle. Then I couldn't let go. I tried to tell him, but I couldn't talk. Couldn't even open my mouth. He kept on cranking.

Mother called from the living room, and when she didn't hear an answer, she came running down the steps.

"You kids will be the death of me yet," she screamed, grabbing me up in one arm. "Tilghman Blevins, what are you doing to your sister now? She's turning blue. You've all but electrocuted her. Get in the house this minute. And be quiet. Granny's asleep," she said, and walked into the house carrying me and muttering to Til, "Your daddy can take care of you when he gets home."

Mother rubbed my face and hands until the feeling came back. "I'll tell you one more time, Cass. You are going to get your killing if you keep messing around with Til. I don't want to run your daddy's people down, but some of them are prone to be a little wild and Til has a streak we've got to discourage."

She sent me to Leeper's for a box of epsom salts. "I think if we can get Granny's bowels to move, she'll feel better. Poor old thing hasn't had a movement in three days. And here's a nickel for a cone of ice cream."

When I got back, Til was lying in the front-porch swing pretending to read a Big-Little Book. Mother sat there in a kitchen chair, stringing green beans, with her legs sprawled apart. Til kept contrarying her.

"No wonder they call me Runt at school. No wonder I weigh half as much as the chart says I ought to. Makin me read when you know a boy my age ought to be developin his muscles." He turned on the other side, facing the back of the swing, and kept muttering. "Ought to be givin me a pair of boxin gloves instead of this dumb book. And boxin lessons instead of violin lessons. Next time I'm born, I hope I get me a daddy bigger than two bits."

Mother narrowed her eyes at him. "That's enough out of you, Tilghman Blevins. Your daddy's still big enough to take the hide off you when he gets home."

Til sat up and slumped in the swing. "That's another thing. When he gets home, when he gets home. That's all I hear. One man in this house, and him part-time. Five females and all of them full-time, and three of them all the time tellin me what to do."

"You're not helping matters," Mother warned him. "Now be quiet. Here comes Mrs. Simpson."

Mrs. Simpson hiked her dress and apron up above her knees to climb the steps. "Mr. Blevins told me down to the store that Granny is ailin. I thought I'd drop by and see is there anything I can do." She wiped her face with her apron.

"Come on in, Mrs. Simpson, and pull up a chair. Get that rocker there and rest your back. Bet you've already put up beans this morning."

"No, I been workin up some early apples Ed brought from the farm last night. Go to the bad so quick you got to screw the cap on em soon as you pick em, what with it bein so hot and all."

Til flipped the pages in "Dick Tracy," and I sat down on the porch steps. Mother handed Mrs. Simpson a newspaper full of green beans from the bushel basket.

"Granny's just lost her appetite. Appears to be a little bloated. Probably nothing serious. It can't be hard work, and she's not been in a crowd to catch anything. Albert asked Dr. Shaw to stop by at dinnertime."

Mrs. Simpson shook her head. "You don't mean to tell me you put your strings right back in your lap with your beans, Mrs. Blevins?"

"You'd learn to take a lot of short cuts if you had more children, Mrs. Simpson."

Mrs. Simpson sighed. "The Lord never saw fit to give me none but Maxine, Mrs. Blevins." She put her strings in the galvanized bucket.

Mrs. Simpson was not one of my favorite neighbors like Mrs. Diggs had been. But Mr. Simpson was, or had been until last week. Sometimes he gave me a penny for nothing, but what happened Wednesday night got me all mixed up. When I was skipping down the street in front of their house just before dark, he called me up to the porch. I thought he was going to give me a penny, but he gave me a nickel and took me by the hand and led me into the living room.

"I've seen some of your art work, and thought maybe you'd like to see some of mine," he said. He was talking about when I was just four and drew pictures of the moon over the ocean and put them under neighbors' doors. I always initialed them CB in the corner. But that was a long time ago. He led me to the back bedroom and got a drawing pad off the closet shelf. He held up a picture of a man, bald like him, in a bathing suit, walking on the beach in front of two girls lying in the sand. The next picture showed him naked as a jaybird, peeing between the girls, and the next one showed him lying between them. One had hold of his peejabber while the other one kissed him on the mouth. They were all naked. In the next picture he was planting a baby seed in one of the girls while the other one watched. All of the pictures had titles printed under them. He said the last one read, "Home, Sweet Home."

My face got hot. "Where's Mrs. Simpson?" I asked.

"Prayer meeting. Can't keep her away from there on Wednesday evening."

He sat down on the bed and pulled me onto his lap, and before I knew it, he had unbuttoned my overalls at the side and slipped his hairy hand between my legs. I jumped down and ran out the door, buttoning my overalls. When I got home, I wondered if it had really happened. Mother was always telling us to stay away from strange men, but she never said anything about staying away from neighbors. She like Mr. Simpson. She told Daddy once, "There's a saint if I ever saw one." So I wondered some more if it had really happened, but the nickel was in my pocket. I decided I'd better not say anything about it. Even Til probably wouldn't believe it. But when I watched Mrs. Simpson string beans, I could still feel Mr. Simpson's cold hand between my legs.

Mrs. Simpson always talked about her bad teeth and the niggers in the alley.

"Those chilrun oughtn't to be allowed to play with those black niggers," she said.

I had heard her say it a hundred times and knew that she was talking about Til and me. She looked over the top of her glasses at Mother.

"Why, I never seen anything like the way them black bucks strut in front of our white girls. I told Maxine to cross the street to keep from meetin one. In ten years half the babies born in this country will be brown. Mark my word, Mrs. Blevins."

Mother threw a handful of beans into the kettle. "You're not telling me a thing, Mrs. Simpson. I worry, heaven knows how much, about raising these four children right here in their shadow. Sometimes I wish to the Lord we'd never moved off of the farm."

Mrs. Simpson said, "It all started with Ham when he laid with the cattle on the ark. They're black because of that sinnin on the ark. That's the only reason. And God made you and me and your chilrun white and He put us right here, and He made them black and put em in Aferka, and He intended for em to stay there. That was their punishment. You don't find many white folks traipsin off to Aferka. Ought to gather ever last one of em up and send em back."

"That might be the answer, Mrs. Simpson, but I doubt it. I worry about what our forefathers did to the Indians. Gathering them up in these mountains where they'd lived for generations and herding them out West like cattle wasn't the answer. And sending the Negroes to Africa is not the answer now. They didn't come from Africa, Mrs. Simpson. It was their forefathers, and they didn't come of their own free will. Our forefathers kidnapped them, they tell me."

Mrs. Simpson gave her empty lap a satisfied look. "I don't know nothin about *that*, Mrs. Blevins. That was 'fore my time. All I know is that we were here before them niggers, and if that Democrat Roos'velt moves into the White House, you can bet your boots they'll be a nigger in there next. And this country will be on a head-long collision course. Have you got a fan, Mrs. Blevins? Cassandra, quit bitin your nails and run inside and get me a fan."

Her face dripped. I walked right in front of her to the edge of the porch and, without aiming at anything in particular, shot a stream of spit between my two front teeth into the petunia bed, then looked right at Mrs. Simpson.

"Daddy said there have always been some in the White House," I told her. "Maids and things like that."

Mother narrowed her eyes at me. "Cassandra, beg Mrs. Simpson's pardon. You've been taught better than to walk right in front of a body like that."

I asked Mother, "Where does Woody go to school?" He was a colored boy that lived up the street and was a year older than Til.

"You'll have to ask him," Mother answered.

"Now, Mrs. Blevins, I wouldn't answer that child thataway," Mrs. Simpson blurted out. "Tell her that he goes to a separate-but-equal school over in nigger town."

"What they don't know won't hurt them," Mother said. "I think the less they know about those things, the better off they are."

I hawked up another mouthful of spit and watered the petunias again. "Why?" I asked. "Why can't we all go to the same school so we can walk together?"

Nobody said anything.

"Give me one good reason," I begged, starting toward the front door. I stopped when Til said, "They can't give you one, because there ain't one to give."

The look Mother gave us both made me run to get the fan. Mrs. Simpson wasn't about to go home. Daddy wondered every little bit who wound her up and when, and sometimes why.

"Have you saw who's a visitin over to the McCormicks, Mrs. Blevins?" She sniggered. "He's brought him a young thing in from the country to keep his books straight. Lets on like it's his niece. Picture takin must be a good bidness spite of the Depression."

"You don't say," Mother answered. "I haven't talked to Mrs. McCormick since Mrs. Diggs passed away. Where in the world does she sleep? That house has two bedrooms. Already bursting at the seams with the four of them."

"About fifteen, I reckon, not even reached the age of consent, and I bet she's keepin more than his books straight. If I was Mrs. McCormick, one of us would get a move on. And if I was Mrs. McCormick, it'd be her. First thing you know she'll be blowed up like a balloon, and they'll let on like they don't know who the pappy is."

I stared hard at Mrs. Simpson and dug my hands into my pockets and walked to the edge of the porch. I spotted a dung beetle in the petunia bed and shot a stream of spit against his hard back. She was talking about my new friend, Jimmie Lou. And Jimmie Lou *was* Mr. McCormick's niece and she *was* doing arithmetic for him and sending out his bills.

Mother picked up the pot and shook the beans down. "Maybe the poor old thing needs relief from him. Why, if he's like Albert Blevins, he's on the verge every night of the world, no matter how many quarts of beans I've put up or how big a wash I've done. He has been more thoughtful about protection lately, though. I told him I didn't feel up to carrying another child, and we can't afford another one anyway. Lets on like he wants another boy, but we've got more now than we can educate. He knows that if he brought in a hussy like that, I'd leave him in a minute. Take these four children and go home. It's the dying truth. Mrs. McCormick never *has* got over having Bobby."

"Ed Simpson knows I wouldn't put up with it. Knows just as sure as the sun rises in the East." Mrs. Simpson laughed and slapped her knees. "I told him a long time ago he could ram that thing in a holler log for all I care. Separate bedrooms is the only answer, Mrs. Blevins."

"We don't have room for that, Mrs. Simpson, and Albert wouldn't put up with that for a minute, even if he did keep me after I refused to obey him when we said our vows. I asked the preacher to leave that part out and he did. I just promised to love and honor him. And I don't have time to do either one, with seven to feed and wash and iron for."

"And them McCormicks think those kids don't know what's goin on. Why, that Bobby knows ever'thing they is to know, and him no older than Cassie there. They ain't nothin on God's green earth he don't know."

"Poor old soul doesn't get any help from him in raising them," Mother said. "Why, Mrs. Simpson, there's not one man in a dozen that appreciates a good woman when he gets her. My mother always told me that. But she never knew about the tears I shed between the corn rows at the Blevins' farm the day after we got married."

Mrs. Simpson pushed her glasses up and rubbed her watery eyes with the back of her hand. "Bless her heart, Mrs. Blevins, Mrs. McCormick's been goin with me ever night to the faith healin in the bottom and leavin them there at the house." She put another handful of beans on the newspaper in her lap. "It chills me to the bone to think what they've been up to. Poor ole thing got the spirit night afore last, and the preacher told her, he said, 'Young lady, put them glasses away. By the grace of the Lord Jesus Christ, you don't need them glasses no more.' She come over the next day to bring me a quart of fresh buttermilk and fell out yonder at the curb," Mrs. Simpson said, pointing down the street. "I said to her, I said, 'Mrs. McCormick, you know you can't see your hand in front of your face without them glasses. Get them glasses off that mantel and back on your nose.'"

The beans finished, Mother and Mrs. Simpson folded the newspapers and laid them on the floor between their chairs. Mother got up. "Would you drink a glass of lemonade if I made it, Mrs. Simpson?"

"No, thank you, Mrs. Blevins. I got to be gettin back down to the house. Like as not, some of Ed's folks will stop by, and if I know them, they'll stop just before dinner. They always expect me to have a tableful of vittles ready. They don't think nothin of droppin by at dinnertime and stayin until after supper. And this ole arthuritis has my ole legs so crippled up I can't hardly get around. Strikes me in the middle of the night sometimes like lightnin."

"I've had some of that lately," Mother said. "I think it's my old teeth. Do you still have your teeth, Mrs. Simpson?"

"No," Mrs. Simpson answered, "I had em took out years ago and got me two plates."

"Why don't you ask Dr. Shaw about it?"

"If I ain't beset by them locusts, I just might come back and see him for a minute," Mrs. Simpson said, putting one foot on the second step. It would be another ten minutes before she got to the bottom.

"Might be a bottle of Sloan's Liniment would give you some relief," Mother said, "or some Cloverleaf Salve."

"Been using that Ben Gay ointment, but it don't seem to help none." Mrs. Simpson wiped her face and neck with her apron. "Come on down and see my new hauled-over vacuum cleaner Ed got me for the anniversary. I never had airy one afore, never did ask for none, but he allowed I needed it since I've got so stove up and all."

"Why, without any children running in and out all day long, I wouldn't think you and Maxine would have to clean house more than once a month," Mother said. "He's one in a hundred if he realizes what it takes to keep a place clean, Mrs. Simpson. Albert's a good man, but he's never paid any attention to anniversaries or birthdays. Why, he doesn't even remember how old the children are! But he never makes light of what I do. My mother always said that man's work is from sun to sun, but woman's work is never done. Albert's work is just like mine, never done."

"Well, now," Mrs. Simpson said, "this was a special one, our twentieth, and he offered to get me some munition blinds, but I wouldn't have them things. Don't see for the life of me how a body keeps all them slats clean, leastways in this town, what with the mill and cement plant and all."

Mother walked to the edge of the porch. "Dr. Shaw will be here any minute. I'd better get a bite on the table."

Mrs. Simpson left just before Dr. Shaw parked his little black roadster in the driveway. He got out and straightened his black bow tie, buttoned his black suit jacket, picked up his little black bag and strutted toward the house. He talked to Mother all the way back to Granny's room.

"Same symptoms, I suppose. Short of breath. No appetite. Irritable. Stubborn. But that's not a symptom. That's a characteristic. Never saw a Blevins yet that wasn't stubborn as a mule, and I've seen many a Blevins."

As soon as Daddy came from the store, he went into Granny's room and closed the door behind him. Mother came out to get dinner ready. She didn't say a word to us about what Dr. Shaw said.

After a long time, Dr. Shaw and Daddy came out quietly, and Dr. Shaw hung his jacket on the back of a kitchen chair, put his glasses in his shirt pocket and rolled up his sleeves.

"Known her forty years, I reckon. Have practiced medicine in this family for three generations. She's the heartiest one of the lot, Albert, but she has about played out." He sat down at the table. "Oatmeal for breakfast and a little warm mush twice a day. Keep her bowels open with epsom salts. I'll stop by again at noon on Friday." He talked between mouthfuls of green beans and buttered biscuits. "Water on the lungs just like before. Makes her short of breath. Not but one thing to do when it gets too bad. Take her over to the clinic and stick a needle in between her ribs and drain it out."

Mother got a banana pudding out of the oven. Til got sassy. "I reckon you ought to get used to eatin rotten bananas when your daddy owns a grocery store."

Mother narrowed her eyes at him, but didn't say a word. He planted his hands in his lap and sat there and sulked while everybody else ate. Dr. Shaw gobbled his pudding and wrote out a prescription. "Spoonful couple times a day, morning and night," he said. "It'll ease her breathing."

He got up to go. "Yessir, I reckon I'm responsible for more babies in this town than any other one man. I can count four right here. That's four out of more than a thousand!"

Mother followed him to the door. "Doctor, I want to ask you about Cassandra. She doesn't seem to be able to control her kidneys sometimes at night."

I didn't hear what else she said. My face got hot. When she came back, she said she had good news.

"I've found out what'll make you quit wetting the bed."

Til hooted. "Double the dose before tonight. She nearly drowned me again last night."

Mother ignored him. "Pumpkin seeds," she said, "just plain old pumpkin seeds. They don't taste bad and don't cost much either. Dr. Shaw said you can eat them just like candy."

FIVE

*G*ranny didn't want any of us kids in her room except Emmy. I didn't care, because since she had got bad off, me and Til didn't even have to go into the house except to eat and sleep.

Ralph helped us build a little shack against the side of the barn in the chicken lot behind the garden. Til dug the furnace, a hole in the ground a little bigger than the milk bucket, right inside the grass-sack door. He put a piece of tin across the top of the furnace for us to cook on, and nailed a big tin Coca-Cola sign behind it to keep the place from burning down when him and Ralph cooked dinner.

Daddy said Ralph was growing like a horseweed and probably had a worm or two in him. Daddy went fishing every little bit with the worms he had cut out of horseweed stalks. Better bait, he said, than earthworms. They were a lot mushier. I wondered where in the world they would be in Ralph. Daddy said Ralph's butt was so flat that it looked like two peanut halves. When Ralph was around Mother and Daddy, he was full of "ma'ams" and "sirs" but when he was around Til and me, he was full of "hells" and "damns."

Mother said over and over, "That shack is an eyesore, Albert. You've got to make Til tear it down. It crowds my chickens, and, besides, Cass is going to get her killing hanging around out there with those two boys."

I expected Daddy to agree with her any night, but he never said a word. Just listened to Lowell Thomas and went to bed. I was sure the shack's days were numbered when Mother asked Til where he got all that lumber. He told her he had bought it with his paper route money and that he was practicing to be a building contractor when he grew up. I knew better. I knew he had stolen those boards two at a time from a lumber yard downtown and had nearly killed himself hauling them home on Ralph's bicycle, which he had rented for marbles. Balanced across the handlebars, the boards had hung out so far that the ends kept hitting trees and telephone poles all the way home. He was afraid to ride in the street, because we lived next door to a policeman, and Til knew that he'd never hear the end of it if he got into trouble with the law.

I sat on my heels and watched him saw a hole in the wall above the furnace. He had picked up an old stove pipe in the junk yard.

"We're gonna eat out here tonight, Satch," he said. "Go ask Mother for some potatoes and sausage and lard and milk. I'll fry the sausage and make gravy, and we'll get some cornbread later." I was on my way when he yelled, "And a fryin pan and three forks." They were getting a fork for me!

Mother even gave us a big tomato and some little green onions out of the garden. When the screen door slammed behind me, she yelled, "How many times do I have to tell you how to let that door go?"

"Got my hands full," I answered.

"And bring back everything you don't eat. You kids would carry off everything I own."

When I got back to the shack, Til and Ralph had a fire going and were sitting on the built-in bunk comparing peejabbers. Ralph shoved his back into his overalls when he saw me, but Til told him to get it out again, and they would see who could pick up the biggest pebble.

Ralph picked up one as big as a steelie and hid it, but Til kept dropping his, even when he pushed the skin over it.

"Shoot," he said. "I read about this fellow over in India that could make a fountain pen out of his. Ever hear of that? Sucked up ink."

Ralph laughed. "Hell, that don't mean he could *write* with it. Just means he peed blue."

"Didn't say. But I bet he *could* if he wanted to. He was some kind of holy man."

I asked Til, "Why don't you get it to suck up some red ink so you can pee red?"

Ralph answered, "We'll have to leave that up to you, but you'll have to get about as old as Maude and Jimmie Lou."

Til crossed his lips with his finger. "Shh. She don't know nothin about that yet."

But I had seen a pair of bloody bloomers on the floor in Maude's closet. And I had seen white rags with blood on them in the corner of the closet in Mother's and Daddy's room. She washed them after she put Daddy's work clothes through the Maytag. Surely, I thought, they didn't pee blood on purpose. I'd just have to wait 'til first grade to find out about that.

Til kneaded his peejabber down his leg. "Girls sure got the short end of the stick when they were givin these things out. It's like theirs got broke off. Show him yours, Satch."

My face got hot, but I pulled my overalls down, just to my knees, and my legs stuck together.

"Sit down there, Satch, and part your legs," Til ordered, pointing to the bunk. "He can't see nothin with you standin up like that."

I let my overalls fall to my ankles and sat down. Til took hold of my knees and spread my legs apart. Ralph squinted between my legs. I held onto the board with both hands and felt sick all over, like I was going to vomit. I wanted to be far away with my overalls bib up around my neck. I saw Ralph every day, but he never had looked at me like that before. I knew they would make fun of me if I cried, so I stared at the grass-sack door and not a tear left my eyes.

Til asked, "Reckon that little thing will ever get big enough?"

"Hell, yeah, they always stretch just big enough." Ralph sounded just like Til, like he knew exactly what he was talking about.

"That ain't the way I heard it," Til said. "I heard Daddy say one time that it's like trying to shove a broom handle through a key hole."

"That's just when it's the first time for the girl," Ralph said.

Til buttoned his overalls fly and put the potatoes in the hot ashes against the coals. The heat that had collected inside the shack all day was sickening, but it made the boards have a woodsy smell.

Til took off his shirt and wiped his face with it, then threw it into the corner. Ralph took his off, too, and I took off my dress. It was much cooler, because my overalls didn't touch me hardly anywhere. Sounds of summer dusk filled the air as the sun sank. The shrill screeching of jarflies promised more dry weather. So did the still, hot air that made everything want to go to sleep, whether it was day or night. When a hot breeze stirred the hydrangea bush in the front yard after dark, neighbors sat in their swings and talked into the night, sometimes even called from porch to porch.

"Have you heard?"..."Why, he was a vet'ran, 102 if he was a day."..."They tell me that he brought it on hisself."..."Don't feed that broody hen no corn."

And on those nights sleep overcame me and Til as we lay on the still, dry grass in the front yard and looked at the stars. We talked about how far away a star is and how long it takes the light to get to our eyes, and he told me the difference between stars and planets. And we talked about where words go after they are said. But that was just when Ralph wasn't around. Til was different then.

Til turned the potatoes over, and we climbed the ladder by Polly's winter stall to the hay loft, swapping the clean smell of the new pine boards for the smell of sweet alfalfa, left from Polly's winter feed.

Ralph found Wimpy in the corner, nursing her four kittens.

"Who'd you wrestle with this time, you ole hussy?" he asked her. "Musta been black."

He teased Til. "How many times has that ole boy had babies?"

"How was I to know he was a she?" Til asked. "Her parts was too little to see. Daddy said we'd have to give her away or make her stay in the barn and mouse. He named her Olive Oil, but that's too long. And she was already named Wimpy.

"Don't touch em," Til yelled. "She'll take em off one by one by the nape of the neck and hide em. Which one do you want this time?"

"They tole me if I drag another damned cat or dog in, they'll throw it in the river with a rock around its neck, and me with it," Ralph answered.

We talked about the circus that was coming to town. Tom Mix and elephants and lions. Til knew all about it.

"It's a little circus. Nothin like Ringlin Brothers. The big ones stay in New York in the summer and Miami in the winter." He picked his teeth with a piece of straw. "Did you hear about the Indian chief that drank 40 cups of tea and drowned in his teepee?" Ralph howled with laughter. I had heard it before.

"Tell him the one about cheese and crackers got all muddy," I said.

"He heard that years ago, about the kid who said, 'Jesus Christ and God Almighty,' and when the teacher asked him what he said, he answered, 'Cheese and crackers got all muddy.' I've got a better one than that." Til shot a stream of spit out the window into the alley below and told me to repeat after him real fast, "Polish it in the corner."

I did and they roared with laughter and pounded their knees with their fists.

Til started singing a new song from the radio about Layena chicken mash. He had changed the words to make it sound like all a hen needed to lay big, brown eggs was to have a rooster in the chicken lot. Ralph and me joined in on the chorus. "They're layin eggs now; they're layin eggs now."

Til said, "Now's a good time for you to help Cass grow. Got a rubber?"

"Never leave home without one," Ralph answered. "Got a brand new one out of my old man's coat pocket this mornin. He keeps fussin about the drug store gyppin him, so I been usin the same one twice on Marcella."

"Don't you use no used one with Satch," Til warned.

"Hell, I don't need to waste one with her," Ralph said. "She's too little."

I ran toward the ladder. "I don't want a baby, not nobody's, not yours or Ralph's. Not nobody's!" I screamed.

Til begged, "Aw, come on, Satch, you ain't gonna get a baby. He's just gonna help you grow a little." Then he said to Ralph. "You'd better wear that rubber just in case."

I watched Ralph churn his peejabber. Til started to do the same thing. "Before long it'll be big enough to hold a rubber all by itself," he bragged. "I won't even have to hold it on with my fingers. It'll fit like a glove."

"Then you can wear one all of the time," I said. "But don't forget to take it off when you have to pee."

"You're so bright I bet your mother has to put you under a bushel basket in the mornin to see if the sun is shinin," Til said.

Suddenly he threw his head back and sniffed. He jumped up and looked through the hole to Polly's stall. "Somethin's on fire down there and it ain't potatoes," he yelled.

He grabbed me up in one arm and jumped through the hole. I felt the heat as we landed. Ralph jumped behind us. Til jerked the grass sacks down and started beating the flames as they crawled above the Coca-Cola sign behind the furnace. I ran outside. The chickens squawked wildly and flew against the garage. Til and Ralph couldn't stop the flames from climbing onto the roof of the shack toward the barn. The pine popped and cracked, and the tar paper on the roof curled up under the stinky, black smoke. I listened to the sizzling sound and when the odor came, I vomited. Gasping for breath, I covered my eyes with my hands and crept as close to Til as I could. Black streaks of sweat rolled from his hair across his face and down his neck. I was looking for Ralph, but couldn't find him. I screamed his name, and Til got short with me.

"If you can't help, get out of the way. You'll get hurt and I'll get the blame. Ralph's all right," he gasped. "He's on the other side."

I sat down against the garage and hugged my knees. I remembered how many weeks Emmy had had to wear a white bandage on her hand when she burned it to a crisp one day last winter. Granny had pulled the lid down to poke the fire in the cookstove and Emmy leaned out from her lap to pick up a "pretty" out of the firebox. I buried my face in my knees, and my overalls soaked up the hot tears. I knew me and Til would get a whipping we'd never forget. There wasn't any way to hide a fire. I wished Daddy would come to the door. He would know how to put the fire out.

I heard a siren, and it was getting louder. The fire truck came up the street and stopped in front of the house. We waited for the firemen to come running through the garden with a big hose, but they didn't come. The truck started up again and rolled away. The only help that came ran down the alley. It was Woodrow, one of the nigger neighbors Mrs. Simpson didn't want us playing with. He got there just as what was left of the shack fell to the ground in a heap of flames and smoke.

Til handed him an old broom, and together they ran toward the fire on the ground, choking and coughing. Woody knew exactly what to do. Holding the broom with both hands, he pounded the burning pieces of wood and tarpaper. Sparks flew like fireflies. Til filled Polly's watering pail from the spigot on the side of the house, and poured water where Woody pounded. They took turns until the fire finally went out.

The fire hadn't liked the barn wood; it had taken just a few bites out of a few boards. Nothing had happened to the barn roof because the shack wasn't that high; its roof had met the barn just below the hay loft.

Til and Ralph and Woody, their eyebrows singed and their faces streaked with soot, lay on their backs in the grass. Wiping my face with a dirty grass sack, I sat down beside them.

"Woody, you know what you ought to be when you grow up? You ought to be a fireman. You didn't get half as black as Til and Ralph did."

Nobody laughed. Woody was looking at something beyond the barn.

"Not me, Cass," he said. "I'm going to be a doctor. If I hadn't seen the smoke, I wouldn't have stopped. I've got to tell you Momma said she doesn't want me to hang around Til and Ralph no more. She said they talk too rough and won't amount to nothing less they get some manners."

Daddy came out the back door. He shook his head and jerked Til to his feet; he shook him good by his shoulders.

"I can't believe my eyes. You really are out of something to do, ain't you? I'm gonna get you a patch of corn to hoe if it's the last thing I do. And they's one thing for sure. I'm gonna bust the rind on you tonight."

Me and Woody and Ralph got to our feet slowly.

Daddy walked around the end of the barn, talking the whole time loud enough for us to hear. "You're lucky the whole derned thing didn't go up. You're lucky they wasn't a wind. Why didn't you come and get me? Who in Sam Hill called the fire department? I told that fireman they wasn't no fire at this address."

Daddy walked back toward us. The four of us stared at the ground around our black feet. His voice sounded mad. "Son, how long do you think it will take you to clean up that mess and replace them burnt boards in the barn? It'll take at least three months for you to pay for it deliverin papers." He picked up a charred board and threw it down.

"It's high time you two boys went on home to dinner," he told Ralph and Woodrow.

Til walked over to Woody and held out his hand. "Thanks, Woody," was all he said.

"You're welcome," Woody muttered, shaking Til's hand. "See you."

"Woody saved the barn, Daddy," I blurted out. "He wasn't even here when the fire started. Just me and Til and Ralph. And we were in the loft looking at Wimp's kittens when Til smelled it. Til saved me. He jumped through the hole with me in his arms."

Woody ambled down the driveway, dusting his overalls off as he walked. Ralph followed without saying a word to anybody. He almost waved, but seemed to change his mind.

Mother came out the back door, wringing her hands in her apron. "Lord have mercy, what's happened now?"

"Nothin, Clary, nothin at all. Your son here just tried to burn the barn down, but they wasn't no wind to help him. Derned lucky," Daddy said.

"I took some tomatoes down to Mrs. Simpson and didn't know one thing about it until I came home and smelled smoke."

On her way back to the house, Mother called, "Cassie, I've told you time and time again that you'll get your killing hanging around those boys. You'd better come with me."

Til looked like he was playing statue. He just stood there, staring at the ground with his hands in his pockets.

Daddy muttered. "You two had better get at your chores. Til, lime that henhouse and give those hens some grit before you get washed up to milk."

I overheard Mother and Daddy talking in the kitchen while I was in the bathtub after supper, and it not even Saturday. Mother said, "That fire did one good thing, Albert. It got rid of that eyesore in the back yard and gave the chickens all of their lot back." Then she added loudly to be sure I would hear, "I hope it put the fear of the Lord into those two. They are making me old before my time."

Daddy didn't get a chance to get a word in edgeways. Mother kept on. "Don't you think it's high time to separate those two some? Cass ought to be spending more time with girls. It would be worth a lot more to her to be with Maude more and maybe learn how to sew. Maude's making most of her own clothes now. Did you know that? I don't want Cass to be a roughneck. There's not a one in my family."

Daddy didn't answer.

After me and Til had gone to bed, the light came on and I watched Daddy walk to Til's side of the bed with the razor strap doubled in his hand.

Til was stretched out in his peejays on his stomach on the edge of the bed. I was on my stomach on the other side.

"If you think this is gonna be a birthday paddlin, you've got another thought comin," he said. The strap struck Til's legs above the knees again and again. Til grew rigid and shook the bed with his quiet sobs.

Mother stood in the doorway, crying. "That's enough, Albert. You don't want to draw blood. He didn't do it on purpose. If he had *set* the shack on fire, it would be a different matter."

Daddy didn't stop. I hid my hands in my face and cried, tasting the salty tears that ran down my cheeks. Mother said quietly, "Stop now. It's time to go to bed."

Daddy let the strap fall to his side. "You think it don't hurt me?" he asked quietly. "Cassandry, go in there and get in bed with Maude and quit your blubberin. You're lucky you ain't got a real reason to cry. Could have got your killin out there today."

I snuggled up to Maude. She put her arm around me and held me against her. She said that's what lovers do. They call it "spooning" when two people fit together in bed like teaspoons. She didn't say a word about the trouble me and Til had been in.

I stared into the dark and listened a long time. The night was warm and still except for a catbird's squawk now and then and the whirring of the machinery at the cotton mill.

I never expected Maude to be so soft and warm or to hold me that tight. She was always mopping the kitchen or clerking at the B&B or studying. She never had time to talk to anybody but Mother or Maxine. Maybe one night I would tell her about Mr. Simpson and Til and Ralph. I wondered if it had ever happened to her and if she had ever told anybody.

Suddenly, it got quiet except for Maude's breathing. The machinery in the village was finished for the night and the birds had all gone to bed. I stared into the dark a long time.

Six

*I*n a few days Granny was up and a-round again, still short of breath and patience. One day as soon as Daddy went back to the B&B after dinner, she put on her good black dress and her black cut-glass beads and muttered that she was going up to visit Birdie a day or two.

"Meant to go afore that sick spell struck me down. Been puttin it off for weeks, so you might as well not contrary me none."

She put a towel, a clean shimmy shirt and a flannel nightgown in her valise.

Birdie was Granny's baby girl and Daddy's baby sister who lived just two blocks up the street, but we never saw her. Granny didn't either unless she went up there. Everybody knew she would be back before dark, because Aunt Birdie wouldn't keep her when it got close to suppertime. Granny and Uncle Jay, the one that got mustard on his face in the war, never had got along. Granny thought he was a roughneck. And Aunt Birdie said she plain didn't know what to do with Granny when they had company.

"Jay wants to play cards almost every night of the week," she said, "and that leaves Granny without anything to do."

Daddy said they moved with a pretty fast crowd and called his little sister the highest stepper in the family.

Granny stomped through the house, swinging her cane and sucking her sweet-gum snuff stick. She turned around at the front door.

"While I'm gone, Clary, you can make Albert a cherry cobbler. I heard him ask about a cobbler just last night and all he got from you was complainin. The very idea of not meetin that man's needs and wants and him out workin his hands to the bone ever day for you and this bunch of fittified younguns. All the asafetidy in the world won't cure em." She slammed her cane against the floor. "They don't get their ways from this side of the house. Ain't a drop of fittified blood in no Blevins to my knowance. You do a heap more complainin with them three upstarts than I did with a dozen. Emmy's the only good one to come out of you. I raised twelve. Stood to the rack many a day, hay or no hay."

Mother acted like she didn't hear. She called it a "Blevins fit" when Daddy wasn't around.

Granny slammed her cane against the floor again. "Wish somebody would tell me what it was he married you for. Couldn't forget seein your bloomers hangin down to your knees in the church yard, I reckon. Ever'body saw em. Couldn't stand it till he got back here from Californy where he was making good money and got hisself tied down to you and this bunch of younguns."

The door slammed, and Granny's three feet hit the porch. Emmy leaned against Mother's knee to cry a while. Her best friend was gone. Mother kept seeding cherries.

Til yelled, "Good riddance!"

Maude said, "I wouldn't put up with it for a minute. Why does she have to stay *here* all of the time? You'd think Daddy was her only child."

I liked to hear Maude talk that way, especially since I had been sleeping with her. I liked her better every day. And she said last night that when we got time, we'd make some peanut butter cookies and divinity.

Mother put the colander of cherries in the sink and put the seeds in the garbage can. "You kids shouldn't talk about your daddy's mother that way," she said. "Blood runs thicker than water."

I sauntered out the back door and skipped down the street. Mid-afternoon was as hot as early morning had promised it would be. Birds hadn't sung between the middle of the morning and late afternoon for several days. June bugs had quit stirring soon after breakfast. Nothing moved that didn't have to. Tar oozed up between the cracks in the sidewalk. I rolled a little ball of it down the seam with my big toe. It was all right as long as you didn't step on a seam in a sidewalk; that's what brought bad luck.

Any more I didn't even knock when I went off down to McCormicks on Thursday afternoons. That was when old man McCormick took Mrs. McCormick and the children to the country to visit his mother. That was when Jimmie Lou did the arithmetic and bills.

Jimmie Lou had told me why she never went with them to visit her folks. "The Mrs. has an ornery streak in her as wide as a striped garden snake. She thinks I got my eye on him, and him my uncle. She ain't said nothin to me about it. She don't need to. I can tell by the way she watches us at the supper table. They ain't a thing to it, I swear to God. Course, I can't speak for nobody but myself."

I knew she was telling the truth. Jimmie Lou had shown me a little brown picture the size of a postage stamp with "School Days, 1932" printed on the bottom.

"My curly headed baby," she said, "name of Joseph Parris, Junior. His daddy named ever last one of the twelve younguns out of the Bible, all beginnin with J. He thinks he's earnin hisself a one-way ticket to heaven. How would you like to be a baby named Judas? Thank goodness, Joseph was one of the first ones."

Then she showed me pictures of her mother and daddy and six brothers and sisters. "The baby, Ron, there, he ain't quite right in the head, but a sweeter child God never made."

She looked at Joseph's picture again. "Ain't he handsome, honey? Quit tenth grade in the spring and got hisself a job, tailin the saw down at the mill. First thing I know he up and bought hisself a jalopy. Come up home one day and broke me down like a shotgun by the sink and bearded me in front of God and ever'-body. Just ruint my complexion. Asked daddy could he marry me, and daddy said abolutely not, not till he had a hunderd dollars in the clear."

I had to go to McCormick's every week to find out how much money Joe had saved and how much longer Jimmie Lou would be there. I was glad his jalopy wasn't parked in front. I held the screen door to keep it from slamming and walked down the dark hallway. Jimmie Lou was lying in her petticoat on the day bed they had moved into the office for her. Her petticoat had a lace ruffle around the bottom as wide as Daddy's hatband, and smelled like cinnamon. Mother's petticoat didn't have lace on it anywhere and smelled like moth balls.

Jimmie Lou invited me to sit in the big swivel chair in front of the old desk that was cluttered with envelopes and negatives.

"Saved you some more film spools this week, honey. Don't forget to take em home with you," she said.

She had the whitest skin I had ever seen, and the blackest hair.

"Hot enough for you, honey?" she asked, fanning with a newspaper. "It's already hotter than a firecracker on the Fourth, and it not even the end of June. Them figures got jumbled up in my head, and I had to take me a little nap. Never did catch on to figures too good, even in the tenth. That's what I finished up with last month before he come and told daddy I could help him. Daddy allowed it was time I quit school and amounted to somethin. But I've a good mind to go back to school in September when you go, if Joe don't get that hunderd ahead by then. He didn't have but thirty-eight saved of a Friday, and it already three months since he asked me to marry him." She swatted a fly with a rolled-up newspaper.

I looked at the paper full of figures on the desk. "It still don't make sense. Explain it again, about how you multiply what one picture costs by the number of pictures a customer wants. I understand it when I'm here with you, but when I get home, I don't understand at all."

"Honey, it's easy. They're called prints when it's more than one copy of a picture." She took a negative out of the envelope and held it up to the light. "Let's say a feller wants six prints of this picture." She squinted at the negative. "That's them triflin Fletchers. Now, say they want six prints of this at a dime a print." She leaned over my shoulder and wrote down 6X10. She put the end of the pencil back in her mouth. "If you write down ten six times in a stack and add it up, what do you come up with?" She added out loud, pointing from one ten to the other with the pencil, and wrote down sixty cents. Then she went back to the top of the page where she had written 6X10 and added = 60. "Now, that's the sum total of what old man Fletcher would owe. That's the way you'll do it when you learn your multiplication tables, but that's higher math, and you don't have to worry your perty head about it for a couple more years."

She wet the end of the pencil again with her tongue and wrote down another stack of ten's. "Look at it like this. Say old man Fletcher wants six loaves of salt risin bread for the church picnic and each one costs a dime. He would owe your daddy sixty cents."

"How long did it take you to learn how to do it?"

"Smart as you are, honey, it won't be no time before you can take over your daddy's books."

I picked up a pencil and an order blank. "Show me how to do it on a real one. After September, I can help you do it all."

"Is your momma sure you're supposed to go to school in September? You ain't as big as a nickel, Cassie. Reckon they could of got you mixed up with another kid at the hospital?" Jimmie Lou laughed.

"None of us was born at the hospital. All born at home," I answered. "So I reckon I'm me, and I'm going on six."

"What are you gonna be when you grow up, Cassie?" she asked. Nobody had ever asked me that before. I squirmed in the big chair and pushed myself around and around, shoving the desk with my dirty, bare feet.

"Might be a missionary and save all the heathens in Africa," I said. "This preacher said last Sunday that they parboil girl babies and eat them. What does parboil mean?"

"That means they just barely cook em."

"Mother said it ain't true, and she didn't see why he wanted to talk that way in front of us. Daddy said he didn't know how she would go about proving it one way or the other, that the preacher had been there and she hadn't." I slid in beside Jimmie Lou on the dresser stool. "I might quit school when I'm sixteen like you. Til says I can."

"Don't go gettin too big for your britches. You got a lot to learn, honey. To my way of thinkin, we all need at least twelve year of learnin, and you, specially, little as you're gonna be. My friends that quit school at sixteen don't waste no time addin to this country's poor white trash. Next thing you know after they quit school, they have one crawlin on their floor, one bawlin on their hip, and one kickin in their belly. Me and Joe, we don't aim to have no kids for a while. Aim to take us a trip to Californy in his jalopy." She pulled a freshly-ironed cotton dress over her head and buttoned up the front. "Don't want no white-trash babies trailin after me. When that Fletcher bunch come over here last week to get their picture took, my uncle couldn't even get em all in the finder. I thought we'd have to knock a wall out, but he finally took the tripod out in the hall and managed. Cut off one kid's arm at that. I'd thin that bunch out like a patch of early corn if they was mine. Give em all a nickel and tell em to go play in heavy traffic."

I wanted to talk to her about other things. I wanted to know if a baby seed sprouted every time a peejabber exploded inside you, and had she ever bled in her bloomers and did it hurt and what caused it, and if the Virgin Mary was really a virgin like me, how did Baby Jesus get inside her, and then how did He get out, and why did Mr. Simpson show me those pictures and touch me, and why did Mrs. Simpson hate Woody, and why didn't he go to the same school as Til, and why did they have one fountain marked WHITES down at the S.H. Kress Store and one marked COLORED right beside it, only a little lower? They were on a brown marble wall.

"Guess what, Jimmie Lou, I didn't wake up black at all," I blurted out.

"What are you talkin about, Cass?" Jimmie Lou asked, polishing her nails with a little eye-shaped brush that looked like velvet. Aunt Flossie was the only other person I ever saw polish their nails. She said it made them shine and brought out the half moons.

"I just mean I didn't turn black like Daddy said I would if I got a drink of water out of that fountain that says 'colored' down at the five-and-ten-cent store."

Jimmie Lou laughed.

"How do you know you won't turn black?" she asked. "How long ago did you do it?"

"Saturday night, three days ago," I answered. "I expected to wake up black on Sunday morning. Didn't though. Nobody knows I did it. Not even Til. I just got me one good swallow. Didn't taste any different."

"It's the same water, darlin. The fountain for whites has a pipe that runs a little higher, but the water comes from the very same place. Just another way for us to tell em that we're better than they are. But drinkin clear water don't have nothin to do with your color. If it did, don't you reckon they would all be drinkin out of the one marked 'whites'?"

I never had thought of it that way.

"Sure," I said, "if I was black like Woody. If Woody was white, I bet Daddy would have thanked him for helping Til put out the fire instead of telling him to go on home. Maybe he would have even asked him to stay for supper." I thought of Sadie and Joe.

"Do you know Sadie?" I asked.

"Is her husband the junk man?" Jimmie Lou asked. I nodded.

"Sweet ole feller," Jimmie Lou said. "But I don't know em personally."

"If I was Sadie, I probably would go on drinking out of the 'colored' fountain," I said. "Wouldn't it be hard to change colors at her age? You know what I mean," I said.

"You'll hear that foolishness the rest of your life," Jimmie Lou said, "but don't let it get you confused. That means mixed up. Why, Daddy says us white folks were born first and that makes us better. Pure, he says. No other color is as good in the sight of God, he says. Black is the worst, the last He made, Daddy says."

Her black eyes softened and she took my hands in hers. "Don't listen to it, darlin. Nothin to it. It don't make no sense. Don't stop lovin Sadie and Woody. Don't stop playin with Woody. You won't feel right in your heart, and if you don't feel right in your heart, you won't feel right nowhere."

I watched in the mirror while Jimmie Lou brushed her hair. It fell down to her shoulders. She looked at me in the mirror. "Cassie, when's your momma gonna let your hair grow out? I'd wash it and iron it for you."

I laughed. "Iron it?" I didn't tell her that Mother had already laid down the law about letting it grow out before school started.

She held my chin in her hand and parted my hair. "Honey, it would be really perty if you'd let it grow out," she said. Her hand felt strong, but was soft and smooth.

"Don't slick it down, honey, like a boy's. It looks softer without all that water on it. If you don't let it grow out, how is the teacher gonna know which wash room to send you to?"

"If I let it grow out and wear overalls, will she know?"

"Honey, you might not want to wear overalls. Little girls wear dresses, you know. And when I say 'iron it', I just mean put it up on kid curlers at night so it will be bent a little in the morning," she said, laughing.

"You mean I have to sleep in them things like Maudie does?" I asked.

"Sure, honey. You're gonna be the pertiest girl in the first grade."

I thought of my flat nose and felt my face get hot. "I'd better be getting on home," I said.

Jimmie Lou didn't answer. She just picked up the mirror and looked at the back of her head and laughed. "It always looks like it's been combed with an egg beater, no matter how long I brush it."

I didn't know what she meant. "Never heard of anybody combing their hair with an egg beater," I said. "Let's see you do it."

"Just teasin again, Cass," she said. "But it's so long I can't do a thing with it, specially right after I warsh it."

She cocked her head to look at the back of the other side. "Don't ever let your hair get this long, honey. Daddy says long hair is a woman's crownin glory, a symbol of her purity. He won't let me cut it off. Momma's is so long it's hardly ever dry, and she warshes it just oncet a week. I warsh mine twice and I swan it takes half a day to dry."

She picked up the blue glass atomizer and put a squirt behind each ear. "And what do you want to smell like today, honey?"

"You," I answered, softly.

"Evenin in Paris? Joseph gave it to me for Christmas." She put two quick squirts behind my ears. It felt cool running down my neck.

"I never heard of that kind," I said. "Maude got her some Radio Girl, but she won't let me touch it."

"This here is better than Radio Girl, honey. Cost him a perty penny, but I like good stuff and he knows it." She put on her tennis shoes. "Come on. Let's go get us a sno-jo."

"I don't have no money," I said.

Jimmie Lou took a dime out of the tray on her dresser and grabbed my hand.

I felt uneasy when we crossed the highway that ran in front of the B&B, because I knew I'd get a whipping if Daddy saw us, even with Jimmie Lou holding my hand. When we got inside the drug store, I felt safe. I felt a hundred miles from home, even if Daddy was on the other side of the wall.

Jimmie Lou rolled the dime down the counter to Mr. Ball. "Fill er up," she called, and lifted me up on a stool.

"It wouldn't take much, would it? Mr. Ball's brown eyes twinkled. "What'll it be?"

"Two sno-jos, please, pineapple." I watched him fill the glasses with ice chips, then shoot the flavoring in.

Jimmie Lou slid off the stool to look at the little bottles of perfume in the counter. "I can't get this kid off my hip, Mr. Ball. All the time interferin with my work." She winked at me. "Reckon if I was to stuff a wad of cotton in the screen door she'd go away?"

"Might be," he answered. "She ain't much bigger than a fly."

I felt relieved when we got back across the highway without anybody coming out of the B&B. She asked me for my hopscotch rock and jumped in and out of somebody's old squares in front of the McCormicks' house.

We skipped to the front door. "Come on in," she said. "I'll teach you another thing or two about figures you'll need to know if you're gonna be my assistant."

"I better get home."

"Aw, them McCormicks won't be home for another hour or two. Separatin him from his old lady is like separatin a suckin calf from its momma."

I dug my hands into my pockets. "Tell me when ten minutes is up."

The screen door slammed behind us, and we went into the office and sat down on her bed. She took off her tennis shoes and rubbed her feet. "Shoes will be the death of me yet," she moaned. "If tennis shoes make my feet ache like this, what kind of shoes do you reckon I could wear?" she asked. "Some people are born with good feet, but me, I got knots.

"Did you know we weren't meant to wear shoes, Cass? And walk standin up? We were made in the beginnin with four legs and four feet, and who do you reckon got the idea for us to be above animals? Daddy says it comes from the first chapter of Genesis where it says that God gave man *dominion* over the fish and fowl and cattle. That means the same as *own*. Reckon that's why we have to stand up? To *rule over?*"

"Is that what Daddy means when he talks about pecking order?"

"I don't know, Cassie. This stuff is too deep for me. When you go to school, maybe you'll find out and tell me all about it." She pulled her dress above her knees. "Ever seen anything like them kneecaps? Just like jar lids. Don't know whether I inherited that or whether it's from walkin on two instead of all four."

We both laughed. Her skin was white and pretty, even above her knees. She took my hand. "Want to see my jewels again?" she asked.

I tried to pull away when she looked at my hands. "What in tarnation are you doin with all them lie spots on your nails, honey? They tell me them little white spots come from tellin lies."

I clouded up to cry. "I don't remember telling a story," I said. "I just didn't tell the truth." I thought about the barn fire and the boards in the shack.

Jimmie Lou put her arm around me and pulled me close and held me there and rocked back and forth. She was even softer than Maude. "Aw, honey, I was just teasin again. Can't be nothin to that. Ever heard of an old wife's tale? Why, them spots comes from hard work."

She pushed my cuticle back until it hurt. "We'll take better care of them nails when you stop bitin em and shootin marbles. I've always heard that people is judged by their hands and their heels."

She opened the little wooden glove box with two pink roses painted on top and took out a silver bracelet and a pair of rhinestone earrings and put them on me."

"Presenting Miss Cassandra Blevins!" She announced my name like we were in a big room full of people in a castle. Then she whispered in my ear, "Curtsy to the queen, honey."

I bowed from the waist. I had seen Til do it at his violin recital.

"No, honey, not like that. Boys do it that way, but girls don't. Looky here." Jimmie Lou put one foot behind the other and held her skirt out on both sides as she went down, covering her feet. She bobbed up and down several times. "Nothin to it. Come on. I seen Maureen O'Hara do it in a picture show."

I stepped out beside her on the worn linoleum and took her hand. When I got my feet fixed like hers, I took hold of the seam in my overalls and went down, shaking. The boys' way was a lot easier.

I could still feel the softness of Jimmie Lou's hand on my face as I ran up the street. I liked Evening in Paris until Til smelled it.

"Wash your hands in skunk pee?" he asked.

"No, Evening in Paris," I bragged.

"Midnight in Hong Kong if you asked me, and you would of got a whippin if I'd told Mother where you were. But I didn't let on. Pretended to look all up and down the street. Reckon you owe me a couple of marbles for that." He took two out of my fruit jar.

"If you knew where I was, why didn't you come and get me?" I asked.

"Look, there's just one place you could go and come home smellin like that, and I wouldn't want nobody to catch me goin in down there. They got words for girls like her." He sniffed again and made a face. "Reckon you won't be goin with me to milk ole Pol tonight."

"What's that got to do with it?"

"Tell you what. You can go for two more marbles, but I get to pick em." He picked two more marbles out of my fruit jar, and said, "But you'll have to steer clear of Pol. She's liable to kick the bucket over if she gets a whiff of that stuff."

The sun had long since dried up the mud in the cow bottom, so Polly was easy to get. After Til gave me another milking lesson, we carried the heavy bucket up the hill between us. He shouted, " 'Red sky at night, sailor's delight,' " then added in a low threatening voice, " 'Red sky in the morning, sailor's warning.' " He didn't even say a cross word when I let my side of the bucket drop so I could poke a blade of grass at a praying mantis, who unfolded his long front legs and twisted his knobby head around to stare at me with green eyes that looked like big beads.

"What do you reckon he's praying for?" I asked Til.

"Probably for you to go on off and leave him alone," Til answered, and walked ahead with the milk to talk to Sadie, who was standing outside her tar paper shack.

"Hurry up," he called. "Sadie's got us some applesauce cake."

Opening the door to the one-room shack was like opening a big oven. Hot apples and cinnamon and brown sugar smelled a lot better than Evening in Paris. The old cookstove and a porcelain-top table and two chairs stood on a scrap of faded, cracked linoleum in one end of the room. A bed sagged under a naked light bulb in the other end. A rickety table against the wall held a white pitcher and wash bowl rimmed in gold here and there. The wall, covered with old newspapers, held a jagged plank which told Sadie and Joe to "Prepare to Meet God." Sadie had read it to me a long time ago.

Sadie jingled some loose coins in her pocket as she walked toward the table with a knife to cut the cake. "Told me a fortune this here afternoon," she said. "A banker. Been comin reg'lar of late. Got hisself a worried mind, all right." She cut big slices of cake for me and Til and a little one for herself.

"Sadie's gettin too fat," she teased. "Want a little milk with it? Make it better, even if it be warm." She lifted the bucket and poured two little jelly glasses full. "Little tads like you needs lots of milk to go to school."

Til pointed to the bucket. "Pour you and Joe out some. Ole Pol don't slack off none, even in hot weather."

Sadie looked at him, standing there at the table, cramming cake into his mouth. She walked over and put her arms around his neck and brushed his forehead with a kiss. Til held her tight around the waist.

Sadie poured some milk into an old pitcher. "Reckon that dent won't hurt it none. Dropped my good alumi'um pitcher the other day and can't get Joe to fix it. Can't get my man to do nothin round here no more, seem like. Act like he don't feel good, but he don't complain none. Just get up early and hitch hisself to that ole cart and go all day long, collectin junk." She nodded toward the cornbread on the stove. "I waits for him ever night to eat, and ever night dark come 'fore he do."

I spotted Sadie's coffee cup on the stove. "Tell my fortune, Sadie. Please tell my fortune."

Sadie laughed out loud and slapped her knees. "Little tyke like you don't need their cup read, don't need to know what tomorrow hold. Can't hold nothin but good for a good chile." She poured a few drops of water from the teakettle into the cup and swirled it around and around and held it close to her eyes. Finally, she began to talk slowly.

"Well, now, all right, let me see, lamb. Them grounds say you is made a new friend that give you perfume and riches untold."

My face got hot. Til laughed. I wanted to ask her if Jimmie Lou would really marry Joe, but asked, "What will school be like?"

"All right, the question ain't what will school be like. The question be will you like school." Sadie laughed and swirled the grounds again. "Honey, the grounds say you'll take to school like a bee take to clover. Don't you worry none."

"I get three questions?"

"All right." Sadie laughed. "That be two."

"Aw, Sadie, that don't count as two. Just one."

"What else you want to know, lamb?"

I cleared my throat and blurted out, "Why do I have to let my hair grow out for first grade?"

"All right, now, that a question? I don't have to look in no grounds to answer that. They ain't no law nowhere, I reckon that say you *got* to let your hair grow out. But it do say in the Bible, lamb, that if a woman have long hair, it be a glory to her. It a knowed fact that long hair make a girl pertier, all right, and if she be pertier, she be happier."

Til squirmed. "Why didn't you ask me that and save one? Do I get to go to the circus, Sadie?"

Sadie swirled the grounds again and looked into the bottom. She squinted her eyes and frowned. "Yes, you go all right, but they be trouble in them grounds. Can't tell what kind of trouble it be, can't make no head nor tail of it, but they be trouble, all right."

"Runaway horses?" Til galloped around the table, slapping his hand against his hip.

"Can't rightly say. Can't say what the trouble be, all right, but them grounds be muddy." She set the cup back on the stove. "Better run along home now, lambs, or they'll be out lookin for you."

Me and Til got home at dinner time. Granny was back. I could hear sounds of "Home, Sweet Home" through her bedroom door. I knew she had taken Em and Mother's music box into her bedroom. I knew, too, that Granny had stopped by Leeper's for a nickel's worth of cinnamon hearts. She always did when she came home from Aunt Birdie's, but she never took me in her room to hear the music or eat the candy. Granny said Em was the smartest one in the whole family, smart enough not to have to go to school, ever. Em could stay home with her and learn all she'd ever need to know and more.

Mother strained the milk. "Polly's falling off a little. Seems like there's nearly half a gallon less than there was this morning. Sign of hot weather."

SEVEN

*D*addy always left us some jobs to do when he went to the B&B. "Now, Tilghman, remember what I said," he warned. "I'll wear you out when I get home if you put Cassandry to choppin that wood. She can rick the kindlin, but don't let her go near that hatchet. I just sharpened it. And *you* be careful of your feet and legs. And don't dawdle with your mind on other things. If you do, you're liable to hurt yourself."

Chopping wood wore my birthstone ring in two in no time, and I ran into the kitchen crying, to show it to Maude. She wrung out the mop and shook it at me.

"You track through here and you really will have something to cry about." She sloshed the mop around in the bucket of suds, wrung it out again and slapped it against the faded flowers on the linoleum.

"That was fourteen-karat gold. Genuine sapphire. See if Santy Claus brings you another one," she said, pushing me closer and closer to the back door with the mop. "If it's sympathy you're looking for, I don't have time right now. But let me tell you one thing for sure. Mother's right. If you don't quit hanging around Til and Ralph, you'll never live to be grown."

Like my locket with the pictures of Mother and Daddy, I never took that ring off, even to sleep or take a bath. I squeezed the two ends together and handed it to Maude. "Help me to find something to glue it together with."

Maude looked at it and handed it back. "Mop water won't do it, Cass. Take it out there to Mr. Thomas A. Edison and see if he has any bright ideas. He happens to be the one that caused it to break."

I didn't tell Maude, but I knew Santa Claus did *not* bring me that ring. Til showed it to me in Mother's sewing box at Thanksgiving and dared me to say anything about it. And he told me I might as well quit getting Mother to write to the North Pole because there wasn't even a post office up there, much less Santa Claus. Nothing but icebergs and penguins. His geography book said so. Til said he could predict the future better than Sadie, and he didn't need any coffee cup or crystal ball or anything. He even knew where that ring came from and how much it cost. Page 246 in the Sears Roebuck catalog: "Ten-karat gold, dainty oval-cut s-y-n-t-h-e-t-i-c sapphire. $2.95." Then he looked up "synthetic" in the dictionary and told me it meant fake, not worth diddley squat.

I ran out the back door to the corn patch. Til leaned on the hoe and shook his head.

"Now's as good a time as any to learn that you don't chop wood with a ring on. You could still get a good case of blood poisonin if it didn't bleed enough where it scratched your finger." He held the ring up and looked at it closely, "Nothin to that. I can fix it in no time with Dad's solderin iron."

"Now?" I stopped crying.

"Keep your shirt on." He handed the ring back and I slipped it on my finger. "I've got three more rows of corn to hoe."

"When?"

"Take it easy," he said. "I'll fix it for you."

He loosened the dirt around the last stalk of corn about the time Daddy got home from the B&B. Daddy hadn't been in the house more than ten minutes when Mother gasped that not a breath of air was stirring and that she felt like a cooped-up dominecker hen.

Daddy hiked up her dress tail with his foot. "Now, Clary, don't fly the coop yet. We'll crank up the car and go to the circus tomorrow."

At the supper table I kept looking at my ring in my lap, and twisting it off and on.

Mother asked, "What's wrong with your hand, Cass?"

"Nothing. Why?" I put the ring on, then held both hands above the table and turned them around.

"Let me look at it," Mother said. "If you've hurt it, I'd better put some Cloverleaf Salve on it. It might get infected."

"It ain't hurt."

"Then what's the matter? Bite your nails to the quick again?"

Til talked fast. "Boy, that corn is really growin. Some has got silks already."

I began to cry, and blurted out, "Broke my ring in two."

Daddy asked to see it. He didn't say a word for a minute, then asked, "How in the world did a thing like this happen?"

"Just broke," I answered.

"You mean to sit there and tell me you don't know what made it come in two? You wasn't choppin wood by any chance? It just broke of its own accord?"

"Can you fix it?"

"Could of hired a man to come in here and do that little bit of choppin cheaper than it will be to get this fixed. Have to take it to the jeweler and get it soldered with gold."

"How much will it cost?"

"Don't have no idea, but can't you ever learn that you'll stay in trouble as long as you mess round with Til?" He pushed his chair back and unbuckled his belt. That was always the first sign that somebody was going to get a whipping.

"Tilghman, when I leave you a little job of work to do, I mean for you, and not your little sister, to do it. You're goin to start mindin me, and I don't mean maybe. I ought to bust the rind on you, taking advantage of her like that, and her not even old enough for school yet. She could of cut her finger off, or her foot, for that matter."

Til finally looked up. "She didn't do nothin she didn't want to do."

Mother sighed. "*Anything*, Tilghman, didn't do *anything*. Didn't do nothing is a double negative."

Daddy buckled his belt. "Son, in a few short years you'll be a man. And it's up to us men to take care of the womenfolks. Diff-'rence between a boy and a man is his attitude toward womenfolks. Real men don't take advantage of womenfolks in no way. Womenfolks rock the cradle of civilization. Your mother rocked your cradle, and some day you'll find the woman you want to rock your son's cradle. It's nothin to take lightly, son. It's what makes the world go round."

Everybody was quiet. Daddy usually didn't even try to get a word in edgeways at the table. He usually just ate and told us what jobs he expected us to do and then went into the bedroom to hear Lowell Thomas or back to the B&B or to bed.

But this time he kept on talking. "Can you imagine me lettin your mother do my work? It's nat'ral for her to take care of you children and the house and put the meals on the table. It's up to me to provide the house and somethin to eat three times a day. That's the nat'ral order of things."

Til interrupted. "Cass don't do nothin she don't want to do. You talk like I *made* her do it."

"The point is you shouldn't let her do it even if she wants to, son. Womenfolks has got to be protected, even from theirselves. They're the weaker sex. Let her carry the kindlin, let her rick it, but don't let her chop it. That's man's work. And soon as you sense the diff'rence, you'll be a man."

He leaned his chair back on two legs.

Mother asked, "Albert, why do you treat our good chairs like that?"

He didn't pay any attention to her, just kept talking to Til. "They's one other thing, son, and I don't want you to forget it. You're the only one to carry on the name in this family. That makes you more than ordinary responsible."

Granny got up, her black eyes glistening as she hobbled across the kitchen. "With a daddy like that, there's no sense in that boy goin to the bad. Albert, I never oncet heerd your daddy talk to you like that, but then you was just a tad when he died."

Daddy dropped the ring into his shirt pocket. "Now, quit that snubbin, Cassandry. Next time I'm in town I'll see 'bout gettin it fixed.

The next night Mother decided that it would be a waste of money for her to go to the circus. Said she didn't like crowds except at church, and certainly didn't have to go to the circus to be entertained. Said she could go downtown any Saturday night and see enough white trash to suit her. For once, Granny agreed with her. Besides, it looked like it was about to rain. Daddy closed the B&B early, but by the time we ate supper and got ready to go, the thunder was right over the chicken lot. Daddy said it was rumored that the circus had been called off because a storm was brewing. But, although big clouds hung like train smoke over the whole town, the man on the radio announced every few minutes that the circus would go on as scheduled.

Toward dusk Daddy took me and Til and Emmy to the circus lot, past the Baptist, Presbyterian and Methodist churches huddled around Broadway Circle, their steeples reaching for the same black cloud. The first big drops of rain fell as he parked the car. We ran across the stubble to the ticket booth.

Rain drops hammered the top of the tent as we found our seats. When the dogs lined up to jump through the hoop, I wished we were down on the front row, but when the lion growled and stomped into the center ring, led by a man holding a big whip and walking backwards, I was glad to be near the top row. And when Tom Mix rode in, sitting tall on his big black horse that the announcer called Tony, he was small and wrinkled, and dark like Woody. He looked a lot older and littler than the picture in last night's paper. Tony's saddle had two rows of silver buttons around it that sparkled like stars as he pranced from one side of the ring to the other. He wore a necklace, too, that had silver buttons on it. When Tony bucked, Tom Mix rared back and yelled and waved his ten-gallon hat in the air and played like he was roping a calf with his lasso. Then he stood straight up on Tony's back and threw his hat in the air and caught it while Tony ran around the ring. The crowd jumped up, clapping and yelling, and drowned out the thunder. Daddy said something about what a fine horse Tony was with his four white socks.

"See how high he carries his tail?" Daddy said. "That's one sign of a fine horse. And the way he prances with high spirits. I'll have me a saddle horse again one day," he said, as though he was talking to himself.

Tom Mix slid over Tony's rear end and grabbed his tail and disappeared in a cloud of sawdust as the horse dragged him around the ring. He was still flying around in the sawdust, barely touching the ground, when a firetruck came in with a man who pushed a ladder near the top of the tent. Everybody's eyes turned toward him. The man behind us yelled out, "Who in hell needs a firetruck when it's rainin cats and dogs?"

The crowd got quiet. A fireman climbed to the top of the ladder and slashed the canvas with a big knife. Tony galloped out with Tom Mix standing up on his back. Tom Mix waved his big hat as water filled the ring where he had been bouncing in the sawdust, holding onto Tony's tail. Women screamed and started running to the doors, knocking each other down on the way.

Daddy didn't even get up. He just sat there with his hands under his legs like he was in a straight-back chair at home. The firemen moved to the other two rings and slashed the tent top. Water splashed to the ground in front of us. Emmy started to cry, and Daddy held her in his lap.

"It's all right now," he said gently. "See, the tent's not goin to cave in. All that water is gone from the top now. Cuttin them holes kept it from collapsin under all that weight."

A man with a big horn raced from one end of the tent to the other yelling that the danger was over, that the show would go on as soon as folks returned to their seats. A few people sat back down. Some muttered that they wanted their money back, and others complained because the trapeze act had been called off. The rain kept pouring, and the clowns sloshed around in the sawdust which had turned to slippery mud.

The man with the horn came back and yelled that the circus was ending early since the performers had to put on a show over in Virginia the next night, and he explained, "They ain't no way to get them fancy costumes cleaned between now and then. I know you folks understand." He warned everybody to watch their step on the way out.

"They ain't no cause for alarm," he yelled. "You men step back and let the women and children go first, just like they did when the mighty Titanic hit that iceberg 20 year ago. Let's don't repeat that awful night when all of those little bitty children went down to a watery grave."

I started crying then, because Mother wasn't with us and Emmy and Til and me couldn't go first without Daddy. Daddy didn't pay any attention to what the man said. He just got up, still holding Emmy, and took my hand and told Til to take the other one.

The man kept talking. "You'uns can get half your money back by mailin yore ticket stubs in."

Til broke away from me and crawled under the seats. I wondered if we would ever see him again when he came out grinning with five soggy stubs in his hand. He didn't realize until we got home that the man never said where to mail the stubs.

Mother made us a pitcher of lemonade, even if it was after 10 o'clock. I was afraid Til wouldn't let me sleep with him after I drank a big glassful, but I ate a lot of pumpkin seeds, and he let me hold the flashlight under the tent sheet while he glued the stubs together. The thunder and rain didn't bother us any more.

"We'll go to the picture show," Til whispered. "They never even look at the tickets. They just tear em in two. I need to see all of the shows about cowboys, cause I may want to be one like Tom Mix when I grow up."

"Remember what Sadie said the other night about seeing trouble in those coffee grounds?" I asked.

Til's eyes got big. "Heck, yeah, that was it!" he said. "The storm! Gosh, that's spooky. I hadn't thought of that! What if she has one of those minds that can look both ways?"

"What do you mean?" I asked.

"She can see tomorrow as good as she can see yesterday. Gosh, she ought to join the circus and get rich tellin fortunes."

"She wouldn't leave Joe."

"He could quit collectin junk and go with her," Til said.

"Maybe she'll teach us how to see tomorrow," I said.

"No way," he said. "She couldn't if she wanted to. That's a special birth gift. Special power."

When we walked to Sunday School, we talked more about the storm than we did the circus. Water was still standing in the streets, and tree branches were down all over town, the radio said.

Mother gave up going to church, because Granny couldn't even get out of bed. Daddy tried to put her bedroom shoes on her feet, but they were so swollen he couldn't.

After Sunday School, I found Daddy talking to the Simpsons. My face got hot when Mr. Simpson looked straight at me and said that I was growing like a weed and getting prettier every day.

I made up my mind I would not walk down the street after sundown on Wednesday, even if Mr. Simpson might give me another nickel. But I didn't have any choice. Mother had more tomatoes than we could use, even on the kitchen table and the vegetable counter at the B&B, and she sent me to take some to the Simpsons.

"Mrs. Simpson may be gone to prayer meeting," she said. "She can do what she wants to with no little children tugging at her all day long."

"Can Emmy go with me?" I asked.

"Why, you never asked her to go anywhere with you before in your life. She's in with Granny."

I couldn't tell her why I wanted Emmy to go. She'd probably just wash my mouth out with Octagon soap again and say I'd been imagining things and that Ed Simpson was a saint if she ever saw one. She'd probably say that she didn't want to hear another word of such foolishness and "Why, Mrs. Simpson would never get over it!"

Mother yelled after me. "Don't dilly-dally and forget to bring my good pan back, and don't go over to the McCormicks. It'll be dark before long, and it's not safe for you to be out by yourself after dark. Lots of bad things can happen to little girls. I ought to send Til. Where *is* that boy?"

Sure enough, Mr. Simpson was sitting on the porch behind the evening paper. All he said about the tomatoes was, "My, those are good eatin." Then he asked, "Have you been doin any art work lately?"

We went into the kitchen to put the tomatoes in the ice box. Then we went to his and Mrs. Simpson's bedroom so he could show me a new picture done with color crayons. A bald man was sitting on the bed with a naked woman facing him in his lap with her legs wrapped around him. They weren't much better than my stick figures.

"What are they sitting like that for?" I asked.

"They're jist havin a good time," he said, and put the picture upside down under the drawing pad. I thought we were going to play Old Maid when he got a pack of cards off the closet shelf, but he didn't shuffle or deal. He just flipped the cards so fast that the man and woman painted on them moved. They didn't have anything on. They were dancing, then he twirled her around on his peejabber. I bet Til never had seen anything like that!

"That beats all," I said, trying to sound like Daddy. But I was scared. My heart pounded when he reached to unbutton my overalls gallus.

"Don't be afraid," he said. "I wouldn't hurt you for the world." My overalls fell to the floor, and I saw us both in the mirror. My dress was too short; I had outgrown it last year. It was an old one of Maude's. And Mr. Simpson was too white even where his clothes didn't cover him.

"But I don't want a baby," I blurted out.

He laughed. "You couldn't have a baby, Cass, even if I tried. Anyway, I promise not to try. You're too little. It will feel good. And I'll give you a nickel." He took my hand and sat down on the bed and began to breathe loud. When he tried to pull me onto the bed, I jerked away and jumped into my overalls and ran out on the porch, hooking the galluses.

I was glad dark hadn't come. I jumped down the steps two at a time and ran home.

Mother was waiting for me in the swing. "What made it take you so long? Mrs. Simpson there? And where is my good pan?"

I was glad it was almost too dark for me to see her, because I didn't want to look her in the face. "I went in to see Mr. Simpson's art work," I answered. "He draws. She wasn't home. I forgot to get the pan out of the kitchen when I left."

"Why, Cass, you are usually more dependable than that. You can just march down there in the morning and get it," Mother said, sternly.

I was relieved, because Mr. Simpson would be at work then.

"Why, I never knew Ed was an artist," Mother murmured, like she was proud to know him. Then her voice changed. "It's getting late. If you want to, you can help Til get in the coal and kindling. I'm going to rest here a minute before bedtime. Your daddy's already gone. Did we tell you children that your Aunt Flossie and Unc are coming for the day tomorrow?"

I wished that Daddy had a farm instead of a grocery store. Then we could go visiting on a week day. We never went out of town except on Sunday.

EIGHT

I shouted with glee when I saw Aunt Flossie and Unc pull into the driveway in the dusty, green Chevrolet coupe the next morning. Even if they were sisters, they didn't look much alike. She was older and plumper than Mother. But then Maude and me and Emmy didn't look alike either. He was a patient, stringy man with a twinkle in his eyes. As they got out of the car, Mother bragged on Aunt Flossie's good, navy-blue voile, and Unc's new, blue serge suit. Within seconds, all of us except Granny were in the yard with them. Granny no longer stomped through the house or yelled at me and Til, and she had to stop every three or four words to catch her breath.

Aunt Flossie and Mother visited in the kitchen while they got dinner ready, and Maude and me set the table. But I didn't stay with them long, because I wanted to go out in the yard where Daddy and Unc were sitting in straight-back chairs under the wormy umbrella trees. The worms had eaten the green from most of the leaves until they looked like lace. Me and Til sat on the ground and listened to Daddy and Unc talk about the Depression and politics.

After dinner, Mother gathered the watermelon rinds to make pickles.

"I still use Mother's recipe," she told Aunt Flossie.

"Clara, you can make them just as good in half the time," Aunt Flossie said.

"The old ways are still the best," Mother replied. "I don't have much use for short cuts. Don't even like that old pectin in my jelly, do you?"

"Can't tell the difference," Aunt Flossie answered. "You need to have some short cuts. I'd lose my mind if I had as many to feed and wash and iron for as you do."

Unc interrupted, "It's high time we got started home, Floss." He consulted the big gold pocket watch, chained to another pocket across his vest. "Already half-past three."

We gathered around them on the porch. Aunt Flossie asked, "Who's going home with me this time?"

I had spent two months in Holston Valley when Emmy was born. I wanted to go, but for just a week. Two months was too long. I got those old fall sores all over my legs and didn't really like being the only child, even if I did get to take my afternoon naps on two dining room chairs pushed together in front of the fireplace. Besides, I had to wear a dress all day on Sunday, even after dinner.

"Now, Florence, you don't have to bother..." Mother murmured, but Aunt Flossie interrupted her. "Nonsense, Clara, you have your hands full. Why don't I just take me two chirrun this time?"

"Well, I need Maude to help around the house while I'm at the store, and Granny would be lost without Em."

She packed one bag between me and Til and said in a low voice that she didn't believe Albert had any idea how fast his mother was failing. Aunt Flossie agreed and promised to take good care of us. They hugged each other, and Mother said, mostly for our benefit, "Now, make them mind, Florence. Don't hesitate to use a little hickory tea now and then."

"We'll get along just fine. Til knows he has to mind Roland and me."

She looked over at me, standing there with my hands in my overalls pockets, and said, "She's not very p-r-e-t-t-y, but she sure is s-m-a-r-t. But pretty is as pretty does, and she's easy to get along with. We need to get a little meat on those bones and begin to make a little girl out of her. She'll be happier in school." She laid a hand on my shoulder.

I pulled away and walked to the edge of the porch, pretending not to understand. I rammed my fists deeper into my overalls pockets and spied a dung beetle shoving his perfect ball of dung along a crooked path. I pushed my hair back, took careful aim, spit and missed. I hawked again and hit a bull's eye. The beetle let go his prize and struggled, wet and heavy.

I felt a pang of guilt, but muttered, "You no account bug. Ugly thing you."

Aunt Flossie said, "She won't have a bit of trouble in school, in my opinion, but we have a couple of habits to break before fall, haven't we, Cassie?"

I didn't look at her.

"Little girls don't spit. That's a nasty habit, even for men and boys. And little girls do not bite their finger nails."

Unc hurried us from the yard. "It's a good three-hour trip even if we don't have no bad luck on the road, and I don't want to have to change one of them ole tires after dark. Spare's slick as a ribbon. Flossie, if you don't come on, dark will catch you doin the milkin."

Me and Til kissed Felix goodbye and climbed into the rumble seat. Picking at her nails under her apron, Mother called, "You kids stay down in that seat. You hear me? I'd never forgive myself if one of you fell out of there. Til, you watch after her. You hear?" She was still talking when the little coupe headed toward the highway.

Two hours later we were in Bristol, 25 miles from home, and soon Unc turned off the highway onto the gravel road. Aunt Flossie unsnapped the isinglass flap that separated us from her and Unc, and yelled, "There's Pemberton Oak, the biggest country estate in the Valley, fit for a king."

She told us again how she had been there once for circle meeting when Mrs. Pemberton was alive. Although it was no longer in the family, the big brick house probably would be called Pemberton Oak forever, because an ancient, gnarled oak tree shaded most of the big front yard.

Aunt Flossie turned around and yelled again, "Our boys bivouacked right there under that tree a hundred and fifty years ago before they marched off to fight the redcoats at Kings Mountain over in North Carolina." She shook her head. "Just think. Your forefathers marched right down this very gap to beat the British in the battle that turned the tide in the Revolution. Til, have you studied about Nancy Ward in history?"

"Any kin to Montgomery?" he shouted.

"What they're teaching you chirrun nowadays astonishes me," she said. "She ought to be in your history book. She paved the way for our boys to win the Revolutionary War and get our independence from England. Have they taught you how George Washington got to be our first President?"

When Unc turned onto the red clay road, we knew we were almost there. It would be ten miles more. We couldn't hear Aunt Flossie any longer; the car made too much noise on the rough road. We went past Darter's Store and the King place and long, green meadows where bulging cows stood hip to hip in shallow ponds, then across the little creek at the edge of Unc's property by his mailbox. "Roland Willett, Route 4" was painted on one side in big black letters. We went around the bottom of the hill, below the big white clapboard house that stood on the very top and had four lightning rods sprouting from the roof. Unc shifted gears to get up the hill and pull into the back yard close to the concrete porch where the cistern was. When he was in a hurry, he parked there, but usually, he went through the gate and parked in the barn hall.

When Unc shut off the coupe's motor, the only sound in the valley came from the tree frogs down in the thicket. Night air, cool and damp, already rising off the river just across the knob beyond the piney woods, made me shiver. I felt warmer when Aunt Flossie put her hand on my shoulder.

"Come along, chirrun," she said, "and hurry. I've got to change into my milking clothes."

Me and Til raced through the living room up the stairs with our bag. We got our sweaters out and changed to our old shoes. Til went to the pasture with Unc and old Shep to herd the cows into the barn lot, and I followed Aunt Flossie to do the milking. Three kittens crawled out from under the house and went with us. I picked one up. Aunt Flossie shook her head.

"You can't carry that cat if you're going to carry my milk pail. That's Tinker Bell. He goes with me every night. You'll see why." Aunt Flossie went through the gate into the barn lot where six cows waited.

"Tinker Bell a boy?" I asked.

"Yes, but I thought he was a girl. I named him after a little girl fairy in *Peter Pan*. Do you know that story?"

She reached inside the feed-room door and got her milking stool. I sat on the rail fence and wondered how in the world, as old as she was, she could get a boy mixed up with a girl, and why Unc didn't help her with the milking. Maybe that was woman's work. Maybe that was why Til wanted to teach me how. Aunt Flossie talked about Peter Pan as the white foam rose in the bucket. I told her I had never heard of him.

"What kind of stories does your mother read to you chirrun?" she asked. "I should think *Peter Pan* would be one of the first. And you're almost ready for *The Secret Garden* and *Girl of the Limberlost*. Til should be reading *Dr. Doolittle* and *Tom Sawyer* and *Freckles*."

I didn't answer for a minute. Then I said, "Maude reads to me once in a while from *The Rains Came* and Granny reads the Ten Commandments from the Bible, but Mother doesn't have time to read to us."

"She works too hard. Should be spending more time with you chirrun. If you were mine, by now you would know how to embroider pillow cases and bake a cake and set a table."

"Til teaches me lots of things, like where ice comes from, what makes the man in the moon, and how Felix barks," I said.

"Speaking of Til, he reminds me of Peter Pan," Aunt Flossie said. "Always acting like he knows what he's doing when the disaster that he has engineered is just around the corner."

She was already milking Old Jers, and just had two more cows to go. I wondered if she would ever get around to Peter Pan and Tinker Bell.

She took a deep breath, straightened her back and began.

"It's an English story about a little boy who refused to grow up. He ran away the day he was born, because he heard his mother and father talking about what they wanted him to be when he grew up. And he learned to fly and taught other boys to fly away from their homes to an island called Neverland. He found the Darling children one night when he and Tinker Bell were looking for his shadow, and they followed him away, bobbing out the window and across the sea."

I could see the parade in the sky, going higher and higher toward the stars that Peter said couldn't do anything but stay there and twinkle, because they were being punished for some wrong that they did long ago — so long ago that not one of them remembered what it was. And so Aunt Flossie told how they lived in Neverland with Wendy Darling as their mother, cooking and cleaning house, and Peter as their father, making all the decisions. And the lost boys were little boys who had fallen out of their prams. There were not any girls there, because girls are too clever to fall out of their prams, Peter said, but the lost boys needed a mother and Wendy made a good one.

Aunt Flossie told how the redskins became friends of the children, because Peter had saved Tiger Lily, the chief's daughter. The saddest part of the story came when Tink drank the poison medicine that Captain Hook, the pirate with the iron claw, had fixed for Peter. And Tink's light grew fainter and fainter. And the little golden bell that was her voice couldn't ring. Peter said she couldn't get well again unless children believed in fairies. He asked them to clap if they did.

I sat on the rail fence and clapped and clapped, and Aunt Flossie said that Tink finally opened her eyes and spoke and her light grew brighter and brighter.

"Well, to make a long story short," Aunt Flossie said, "the Darling children got homesick and went home and found the window open. And guess what?"

The stars began to twinkle and I wondered who they were and what they did so long ago to deserve being stuck up there in the sky every night, silent and helpless.

"They went to bed and lived happily ever after," I guessed.

"Wendy got married and had a daughter, and Peter flew into her room one night. He was still a little boy and he wanted to take her away to Never-Neverland to cook and clean for him. But when he saw that she was grown up, he took her daughter Jane out the window."

"Did Jane come back?" I asked.

"Of course, and Jane's daughter came back, too, many years later, after cleaning Peter's house.

"Cass, do you think that every time a child says, 'I don't believe in fairies,' a fairy somewhere falls down dead? That's what Peter said."

"Maude says fairies live in Mother's big sugar bowl. I believe her," I said.

Hearing Aunt Flossie tell a book was almost as good as being able to read it myself. She had taught school so long that she knew how to answer my questions even before I asked them.

Maybe if I left my bedroom window open, Peter would come and teach me to fly. Then I could teach Til something. As night pushed closer and closer through the pine trees, I made a wish on the star twinkling over the smokehouse. What could it have done to be jailed in the sky at night? Where did it go during the day? Til told me once, but I couldn't get it straight. Aunt Flossie poured some milk in the pans in the corner of the barn, and the kittens purred and strung white beads on their whiskers. Old Shep gulped his milk down in fewer swallows and begged for more. Even with all of the stars, it was darker outside than at home.

Aunt Flossie aimed the lantern's light carefully in front of us on the path. I wished for swimming weather tomorrow so me and Til could dam up the creek and wade up to our waists.

"You're not afraid are you, Cass?" Aunt Flossie asked.

"No ma'am," I lied.

"There's nothing to be afraid of here," she said. I thought about how far away I was from Mr. Simpson, and sang, "Home again, home again, jiggety jog," when I saw the coal oil lamp flickering in the kitchen window. "That's what Daddy says when we get home. Do you know the rest of it?"

"It's an old nursery rhyme, 'To market, to market to buy a fat pig, home again, home again, jiggety-jig.' Your daddy jogs where he ought to jig." Aunt Flossie laughed as she set the milk on the table and turned the lantern down.

"Do you want some bread and butter before we go to gather the eggs?" she asked.

"No ma'am," I answered. Til had already come in and got him some milk and bread.

"Don't eat too much, Til. You'll spoil your supper," Aunt Flossie warned gently. "We're going to have fried chicken and cornbread."

Til gave her one of his chicken-every-Sunday looks. I was glad she didn't see it. She was turning the lantern back up.

When we got to the henhouse, we heard a soft cluck or two, but when we opened the door, the old hens fluttered and fussed like a possum had stolen their last egg. I counted fourteen eggs into Aunt Flossie's apron.

"They're falling off. Must be this hot weather." She fed a few pullets that were fenced off from the others. "These young domineckers are a little puny. I hope they don't have the gapes." She picked one up and held the lantern close to its eyes. "Granma used to stick a horsehair down their throat and pull out the worm when they were yawning and blinking that way, but I can't bring myself to do it. What does your mother do with them?"

"Ours get the pip sometimes," I answered. "Is that the same thing? Mother don't know what causes it, but they are as good as gone when they get it."

"Mother *doesn't* know," Aunt Flossie corrected me. "I don't believe you are talking about the pip. That doesn't kill them. That just means they have mucus in their throat, like when you have a cold. Now, coccidiosis is another matter. They get diarrhea like *you* do when you eat green apples, and their feathers droop. They stand a good chance of dying when they get that." Til said Aunt Flossie couldn't resist teaching whoever was around. She thought they were in a school room whether they were in the barn or the kitchen or the garden.

We walked back to the house, and Aunt Flossie mixed the cornbread and spread a few cracklings in the bottom of the skillet. After she put the skillet in the oven, she strained the milk and took it to the cellar, which she said already held 56 quarts of early apples and would hold twice as many quarts of tomatoes before the first frost. And there would be green beans and corn and peaches, blackberries and cherries.

We hadn't even left the table with the big coal-oil lamp in the middle when our eyelids were as heavy as pot lids, and the next thing I knew I was climbing the stairs behind her and Til by the light of the lamp. I scrouged down into the feather bed in the guest room where the big white pitcher and bowl sat on the marble washstand against the wall.

Aunt Flossie said we wouldn't open the window because she didn't want Peter to come in and take me off.

I couldn't get any colder. Before she left, she said, "Now, if you have to 'go' in the night, use that chamber pot under the bed. It takes a lot longer to dry out that feather bed than it does one of your mother's mattresses, and I have to do all of my washing by hand." That meant she didn't have a washing machine, because they didn't have any electricity.

Til was in the room across the hall.

"Don't raise Til's window," I reminded her as she went to tell him goodnight. "Peter might come in and take him to Never-Neverland."

Aunt Flossie said we were entirely too big to sleep together, even if she did have to heat all of the water on the cookstove and do a week's wash on a scrubbing board.

"Your mother always has had it easier than I have," she said, "but I wouldn't swap places with her, even if she does have electricity and hot and cold running water and a Maytag."

When she had taken all of the light downstairs with her, I lay and thought about important things, like going to first grade and going to the doctor for typhoid and smallpox shots and getting saved and telling somebody about Mr. Simpson and me. But who would that be? Til wouldn't ever stop thinking long enough to listen, and Aunt Flossie would just worry and say I had better talk to Mother.

Mother and Aunt Flossie didn't act alike any more than they looked alike. Both of them had been to State Normal School for teacher training, but Mother married Daddy before she got her teaching certificate. Married women couldn't teach. Anyway, Daddy said no wife of his would teach even if the state would allow it. Aunt Flossie taught for two years before the war, then went to Washington to work for the government. She liked to talk about being a Red Cross volunteer with coffee and donuts at the train station when our boys came back from the front lines. She might have been there when Uncle Jay got off the troop train with his gas mask and red eyes. She voted in every election and fussed at Mother for not casting her ballot every time she had a chance. Mother said if Aunt Flossie had children, she'd find better things to do with her money than to pay that old two-dollar poll tax.

Everybody wondered why Aunt Flossie had come back from Washington and married Unc after meeting all those boys who got off the train in Washington after they had served their time across the ocean. Mother said he couldn't hold a candle to her. Mother said she let three good chances slip through her fingers before she married beneath herself. I didn't think she had married beneath herself at all. I liked Unc. I liked him a lot better than I did Mr. Simpson.

I tip-toed across the hall and got in bed with Til. It felt good to lie down next to him. He rolled over against me.

"What's the matter? 'Fraid of the dark?" he asked, and put my hand on his peejabber, but it stayed limp.

"Ain't growing much," I whispered.

"Gettin the wrong kind of exercise, chasin them blamed cows," he muttered.

I wanted to stay beside him, but didn't dare. I tip-toed back across the hall and slid in between the cold sheets and stared into the dark. I missed the whir of the machinery at the cotton mill, Felix, and Maude, and Jimmie Lou and Emmy. I missed my ring, too, and almost got mad at Til when I remembered that he had made it come in two. I pulled the heavy comforter over my head.

The sunlight splashed a yellow patch across the pine-board floor the next morning. I jumped out of the feather bed and ran into Til's room, afraid that he had gone off early with Unc. But he was curled up under the quilt, still sound asleep.

After breakfast, we bolted out the door toward the creek. Wiping her hands on her apron, Aunt Flossie watched us from the porch.

"Stay together, now. Til, you take good care of her, and come back by dinnertime. Keep an eye on the sun."

When we got into the piney woods, we rolled up our overalls legs and ran down the hill.

I stacked rocks from one bank to the other while Til packed mud and sticks and pebbles around them. Pretty soon the water was up to my waist. All of a sudden, Til pulled me up on the bank. He pointed to a snake. It didn't stir from the very spot where I had been standing. It stuck its head out of the water and wiggled its whole body. Til dangled a twig above it. Its eyes moved back and forth; its mouth opened and clamped shut on the twig.

"Cottonmouth!" Til screamed. He grabbed my hand. "Come on. We got to get outta here!"

We ran back up the hill without stopping and fell, exhausted, on the steps. Til gasped for breath. "Don't mention it, or she'll never let us go swimmin again."

"What would happen if he bit you?"

"You wouldn't last two minutes, little as you are."

"Why didn't you kill him?"

"I'd like to see *you* kill him. Talk is cheap."

A hummingbird with a red breast darted in and out of the hollyhock blooms by the porch, shoving his needle-like bill into the bottom. Til said, "You can catch him by pourin salt on his tail."

"I'll get the salt if you want to go back down there," I said.

"Not the snake, dummy. The humminbird." Til spread-eagled into the grass and lay motionless.

"How do you know the hummingbird is a boy?" I asked.

"Girl humminbirds have white throats," he answered.

I ran to the kitchen to get the salt box and held it open over the hummingbird as he darted from bloom to bloom. A stream of white salt poured to the ground. Til lay in the grass and laughed.

"You're in for it now," he warned.

When Aunt Flossie came out and saw me holding the salt box, I told her why it was empty, and she didn't think it was funny. She said we could just walk to Darter's Store and get another box.

"You can't believe everything you hear, Cass, particularly when Til is talking. You should know that by now," she said. "I doubt that anybody could ever prove him right or wrong about that one."

"Walk?" Til asked. "All the way to the highway?"

Unc was sitting on the porch reading the weekly newspaper. "Eight mile, round trip," he mumbled.

"We could ride Lady," Til offered.

Aunt Flossie shook her head slowly from side to side. "You can carry my eggs to Mr. Darter. Leave early tomorrow morning. Be back by early afternoon if you don't dawdle. You can't get lost. Just follow the gravel road. But I don't want to hear of you going near that old swinging bridge."

After supper, she got out the box of tintypes while we got ready for bed. When we gathered in the parlor, it was like she was teaching school again, telling us who everybody was and whose side of the house they were on and how much kin.

"That's your Great-Great-Grandmother Kuehn." She pointed to a woman holding the Bible on her knees with both hands. "She came from Germany with the Bible under her arm to preach the Methodist Gospel to the heathens. She's on your grandmother's side." Her hair, parted in the middle and pulled straight back behind her ears, framed the old lady's unsmiling face.

"And that's your great Uncle Dow Rogers. Granma and Uncle Hod have his eyes."

"How did Uncle Dow get along without them?" Til asked, and got Aunt Flossie's yardstick out of the corner by the sewing machine and tapped it around the room with his eyes closed. Looking at the picture again, he said, "He looks like Ichybod Crane to me."

"Tilghman Blevins, you are sure to come to want if you don't learn some reverence, and that right away," Aunt Flossie said sternly.

She showed us a picture of Mother's family taken in front of the big white house when it was new. Granpa had scratched out his face, because he didn't feel worthy to keep on living after they had to come back from Kansas where he gave up religion because the crops had failed in the dust storms and their first baby, a boy, was born dead. He and Granma were sitting in straight-back chairs with their poker-faced children lined up beside them. Mother held a doll, and Aunt Flossie held a post card of a dog.

"How old was Mother when that picture was made?" Til asked.

"The date's on the back," Aunt Flossie answered. "Twenty-eight years ago. How old is your mother now?"

"Thirty-six," I answered, "so she was eight."

"Good, Cass, and you didn't even count on your fingers. Arithmetic is usually a boy's subject, but it never gave me a minute's trouble. And don't let it give you any."

We couldn't go to Darter's store the next day because it rained. Til made Daddy a bead belt with Indian designs on his Boy Scout loom, and I learned to embroider. Aunt Flossie traced a map of Palestine in the Time of Christ on a piece of muslin and started outlining Judaea in black thread to show me how. I finished it, and did the Jordan River in blue, because blue was the color of water. Aunt Flossie said that the river made Canaan flow with milk and honey. It probably should have been done in white, because milk and honey mixed up would probably be white, not blue. Anyhow, I put a red X for Jerusalem between the Sea of Galilee, done in blue, too, and the Dead Sea, but I didn't have any black thread for the Dead Sea. And I ran out of red for the names of countries and had already finished Samaria in green before Aunt Flossie told me to put it up and wait until I got a skein of red and black from Mr. Darter. She showed me where to put Bethlehem, just below Jerusalem, where the Baby Jesus was born in a manger full of straw, because the inn was all filled up. She said we were lucky that the Baby Jesus lived to be grown, because it was very cold that first Christmas night. It's always cold at Christmas time.

Aunt Flossie bragged on my mountains, green X's, and said we'd frame the map when I finished it. Maude had made a sampler last summer and embroidered "Maude Blevins, June, 1931, 13 yrs. old" down in the corner in black. I wanted to embroider my name in blue in the corner the next time it rained.

When the sun came out in the afternoon, Til and me went to Unc's barn to play. His barn was about three times as big as ours, and the loft was open, like a porch hanging out over the first floor. Til tied a loop in a big rope hanging from the ceiling. He grabbed it and swung from the loft across to the wall, then pushed away from the wall with his feet and swung back. Sometimes he'd let out a holler and drop into the hay.

It looked like fun. He told me, "No way for you to get hurt with all that hay under you less you hit that wall backwards. It'll knock the livin daylights out of you if you do. You got to hit it with your feet."

I grabbed the rope and sailed through the air, twisting around and around.

Til screamed, "Turn around and hit it with your feet!"

I slammed into the wall. When I came to, Til was straddling me in the hay. I looked up at him.

"Get off! Leave me alone."

"Be quiet and let me get the hang of this. Just givin you artificial respiration. Might be a doctor when I grow up."

I squirmed out from under him. He brushed off his overalls and walked behind me to the house. "You could have broke something. Next time, push yourself away from that wall with your feet, like I told you to."

The next morning after breakfast we put on clean overalls and left for Darter's, barefooted and carrying two dozen eggs apiece. Til stopped by the gate and picked up another eleven he had taken out of the henhouse a few at a time. We waded in the creek that the road followed, then climbed a fence and watched a nest of naked field mice. They looked like the end of a baby's little finger, red and bare. Cattle grazed all around. I yelled for Til to come quick when I saw a cow with a bloody rope hanging out of her back end. The baby calf under her looked dead. Til squatted close to it, and crept closer until the cow's glance stopped him.

"What killed it?" I asked him.

"It ain't dead," he answered, softly. "Just looks dead. That calf couldn't be more than five minutes old."

The cow licked its face, then nudged its rear end with her nose, and licked and licked, eating the inside of the egg the calf came in.

"Boy, how big was that egg that calf came in?" I asked.

"It's hard to believe how much you don't know," Til said, in his old voice. "Calves are born, like dogs and babies. Cows don't hatch out of eggs, like chickens and grasshoppers."

Pretty soon, the calf's red fur looked silky and it shook all over when it tried to stand up, and fell back down into the soft grass. Its mother helped with her nose until the calf got up, sprawled on all fours and found a nipple. I wanted to stay and watch, but Til said that the cow and her calf weren't going anywhere and we would see them on the way back. He stuck out his tongue at the black bull across the fence, then broke into an Indian war whoop. The bull looked at us with a blank stare until we walked off. Til said it was a good thing I didn't have anything red on, because if I did, that bull would come right through that fence and stomp me to death.

We ran by Billy Jack King's place, because if Mrs. King saw us, she would make us come in and recite a few Bible verses. She was as crazy about making children learn Bible verses as Preacher Thomas at Aunt Flossie's Presbyterian church. I didn't see any difference between her church and our Methodist church at home. She said Presbyterians believe in predestination, whatever that is. Only thing I could gather was that we didn't have much to do with what happened. It was all determined by God. Til said if that was true, and there was a good chance that it was, then it wouldn't matter whether we were good or bad. But I was afraid it wasn't true, because we weren't Presbyterians, and Methodists didn't agree with that, Mother said. Anyhow, Til reminded me often that he had been saved and said that once you got saved, it didn't matter what church you went to. He said he hoped that God would give me time to get saved, and the chances were good that He would.

Dusty and thirsty, we climbed the rickety steps to Darter's. Mr. Darter stuck a dark hand into the dirty bowl on the counter and handed us a lemon drop. Where his skin showed, he was dark like Granma, and I wondered if he had any Indian blood. Rheumatism had bent him over and turned his knuckles to knots. He used a cane to go any distance, and kept his overalls rolled just above his boot tops, summer and winter. His store smelled a little like the B&B, but, being a country store, it didn't have electricity, so he couldn't keep much in the way of meat. The meat counter was bare except for some slab bacon and fatback. Hams hung from the ceiling in greasy burlap bags.

"I ought to know you younguns," he mumbled. "You come a visitin folks in the valley ever year, but for the life of me, I can't place you."

Til set the eggs on the counter and stuffed his hands in his overalls pockets. "We're from Clarksport, visitin Uncle Roland and Aunt Flossie Willett a few days."

"Mighty fine folks," Mr. Darter said. "Mighty fine. Pity they ain't never had no younguns of their own."

Mr. Darter weighed us on the big scales in the feed room. Til weighed sixty pounds, twice as much as I did, but Mr. Darter said boys always weigh more than girls, even when they were born. He gave us a penny apiece for the eggs, but didn't want the four that were cracked, so him and Til sucked them and offered me one. I said I'd rather have a lemon drop, so Mr. Darter got me another one, then I bought some for Aunt Flossie and the red and black embroidery thread. Between that and the box of salt and a pack of Camels, we had six cents left to take home to Aunt Flossie. Mr. Darter walked to the front door with us and shooed the flies off the screen. There wasn't any room left for them on the fly paper that hung from the lamp above the pot-bellied stove. Men still sat round it and chewed tobacco, even in summertime. Mr. Darter said he left it there so they'd have a place to spit. Everybody knew he was too do-less to move it for a few months.

As we jumped off the porch, he yelled, "Now don't you younguns step on any road apples on the way home."

I did, first thing, and ran through a mud puddle to wash the horse manure off my foot while Til lit up a Camel.

"You can have one of these if you'll keep your mouth shut when we get home," he said. "Better than corn silks or rabbit tobacco."

"I quit smoking. Burns my nose and throat."

He coughed and shot a stream of spit between his front teeth.

"You oughtn't to do that," I said. "You got your permanent teeth and they'll never go back together. How are you going to explain the yellow stains between your fingers?" I shot a stream of spit at a grasshopper.

Til blew out great puffs of smoke and kept spitting. "Lots of men have gaps between their front teeth," he said, "but I don't know of a single lady that does. In fact, I ain't even never seen a *lady* spit. You'd better kick that habit before school starts."

"You'd better kick it first. My teeth are temporary. I asked how are you going to explain the yellow stains between your fingers."

"That takes a pack a day for years. And even if it didn't, I could always say it's tobacco juice from a grasshopper."

We found the cow and baby calf right where we had left them. The calf still stood like it was straddling something and nudged its mother's bag, gulping warm milk from one tit, then another. The spitting image of its mother, it had a shiny red coat except for curly white hair on its face and neck. Its big eyes bulged.

Til squatted to look at her. "Wouldn't you know it! Another heifer! First thing you know she'll come fresh just like her mother and have to be milked mornin and night."

"What does that mean?"

"Means her mother will have more than enough milk for her in a few days and she'll have to be milked mornin and night. And the first thing you know, that baby calf will be big enough to have a calf and she'll come fresh."

Til broke into a run down a path through the woods to the swinging bridge. I held back.

"Last thing Aunt Flossie told us not to do. It's too old to be safe."

"Ain't nothin safe to hear her tell it. She'll never even know unless you tell her."

The woods near the river were dark, and thick bushes grew along the bank. The ground was mossy and cold, and I was afraid of snakes. It was a relief to get to the swinging bridge. I ran to keep up with Til as he raced across it, the cable on either side slipping through his hands. I stumbled after him, clutching the cables, jumping holes where planks were missing in the floor. When Til reached the other end, he jumped up and down to make the bridge bounce and creak. I screamed for him to stop and grabbed the cables so hard my hands hurt. He finally ran to me and took my hand, but I broke loose and ran across fast, trying to look at the trees on the bank instead of at the water below.

On the ground at last, I called, "We'd better go home. Sun is straight up."

Kicking up a bed of pine needles, Til lay down, his hands behind his head.

"I got to take me a little nap," he said. "Godamighty, just look at them two butterflies. That's what makes the world go round." He took off his overalls and pulled me down beside him. "Just a little while," he begged. "Ain't gettin enough exercise."

When we got back, it was the middle of the afternoon, and the lemon drops were gone. Aunt Flossie ran her hand through Til's hair. "Tilghman, did you go swimming?"

"No," he answered.

"Cassandra, did he go swimming?"

"No ma'am," I answered, "but we saw a baby calf born."

"How was Mr. Darter?" she asked. "Did he know who you were?"

"Said he had seen us before," Til answered, "but we had to tell him who we was visitin."

"*Were* visiting, Tilghman," she corrected him.

After supper, Aunt Flossie took us into the parlor to play the Victrola. Unc never went in there. He just lowered the wick in the lamp and folded his hands in his lap to take a nap in the big rocking chair in the living room. The parlor was cooler than the rest of the house and smelled musty. The inside of the fireplace was shiny, like new. The books looked new, too, behind the doors with the glass window panes. We were not allowed to go in there unless Aunt Flossie went with us. She let me hold a piece of wood from the very tree where Daniel Boone had carved "D Boone cilled a bar on this tree in year 1760" when he cut his way through the wilderness into Kentucky.

"You'll study about him in school," she said. "You have already studied about him, haven't you, Tilghman?"

"No, but I know about the Indian Warpath. That concrete marker at the church circle in Clarksport is loaded with real arrowheads. Boy, I'd like to figure me out a way to get em outta there."

"Why Tilghman Blevins, that would be against the law. The Daughters of the American Revolution put that marker there to show all of us how important this area has been to American history." She cranked the Victrola. "We'll listen to a record or two, then I'll tell you about Nancy Ward, the Indian maiden. Want to hear Caruso?" She said that she was determined to teach us something about good music, because she knew we never heard any at home.

"Is he a foreigner?" Til asked.

"You won't understand a word he sings, because he always sings in his native Italian," she said.

"Why?" he asked. "He knows Americans are listenin to him."

"Because he is Italian," she answered. "Shh. Listen. It's the story of a clown saying his heart is broken because somebody has taken his sweetheart, but because he is a clown, he can't be sad. He is paid to make people laugh all of the time."

I squirmed. "Do you have 'How You Gonna Wet Your Whistle?'"

Aunt Flossie turned the Victrola off. "How does it go?"

I sang, "How you gonna wet your whistle when the whole darned world runs dry?"

"That sounds like some of your daddy's foolish..." Aunt Flossie stopped. Unc laughed in the next room. She put "Carolina Moon" on, and Til accompanied, "When the m-moon comes over the cow shed, I'll be waitin for you at the k-k-k-kitchen door." Then we heard the United States Military Band play "Columbia, the Gem of the Ocean." She always played that one. She had bought it in Washington when she was working for the government and meeting the soldiers at the train.

"I'll play you one more, one of my favorites," Aunt Flossie said, "and then I want to tell you a story about how we got the very land we live on from the Indians and how we won our independence from the British."

We heard a movie star called Delores sing a song about bells calling, from a new picture show she was in called *Ramona*. Aunt Flossie said she had read the book. It was about this beautiful girl about Maude's age whose mother was an Indian and whose father was a Scotsman and he was white. She fell in love with the son of this Indian chief, and together they fought the greed of the white people. They ran away and got married, and he got shot and died. Aunt Flossie said that Ramona had heavy, black hair and steel-blue eyes, and didn't have any idea how pretty she was and that helped to make her even more beautiful.

The nearest picture show was more than ten miles away and Aunt Flossie hadn't seen a show since she left Washington, but once in a while she bought a record from one with her butter-and-egg money. They were all sad, like "Indian Love Call" and "One Alone."

She wiped her eyes with the back of her hand and turned off the Victrola. Then she picked up the lamp and started toward the living room where Unc was snoring. We followed her.

She nudged Unc gently. "Seems to me that bed would be more comfortable. I am going to tell Til and Cass about Nancy Ward. Remember her in your Tennessee history?"

Unc yawned. "You know I never got to history of no kind. Went about as far in school as their pa did. And that was the eighth."

Muttering "once a school teacher, always a school teacher," Til settled down on the floor beside me, and we heard about that hot sticky June night in 1776 when the long-haired, dark-eyed Indian maiden about Maude's age helped the colonists to turn the tide of the Revolution.

"Don't get her mixed up with Ramona," Aunt Flossie warned. "They looked alike and were about the same age, but we're talking about Nancy Ward. Ramona was in California a lot later; Nancy Ward was in East Tennessee 150 years ago."

She told about how the British gave the Cherokees guns and liquor to get them to attack the settlers that lived right where Clarksport is. Even her own folks never knew that Nancy Ward, daughter of Tame Doe, raced through the night to tell Isaac Thomas, the white fur trader she loved that Old Dragging Canoe planned to attack in the dark of the moon. Dragging Canoe, Nancy Ward's first cousin, didn't see eye-to-eye with his father, the chief, who had been to England as the king's guest. The English had won him over to their side against the settlers. Dragging Canoe wept and told his father that their land was "melting away like balls of snow in the sun."

Aunt Flossie went on to say that the settlers knew that Dragging Canoe had 350 braves with tomahawks and bows and arrows. They also knew that they would be destroyed, their families killed and their homes burned. But Nancy Ward's warning gave them time to get ready, and they soon killed most of the braves.

Til rolled over toward Aunt Flossie. "How many Injuns got it in the guts?"

"Your mother would be ashamed of you for talking like that," Aunt Flossie said. "History tells us that the battle was over in ten minutes. Forty Indians died, but not one single white man was killed."

Except for Granma, I had never seen an Indian. "Where did all of the Indians go?" I asked.

"That's another story for another night," Aunt Flossie said, "but to make a long story short, the President gathered them up about a hundred years ago and made them walk to Oklahoma to live on government land. Hundreds died on the way. Some starved, and some drowned crossing the Mississippi River. But a few hid out in the mountains and didn't go. There are still a few over in North Carolina."

"Remember mother telling us about that, Til?" I asked. "She said she didn't believe the Cherokees caused the trouble in the first place."

"They didn't," Aunt Flossie agreed. "This was their land. They had lived peacefully for hundreds of years. After the war Nancy Ward herself went to President Washington and told him that her tribe wanted to live in peace with the paleface. Her people named her White Rose when they initiated her into a secret society of sacred persons called Pretty Women. The Pretty Women counseled the chief about when to attack if it became necessary, and they decided the fate of every man who was captured in battle. They usually let prisoners go, because they didn't believe in killing any living thing unless it was absolutely necessary. For example, they didn't kill animals unless they needed food."

"Who believes that?" Til asked. "My geography book says that the Indians were savages and heathens. Says we would be English today instead of American if we hadn't put em in their place."

"The Cherokees were peace-loving people," Aunt Flossie repeated. "They were the only tribe in the country to have an alphabet and print their own newspaper. But that's another story, too."

Unc's snoring got louder by the minute, but she ignored it. "One day I'll tell you about the Battle of Kings Mountain," she said. "That took place over in North Carolina in 1780, five years after the settlers took all of the land around Clarksport from the Indians. Thomas Jefferson said it turned the tide of the Revolution. Now, to bed, chirrun, to bed all three of you." She leaned over and pulled Unc's ear lobe.

He didn't wake up until Til rode the yardstick around the room, giving an Indian war whoop to the top of his lungs.

"Shh," Aunt Flossie said. "You'll wake up the dead. I've kept you up past your bedtime and told you enough to burst your head. You didn't know I was a poet, did you, Cass?"

"Did Nancy Ward ever marry that fur trader?" I asked.

"Like as not, and they probably had a dozen little black-eyed, dark-skinned settlers, called Melungeons, part Indian, part white."

Unc unlaced his boots and took them off, then put his socks inside them.

"Past nine o'clock, Roland," she said, but she couldn't stop teaching school. "The French word for mixture is *melange*. The word Melungeon comes from it, and means a mixture of white and Indian blood."

I wanted to ask her if Mother knew that Granma was a Melungeon, but I didn't. I was too sleepy to talk, but my mind kept working as we climbed the stairs behind the coal-oil lamp. Where had all of the Indians gone? Did Indian children go to a separate school like Woody did? How far away was Oklahoma?

The next morning Unc gave us each a tin can with a little lamp oil in it and took us to the bean patch. "Count the beetles as you drop em in," he said, "and I'll pay you a penny a hunderd."

I made a dime, but Til made eighteen cents. When we poured the beetles out to burn them, the two piles looked about the same size, but Til said most of his were babies. After dinner we rode on the back of the flatbed to help Unc sucker the tobacco. He let us ride Lady around the barnyard, but decided it was too risky when she tried to brush me off against a cedar tree. When he told Aunt Flossie about it at the supper table, they agreed that I'd better spend more time inside with her.

"Good time to try being a girl for a change, instead of a tomboy," she told me.

So the next morning I watched her make gingerbread cookies and looked at some pictures of corseted women and big houses in old magazines, then transplanted some violets and butter-and-eggs and spiderwort from the edge of the woods to the side of the house. Columbine was my favorite flower, but it was down by the creek where the snake was. The days were long, but Aunt Flossie still let me go milking with her every night. Pretty soon I could milk almost as good as Til. But most of the time, I felt like I was in jail.

I knew Aunt Flossie was the boss, and I knew Mother would like me better if I could make my own clothes like Maude. I wanted to show Til how to embroider and make cookies, but he said no real man would pick up a needle and thread even to sew on a button.

"Did you ever see Daddy do that?" he asked. "Heck no, and you never will."

I didn't mind going to bed early. That was the only time Til and me got to be together. I just tiptoed across the cold hall to be close to him for a while and hear him talk about riding Lady bareback and sitting on the back of the flatbed as it bounced to the tobacco patch behind Nellie and Ole Ned, Unc's team. Unc sometimes let Til yell, "Gee," when he wanted them to turn to the right or go faster, and "Haw," when he wanted them to turn to the left. The only thing I was afraid of was going to sleep in Til's bed. Aunt Flossie would be mad if I did that.

On two Saturday nights Unc took a big tub off the side of the smokehouse and set it in the middle of the kitchen floor, then poured in buckets of hot water from the reservoir on the cookstove and added a couple buckets of cistern water. Til scrubbed down with Ivory soap until he passed Unc's inspection, and, then, Aunt Flossie heated the water a little and washed me so hard that I stung all over, and my hair squeaked in the towel.

On two Sundays we put on our best clothes and went to hear the Reverend Thomas. "Don't forget," he told us after church, "a Bible verse a day will keep the Devil away."

Unc kept on his blue serge suit all day, and I had to keep on my blue dress. Aunt Flossie got out her box camera and stood me and Til against the kudzu vine to take some pictures.

"Push your hair out of your eyes, Tilghman, and stand up there straight. You stand just like your daddy's people. You'll have consumption before you're grown. Stand up there tall like your granpa. Cassandra, get your fingers out of your mouth. You're ruining your hands, biting your nails that way. And it won't hurt you to smile a little. Come to think of it, I've never seen a picture of you smiling."

Then she showed us the king in the pansy. She pulled the velvety petals off one at a time and pointed to the little gold head and big fat body. He was soaking his feet in a long, thin, white tub that covered his toothpick legs.

Monday morning I took the post card out of the mailbox at the foot of the hill. Aunt Flossie read it out loud. "Dear Florence, Granny is bad off. Bring the children as soon as you can. Hope they haven't been too much trouble. Love, Clara."

Aunt Flossie spent the rest of the day washing and ironing our clothes. "I meant to make you a dress or two for school, Cassie. That little jumper won't be warm enough for September."

She had made me a pink jumper trimmed in brown with an elephant holding two balloons embroidered on the front.

"Can you go a few days without that little blue dress?" she asked. "I could cut a pattern from it in a day or two."

Unc did the outside chores, like feeding and watering the livestock, and Til pumped a bucket of water from the cistern for Ole Shep. I wondered how long it would be before I would see the chain of little silver cups climb from the bottom of the cistern again to pour the clear, cold water in the bucket hanging from the spout.

"Don't forget your map of the Holy Land, Cass," Aunt Flossie called from the kitchen, "and don't you want to take some of these cookies to your mother?"

She handed me a tin of cookies as Til and me got into the rumble seat of the dusty coupe. Aunt Flossie unsnapped the isinglass window between us, but didn't say a word as Unc drove down the hill in front of the house and past the mail box and the green meadow where the cows grazed with their calves. Sure enough, Til and me saw the little white-faced, red girl calf that was born the day we went to Darter's Store. Til and me didn't even talk when we went by the King place and Darter's, where Unc turned onto the highway. How many days had it been since we passed by Pemberton Oak on the way to the valley? It didn't seem like any time at all, but I would be glad to see Felix and Maude and Daddy and Mother and Emmy and Jimmie Lou. It had been over a week.

Inside I felt like something had changed. Something would be different when we got home. Maybe it would be different forever. I knew Til was right beside me, but I slid over against him just to make sure. I really wanted to go home, but dreaded it at the same time. It reminded me of wanting to go to school and not wanting to go. I knew one thing for sure. It didn't feel right to have on a dress and it not Sunday.

NINE

When we got home, little groups of people clustered in every room. Granny was in Mother's and Daddy's bedroom, because her room was too little for company. I could hear her short, shallow breathing. She looked tiny, lying there swollen and still in a hollow of pillows. An electric fan groaned from the top of the radio where the boy-and-his-dog figurine had stood as long as I could remember. Three straight-back chairs took the place of Daddy's big rocker in front of the radio.

Mother put her hands on our shoulders and guided us down the hall into the kitchen and said loudly, "Here are our other two. They've been up to my sister's in Holston Valley for a few days." She turned to me and Til. "This is your Uncle John and Aunt Evelyn from Walla Walla, Washington. They came in late last night. Been on the road two weeks. Uncle John is your daddy's big brother."

Uncle John shook hands with Til and said he would have known he was a Blevins if he had seen him anywhere. He put me on his lap. I squirmed to get down until he showed me his gold pocket watch that chimed every fifteen minutes and struck the hour just like the big clock down at the depot. When he asked for a little sugar, I slid off his lap between his legs. He kissed me on the forehead and gave me a nickel. He was different from Mr. Simpson.

Mrs. Simpson's voice came from Granny's little room. She was always near a sick room and read the obituary column every night whether she knew anybody in it or not. She was taking on so loud that everybody could hear her.

"Don't see how the poor thing can last through the night. They ought to have a heartgram made. Her goin on 78 in August, and her existence has been low for some time." She lowered her voice. "Do you know if they've had a preacher yet, Mrs. McCormick?" She consoled Daddy. "You've got so much to be thankful for, Mr. Blevins. What with her bein in her right mind and all. It's a shame the shape a lot of folks go back to God in, bodies mangled beyond His recognition from car wrecks and all."

Daddy hugged me and Til and shook hands with Unc. Everybody stood around the kitchen table and ate fried chicken and biscuits, and pretty soon Unc looked at his pocket watch and said they'd better be getting back to the valley. Mother whispered that it was just a matter of time now, and that the death notice would be in the Bristol paper. Then she talked in her usual voice.

"I can't thank you enough for bringing the children home. It gets mighty lonesome around here without them, and Maude's tired of doing all the milking."

Aunt Flossie told her not to mention it and promised Maude that she could come soon for her vacation. She even said that maybe me and Til could come back later and get our visit out. After quick hugs and handshakes, she and Unc were gone.

Back in the kitchen Daddy and Uncle John waited for the rest of their family. They agreed that their brothers and sisters who lived close by would be there the middle of the afternoon, but they waited anxiously for word from Uncle Clint in California and Uncle Jesse in Iowa. Daddy had wired them both.

Daddy held out his arms, and I jumped at the chance to sit in his lap. He pulled a little envelope out of his shirt pocket and told me to hold out my hands. My ring fell into them. I couldn't even tell where it had been mended. I hugged his neck.

"Sugar won't pay for that," he said, laughing. "That will be one dollar, Feisty Britches."

Uncle John said he would stand good for the debt and collect in sugar.

We moved into the yard in the heat of the day. More people came, and the men squatted on the grass and talked while the women sat on the porch and took turns tiptoeing in and out of the house. Old Doctor Shaw came by again and said there wasn't a thing they could do for Granny at the hospital that Mother couldn't do at home. He said her lungs would fill up now as fast as they could draw the water off. He called it dropsy.

Uncle Clint wired that he couldn't come, but no word came from Uncle Jesse.

I crept outside for a minute to sit on the back steps with Felix. I thought about being at Aunt Flossie's and going down Unc's driveway the last time. Suddenly, I understood that feeling that things would be different. I knew what it meant. What would it be like after Granny was gone? After Granny died? Words like "dead" and "died" were hard to think, much less say, but I thought them, even said them out loud to Felix. Did "died" mean forever?

Granny would be the third. Little Charles Lindbergh and Mrs. Diggs, and now Granny. What would Emmy do without her? Granny was not going to get better. Daddy's eyes showed that, and Mrs. Simpson kept saying, "Her time has about come. She's earned her home up yonder."

Nighttime was not any cooler than daytime had been. Stretching out on hot sheets promised no relief. Anyway, everybody seemed afraid to go to bed, afraid they would miss Granny's dying. She might mumble the name of a loved one who had long ago gone beyond the sunset, or she might say something about a bright light blinding her. And that would be the Baby Jesus come to get her. Nobody wanted to miss that.

Felix curled up in my lap. Although the sun had been down for hours, he still panted. I put him down gently and went back into the house to Granny's room, expecting Mother to say "Bedtime," but all I heard was the fan pushing hot air from one side of the room to the other. Granny fingered the bedclothes and moaned loudly from the mountain of pillows. "Mercy! Mercy! Save me!"

I listened harder when the wheezing stopped for a little, then heard her take a deep breath and cry, "Help me, help me, Jesus!" Then her voice reached to the far corners of the house. "Emmy, Emmy, come here, chile."

And Emmy tried to climb onto the bed, but Granny couldn't help her up. Granny's eyes stayed fixed on the ceiling. Daddy held Emmy in his arms, so Granny could see her, but Granny just stared at the ceiling and mumbled, "Promise me...you'll change ...them younguns' names,...Albert."

Daddy didn't answer. I tiptoed out the back door and sat on the steps with Felix again and asked him what there was to cry about. She was old, and her children were every one grown. Mrs. Diggs didn't even have any children, and she wasn't half as old as Granny when she died. Little Charles Lindbergh didn't even live long enough to have any children. I hugged Felix's neck and crept back through the door to bed in Maude's room. She was with the neighbors on the front porch. I stared into the dark for a long time, afraid that I wouldn't be able to cry when the time came.

I wondered if anybody noticed that I didn't go near Granny's room after breakfast. Me and Til sat on the porch steps in the sun and threw a stick for Felix to fetch. After dinner Granny whispered for Emmy again. Emmy cried when Daddy carried her into the bedroom. Coming back into the kitchen a few minutes later, he choked back tears and wiped Emmy's face with his handkerchief, then handed her to Mother.

"She's gone," he said quietly.

Mother bit her lip. Daddy walked to the window, holding his handkerchief tight against his eyes. I never had seen him cry before. Aunt Birdie sat down at the table and sobbed. Uncle Jay patted her head, then took her home. Mrs. Simpson said she'd call the undertaker from her house and rushed out. In a few minutes, she was back, smelling of fresh powder and wearing a clean apron. She washed the dishes while Mother and Aunt Evelyn wrote the death notice. Daddy and Uncle John took it by the newspaper office, then went by Western Union to wire Uncle Clint and Uncle Jesse.

After the hearse came and took Granny away, I couldn't understand why all the people didn't go home. They had come to see Granny and she wasn't there any more. They hadn't even been there to see her after she came to live with us over four years ago. Aunt Birdie hadn't been there but once since Christmas, and that was after Daddy called and told her that Granny was failing.

The next morning the men carried the casket into the front room and put flower racks behind it and set folding chairs around. Daddy lifted me and Emmy up to see her. Emmy cried into his shoulder. I stared at the familiar wrinkled face. Her hand looked little lying there on her chest, and she had on her good black dress

and her cut-glass beads and cameo pin. I had never seen her without those little horn-rimmed glasses before. Her thin, white hair
looked like it always did, in a knot on top of her head. The only
thing different about her was that her eyes were closed. Mother
said all people close their eyes when they pass away, but I knew
better. Til told me the undertaker had to leave everybody lying in
a cold room all night long with silver dollars on their eyelids to
make them stay closed forever.

"Haven't you ever wondered what Mother means when she
says, 'Why, he's so low-down he'd take the silver dollars off a dead
man's eyes.'?" Til asked. "Now, you know."

And he said if you could get back there in the undertaker's
parlor where they drain all of the corpse's blood out and fill their
veins with alcohol or something like that, you could probably get
eight or ten silver dollars, because they always work on four or five
dead people at a time.

The neighbor women came and brought dinner, and then their
families came and ate. The women stood and whispered in the
kitchen, and the men squatted in the yard and chewed match sticks
or tobacco.

Maude kept the register and the flower cards. The flower truck
came every little bit with more sprays and baskets. Daddy's
brothers and sisters waited until after midnight for word from
Uncle Jesse, but it didn't come. Finally, Uncle John and Aunt Evelyn went to bed with me in Maude's room, next to the living room
where Granny lay a corpse.

The next morning a night letter came from Uncle Jesse saying
that he and Aunt Lutie were on their way. The funeral was set for
2 o'clock that afternoon at Muddy Creek Church, but they hadn't
arrived at 1:30 when the cortege lined up. The undertaker said he
didn't see any harm in waiting after they got to the church a few
minutes. He said they might even be there. Sure enough, when we
pulled into the church yard, there they were. Uncle Jesse looked
like Daddy, only stouter.

"We was about to give you out," Daddy said, hugging him.

Aunt Lutie said they had come straight to the church after
stopping to wash up at a tourist home just out of town. It had
been a long, hard trip with their car boiling over every few miles.
Uncle Jesse pointed to the old Ford.

"She's got over 98,000 mile on her, and the first owner wasn't no old-maid school teacher, neither."

The seat of his pants was shiny, and the button holes of his jacket was frayed. Aunt Lutie's black dress, shorter than Mothers, showed great rings of sweat to her elbows, and her heels were run down.

Inside the church, the Sloan Family Quartet sang all three verses of "Good Night and Good Morning."

By the last time they sang the chorus, I knew it and sang along with them.

Good morning up there where Christ is the light
Good morning up there where cometh no night
When we step from this earth to God's heaven so fair,
We'll say "Good night" here, but "Good morning" up there.

When they heard the music, some people sauntered in to be sure to get a fan and a place by the window. Dusty, dented cars kept pulling into the church yard, and men shook hands with other men who stood under the trees, and women rushed quietly to hug women kinfolks and acquaintances before the funeral began.

The quartet invited everybody into the church with "When the Roll is Called Up Yonder."

When the trumpet of the Lord shall sound, and time shall
    be no more,
And the morning breaks, eternal, bright and fair;
When the saved of earth shall gather over on the other shore,
And the roll is called up yonder, I'll be there.

But everybody didn't go. Daddy put off going inside as long as he could, and Til and me were like leeches. Mother and Maude and Emmy were in there somewhere, waiting, and we knew it wouldn't be long.

A bearded man in overalls stuck out his hand to Daddy. "Why, I didn't know you two fellers had a boy," he said, and spit a wad of tobacco by the oak tree he was leaning on.

Daddy shook his hand and slapped him on the back at the same time. "Archie Millsaps, I'm su'prised I reco'nize you. Tilghman here's my only son. I got me three good cooks though. Ain't seen you in a coon's age. What line of work you in now?"

"Drivin one of them big jewel-wheel trucks for the rock quarry. Seen your woman talkin to her folks a minute ago. Hardly knowed her. She's dropped several pounds since I seen her last."

"How long has it been? I bet we ain't laid eyes on you since Aunt Mandy Roller laid a corpse."

"Yeah. Your mammy was as spry as the next one at them services. I don't reckon I need to tell you how sorry…"

"Much obliged, Archie," Daddy said and picked me up in one arm and put his hand on Til's shoulder to point him toward the church steps. He must have known that "Rock of Ages," Granny's favorite hymn, was the last one before the preacher was to talk. The people got quiet as the ushers took us down where Daddy's brothers and sisters sat and put us with Mother and Maude and Emmy in the pew right in front of Granny's casket.

I wondered what the words all meant.

Rock of Ages, cleft for me,
    Let me hide myself in Thee;
Let the water and the blood,
    From Thy wounded side which flowed,
Be of sin the double cure,
Save from wrath and make me pure.

Cleft. Cleft. I knew it was bad, because that was what a little boy up the street had that kept him from talking plain. Mother said over and over again that he was so smart it was a pity his folks couldn't afford to have that "old cleft palate" fixed.

Maybe when I knew what it all meant I could get saved like Til.

I always thought Granny had been saved, but I was glad to hear the preacher tell when.

"Cassandra Hawk Blevins was born on August 18, 1854, in Fordtown, the daughter of John William and Cassandra Baker Hawk, and passed away on July 2 at the home of her son, Albert, at the age of 77 years, 10 months and 22 days. She accepted Christ as her Savior in this church when she was 16, in 1870, and was married to John Robert Blevins in 1872. That union was blessed with twelve children, eight sons and four daughters. Mr. Blevins passed away in the flu epidemic of 1914, the same week that their boy Earl was taken. Mrs. Blevins was also preceded in death by two sisters and three brothers. She is survived by all of her children except Earl and a daughter, Lottie."

Lottie died with pneumonia a few weeks after she eloped with Tom Doran, who Daddy said wasn't worth the lead it would take to blow him up. He had come by night in the dead of winter and taken Lottie out of the upstairs window at the old brick house.

They found her footprints in the snow leading down to the river bank. She never saw a well day after she got in that boat with Tom Doran, Daddy said.

The preacher droned on, naming Granny's children, and added, "Also surviving are thirty grandchildren and eleven great grandchildren and a host of nieces and nephews."

Til whispered, "Grandchildren—that's us." He printed in a hymnal, and whispered to me, "George Washington, His Book. Valley Forge, Pa., 1776. Death be to him who steals this book."

Another preacher got up with a tuning fork and launched into "Sweet By and By" all by himself.

There's a land that is fairer than day,
And by faith we can see it afar;
For the Father waits over the way,
To prepare us a dwelling place there.

The Sloan Family Quartet joined in on the chorus.

In the sweet, in the sweet, by and by,
We shall meet on that beautiful shore,
In the sweet, in the sweet, by and by,
We shall meet on that beautiful shore.

Daddy cried so hard I wondered if he would ever breathe again. Mother took his hand. I had never seen her do that before.

Then the preacher told us in a raspy voice about how "Our dear beloved Sister Cassie was left a widow woman with children to raise. The baby, Birdie, was just three when Sister Blevins had to go out in the fields and work beside the boys. But her trials and tribulations never diluted her faith, and she taught them all to be God-fearing and support the church. Now He has harvested her for His garden up yonder, a rose to bloom eternally."

Sweat bees floated through the windows and bobbed up and down on our legs. Til reached over and killed one on my knee. It stung, but I didn't dare cry. The pianist played "Softly and Tenderly," and the preacher invited those who wanted a final visit with Granny to come forward.

The men who had stayed out in the yard came first, single file down the aisle, clutching their hats to their chests. The floor creaked above the quiet shuffle. Now and then the preacher stopped whispering to those who were viewing the body long enough to say, "As these retire, let others come forward."

We gathered around the casket last. Daddy held me and Emmy up. I didn't want to see Granny again. Til whispered in Pig Latin. "En-way are-a ee-way oing-gay ome-hay? Ets-lay amoos-vay." I pushed my hair back and thought of Mrs. Diggs and little Charles Lindbergh. I wanted to go home, too.

The quartet started another hymn. The preacher screwed the lid down on Granny's casket, and yelled, "Yes, we'll gather at the river, the be-yew-tee-ful, the be-yew-tee-ful river, gather with the sa-aints at the river that flows by the throne of God."

The flower girls, big granddaughters like Maude, held the flowers and lined the aisle for the pallbearers, the big grandsons, to carry Granny out. Til had lifted a corner of the casket all by himself at home, and he sulked at being left out even after Mother explained there were seventeen grandsons and only six handles. The cortege wound around the gravel road to the cemetery. Mother dug in her purse for a mint.

"Got that old dry throat again," she gasped. "Sure pity those back cars, eating all that dust."

The sun was setting when one of the preachers opened the casket again and threw a red rosebud on Granny and talked about ashes to ashes and dust to dust. Aunt Birdie burst out crying when the undertaker handed her Granny's wedding band and cut-glass beads and cameo pin.

Mother whispered to Daddy, "Let's go now. The children are worn out." He picked Emmy up and started toward the car. Mother took my hand. "What makes Birdie carry on like that? She hardly ever darkened our door when your mother was living, and I wish you'd tell me why he gave her all your mother's good jewelry."

Daddy stood Emmy in the front seat. She screamed and locked her arms around his neck.

He said softly, "You wait right here a minute. I'll be back direckly."

Emmy sobbed and stiffened her body against the back of the seat as he left. Mother found another mint in her purse and unwrapped it for her, but Emmy knocked it out of Mother's hand and buried her wet face in Mother's throat. We watched the men lower the casket on big belts, then shovel dirt on it. Mother said it had to be heaped up in a mound and packed down, because a sunk grave was a sign of neglect, a sign that devils had been dancing on the dead.

Then they banked the grave with flowers. Daddy wore a white carnation in his lapel when he came back to the car.

The sun was down when we got home. The kitchen table was full of food, but the house was empty. I looked into Granny's little room. Some neighbor women had already cleaned it up and rearranged the furniture. The front room looked empty without the flowers and casket. And the folding chairs were gone. Even after Uncle Jesse and Aunt Lutie and Uncle John and Aunt Evelyn came, the house seemed empty. Til changed his clothes and counted his coupons from Granny's Red Rooster snuff boxes. He needed eight more to get a steam engine that puffed real smoke. I put on my overalls and slipped out the back door with Felix. The jarflies' raspy chorus drowned out the cotton mill's steady hum as I ran across the brown grass to the sidewalk. The tar in the seams was soft, and I dug out a hunk with my big toe and put it in my mouth. I spit it into the zinnia bed at the McCormicks, because it didn't taste good unless you mixed it with cinnamon or vanilla extract.

Jimmie Lou was at her desk. "Come on in, honey," she called.

I sat down in the middle of the daybed where it sagged, and, even then, my feet didn't touch the floor. Jimmie Lou sat down beside me.

"I've been thinkin about you all afternoon," she said. "You'll miss her for a while, honey, but she was old. The Bible says that three score and ten makes a ripe old age. A score of years is twenty; so that's sixty, and ten more is seventy. She was 78, going on four score. Lived her life and her time come. Her parts was wore out." Jimmie Lou glanced at herself in the mirror. "At the rate I'm goin, mine will be wore out in half that time."

I didn't look up. "I just got one granma left."

"Hon, I don't have none. You can get along all right without none. Did I ever tell you about my Grandma Zenobee? That's what we all called her, but her name was Zenobia. Where they got that handle, Lord only knows and He ain't talkin. She weighed 64 pounds soakin wet and never had her sweet-gum stick out of her mouth until she had drawed her last breath. Her funeral beat anything I ever seen. Lasted nearly all day, noon to sundown."

Jimmie Lou shoved two straight-back chairs together with the seats touching and got behind them. She leaned over and imitated the preacher. " 'Just look at that sweet smile. A better wo-man than Zenobee God never made.' Pretty soon he acted like they wasn't nobody there but him and her," Jimmie Lou said. "He told Zenobee to go on ahead and prepare a place for him."

Jimmie Lou told how he went to see Grandma Zenobee the day before she died, and he knew she was ready, because she had put on her good pink gown to meet her Maker in, the one she'd been saving since her first bad sick spell five years before. Jimmie Lou fanned us both with a newspaper.

"And after he carried on considerable for about two hour," she said, "we went to the graveyard. Cousin Minnie, Crying Minnie we call her because she takes on so at a funeral, she almost fell into the grave sobbin. She always does it, whether she knows the departed or not. And her just Grandma's fifth cousin!"

I squirmed. "I got to go home now."

"Aw, Cassie, don't be like a square peg in a round hole. You just got here and they won't miss you for a while. We ain't even worked none with figures yet." She sat down on the dresser bench to brush her hair. "Did I ever show you how to make a lantern?"

"They won't let us play with fire."

"Sometimes a girl needs a little light to guide her in a dark world. I read somewheres that our most important travelin is done alone on a unknown road in a dark world."

She got a shoe box and cut out some daisies and a moon and some stars, then pasted some crepe paper behind them and punched holes on two sides of one end for a ribbon handle. She stuck a birthday candle holder through the other end, and when she lit the candle, the light flickered through the moon and stars and daisies. Jimmie Lou held the lantern by her side. "Carry it carefully, like this, hon."

I held it up and watched the light glow. I wanted to hug Jimmie Lou, but I couldn't with the lantern in my hand. "You keep it here and we'll watch it together when I come. It'll be just ours." I was afraid of fire after the shack burned, but felt safe as long as Jimmie Lou was with me.

"Okay, Cassie, have it your way. Don't you want no perfume on you today?"

"No, thank you. Got to go. They don't know where I'm at."

"Just a dab right there," she said and touched my neck with the cold glass tube. "There! You'll smell so good they won't make you take your Saturday bath."

I reached up and put my arms around her neck, but when our eyes met, I looked away and stuffed my hands into my pockets. She picked me up and settled in a straight-back chair and rocked. She held me tight against her and dropped her cheek against the top of my head.

"Has anybody but me ever told you how perty your hair is, Miss Cassandra?"

My face got hot, and I jumped down and ran to the door. "Thanks for the lantern. Thanks for the perfume. Thanks."

I slipped in the back door at home just in time for supper. Aunt Evelyn and Uncle John had gone visiting for the night, but Uncle Jesse and Aunt Lutie were spending the night in Maude's room. They planned to leave for Iowa early in the morning. Mother shook her head when Aunt Lutie said they had left their six children alone. Uncle Jesse said the Depression had hit farmers worse than anybody else, and it was likely to get worse before it got better.

"Bottom's fell clean out of the market. Crops is good, but I'm sellin corn at a quarter of what it ought to bring, and my dollar won't hardly buy half the sugar it did two year ago."

Emmy had gone to bed in Granny's little room, and Mother sent me to sleep with her. I heard her sniffle as she wadded herself up on top of the sheet. Then she burst into tears.

"Granny was my best friend," she said, and sobbed and squirmed toward me until we touched. Emmy never had cuddled up to me before.

I stared into the dark, thinking, and finally said, "Granny had lived her life and her time had come. The Bible teaches us that three score and ten makes a ripe old age. A score of years is twenty, so that adds up to seventy. Granny was almost 78, and her parts were worn out, and she hurt all over and was lonesome for her mother and grandmother."

"And Baby Jesus? She told me she was going to see Him."

"Yes, and Grandpa and Aunt Lottie and Uncle Earl."

Emmy rubbed her eyes and nose with the sheet. "Will she see Mrs. Diggs?"

"Yes," I answered. "And little Charles Lindbergh. And if we're good, we'll see them some day, too."

"I want to see Granny right now."

"You can't. She's gone away." I wondered what Jimmie Lou would say. Then an answer came. "She's gone so far away that we don't know how to get there. Don't even have a map. It takes years and years, a long way beyond Aunt Flossie's and Unc's."

I wanted to scoot away from her when hot tears began to leak out of my eyes, but I didn't. I slipped my arm under her shoulders.

Ten

*A*fter supper the next day, Daddy leaned back in his chair, lifting the front legs off the floor, and put his thumbs in his belt. "You wouldn't guess in a hunderd years who came by the store today, Clary. You'd remember them, too, Johnny, but you ain't seen them in a whet." He let the front legs of his chair hit the floor. "Uncle Lige Bridwell and Effie."

Mother said, "Albert, I wish you wouldn't treat those good chairs that way."

Uncle John didn't remember them.

"Uncle Lige is 85 if he's a day, and she ain't far behind him. He said she's got so old and ugly he can't stand to kiss her good-bye, so he just takes her with him ever'where he goes." They all laughed. "He said she ain't never been nothin but trouble and satisfaction." Uncle John still didn't remember him.

"Now you ain't been gone from here that long, Johnny. You're bound to remember his daddy's funeral when we was boys there at the old brick house. He was so big that they had to make a casket for him. Couldn't a bought one if they'd had the money. And they had to take the door facin off to get it through."

Mother spoke up. "Now, you've got it all wrong, Albert. You're talking about Ike. He was the big Bridwell."

"No such thing. I know what I'm talkin about. They was our neighbors for a while."

"I guess I know what I'm talking about, too. My daddy preached at both of those funerals."

The front legs of Daddy's chair hit the floor again. "You'd argue with the Devil hisself, Clary."

Uncle John bragged on the coconut cake Maude served. "You're mighty young to know that the way to a man's heart is through his stomach. That'll help you get a good man. Your pa will have to beat them away from the door," he said, laughing.

Daddy didn't laugh. "Only one I've had to beat away so far is really a good one—good for nothing. That Fred Gaylor. His daddy moved in here last year and opened up a pool hall and beer parlor. Whole family's the last of peatime. Their heads is as empty as pea pods in August, and their ways is as tough."

"Now, Albert, that's enough," Mother said. "Fred makes good grades. There's no reason for you to hold his daddy's line of work against him."

Daddy got up and went into the bedroom to turn on Lowell Thomas. "Come here, Johnny," he called. "They're gonna replay that speech that Roosevelt gave Saturday in Chicago."

That was the day Granny died, one of the few days that Lowell Thomas didn't share the news with Daddy. The radio was not on all day. Of course, the speech was written up in the paper, but nobody had taken time to read it yet. All we knew was that Roosevelt would be elected President and that would make a man named Garner Vice-President. Me and Til followed Uncle Johnny into the bedroom. Mother and Aunt Evelyn cleared the table, and Maude started doing the dishes.

Lowell Thomas said that the historic occasion deserved more than a momentary spotlight, now that the presidential race had begun in earnest. He said that Roosevelt had already mapped out a strenuous cross-country campaign against the advice of party leaders who insisted that he use the radio to save his energy. He said Roosevelt was determined to show the American people an image of action and strength, despite his crippled legs. Infantile paralysis had made him an invalid after he got married.

Lowell Thomas reminded us that Roosevelt, Governor of New York, was the first candidate to fly to a national convention to accept the nomination for President. A flimsy, tri-motored plane took him, his wife Eleanor and an airsick son through thunderstorms from Albany to Chicago, stopping to refuel in Buffalo and

Cleveland. Lowell Thomas said that when Roosevelt finally entered the convention hall, wearing a blue suit with a red rose in his lapel, the delegates stood up, and the cheers easily drowned out the boos.

Daddy clapped like he was at the convention in the Congress Hotel. "He's tellin us how to say his name. What do you want to bet that ole Hoover will have to work for a livin yet?"

Lowell Thomas reminded us again that we were about to hear parts of Governor Roosevelt's acceptance speech made in Chicago on Saturday, July 2.

Roosevelt's voice came on the air. His decision to fly to Chicago, he said, was to show that "absurd traditions" had to be broken.

I was afraid to talk out loud, so I whispered to Til, and he whispered, "Habits," as Roosevelt said, "Let it be from now on the task of our Party to break foolish traditions and leave it to the Republican leadership, far more skilled in that art, to break promises."

I knew what that meant. Everybody older than me had told me what that meant. They told me that if you broke promises, you couldn't get saved and go to heaven.

Roosevelt said that the Republicans had favored a few people while many people suffered, and that "Ours must be a party... of the greatest good to the greatest number of our citizens." He said it was obvious that the prosperity of the few would not leak through to labor, to the farmer and to the little businessman. I knew that Daddy was a little businessman and had always been one or another of those three kinds of men.

Daddy clapped when Roosevelt talked about a shorter work week and planting trees.

Mother and Aunt Evelyn came in and stopped talking to listen when he mentioned "spiritual values." Mother said, "Now, if he really means that, I will vote for him, but talk is cheap."

Daddy stared at her from his rocker. "Why, of course you'll vote for him. You wouldn't kill my vote, would you?"

When Roosevelt talked about hope of salvation and cried out, "I pledge you, I pledge myself, to a new deal for the American people," he reminded me of Aunt Flossie's preacher. Everybody on the air clapped and whistled and shouted, and the organ blared out, "Happy Days Are Here Again," and Lowell Thomas signed off.

Daddy said that the bad times were almost over. I knew what he meant when he read a story out loud from the Clarksville *Tribune* about how just over the Virginia line children without shoes nearly froze to death walking to school last winter, and now they were living on boiled weeds and violet tops and onions. Uncle John told about a four-year-old boy out in Washington whose stomach busted from eating plantain that his mother had boiled for greens. He reminded Daddy that farmers in Kansas and Colorado were ignored last summer when they said that dust storms were burying their wheat and blinding their cattle and blotting out the sun for days on end.

Daddy said that the sun in the valley parched the tobacco so bad last summer that farmers didn't even cut and cure it. "They just let it lay in the fields and rot. And every few weeks another cloudburst warshes more of the rich soil away," he said. "The grass right now is so withered that it don't have no roots strong enough to hold the soil. A man ought to be made to plant a tree for ever one he cuts on a place," he said, crossing his legs and leaning back in the chair. "Ever'body ought to know it's the grass and trees that keeps the water in the soil and keeps the wind from blowin the soil away."

"But they don't give a thought to tomorrow," Uncle John said. "And hundreds of years from now when this land becomes a desert, people will not even know that they are reaping the harvest of their fathers' sins. They'll probably blame it on the weather and blame the weather on God."

Aunt Evelyn agreed. "It gets harder and harder to find a man with the fear of the Lord in his heart."

"Or woman," Uncle Johnny reminded her.

Mother sent me to see what Emmy was doing. She was too quiet, so I expected to find her asleep in Granny's bed. She wasn't there. I found her on her knees on the counter of the kitchen cabinet, holding the salt box over her mouth. Her head was thrown back and her mouth was open, and salt poured from the spout, some into her mouth and some down her overalls bib.

I yelled for Daddy, and he jumped up and grabbed her by her feet and held her upside down all the way to the back yard, pounding her between her shoulders on the way. Mother poured warm water from the tea kettle down her throat. Emmy vomited and strangled and vomited some more.

"She's turning blue," Mother cried as she ran toward the Simpsons' house to call the doctor.

"No need to call him this time of night," Daddy said. "She'll be all right as soon as she catches her breath. I think we've got rid of the salt."

I felt hot tears leave my eyes. Emmy wasn't breathing. It looked like she never would catch her breath. I don't know how long it was before she opened her eyes and whispered, "Granny." Mother carried her into Granny's bedroom and rocked her to sleep with a cold washcloth on her forehead. The rest of us sat quietly and listened to the Grand Ole Opry.

When Mother slipped into Granny's little bed with Emmy, I knew I could sleep with Til. We hadn't slept together since we got home from Aunt Flossie's. I was wide awake.

"You miss Granny?" I asked.

"Miss them coupons," he answered. "Would have had me enough if she had lived eight more weeks."

"Do you think Daddy loved her more than he does Mother?"

Til rolled over on his stomach and propped his head in his hands. "After all, she *was* his mother. One of the Ten Commandments. She left a five-dollar bill in her pocketbook. Found it there today when I was looking for coupons."

"She didn't keep coupons in her good pocketbook and you know it. Where's heaven, anyway?"

He didn't answer.

"Jimmie Lou told me she was three score and ten and her parts were wore out."

"Jimmie Lou? She don't know nothin about it. Poor white trash!"

"Is not."

"Is so. Daddy said so. Have you seen that old jalopy down there? Well, that belongs to a ole boy from down Church Hill. And he don't stop by there to talk. Ralph's been down there, too. He says when she gets knocked up, they'll have to wait for the baby to come to know who the daddy is."

"What does knocked up mean?"

"Hand me that biggest, black book outta the bottom of the closet there," Til said. "That's my dictionary."

He thumbed through it. When his eyes landed, he answered, "Means to make pregnant. Also means to wear out, exhaust, or become worn out or exhausted. But when Daddy says it, it means to make pregnant — to plant a seed that grows into a baby."

"Does it hurt when you get knocked up?" I asked.

"One thing for sure," Til said, laughing. "It don't hurt him."

"Is Ralph telling the truth?" I asked.

"Probably. He gets around."

"I don't believe it. Mother said she don't put much stock in what he says. I'd believe Woody quicker."

"Woody knows better than to go to a white girl. Knows Ralph and me would kill him." He clenched his fist. "Shhh," he said. "Let's listen to what Mother and Daddy are talking about."

Mother asked Daddy if it would be all right for Uncle Lee to stay in Granny's room while he looked for work in town. He was going to get married as soon as he got work, so he wouldn't be there long.

Daddy didn't take to the idea. "He's a big eater," he said, "and I was hoping we could put Cassandry in there with Emmy."

"It'll be for just a little while," Mother said. "Emmy's so heartbroken I think we'll keep her in our room for a few days."

"Wouldn't it bother you to have him around Maude?" Daddy asked.

"Can't believe you'd ask a thing like that about my baby brother after all I've done for your family."

"Better go to sleep. We'll talk about it later."

Emmy seemed all right the next day, but was as white as the inside of a coconut and didn't talk any. She didn't even answer Daddy when he asked, "What in the world made you do a thing like that?" When he laughed and said her eyes looked like two pee holes in the snow, she cried.

Mother made him hush. "Quit picking on her. She just misses Granny."

Uncle John and Aunt Evelyn left most of their things at our house when they went to visit relatives and came back for the weekend so we could spend the night on the fish trap at Daddy's old homeplace on the river.

The weather cock stood as still as the lightning rods on the old brick house where Daddy and Uncle John grew up, about ten miles from town. Hens scratched around in the scrawny petunias below the porch where the renter and his wife rocked in silence.

Daddy said that since the light and power company had bought out the heirs and put that old man and woman in there, the place had gone to rack and ruin. Said they were too lazy to breathe country air. Time was when all hundred acres were in corn, he reminded us.

"Hidy," Daddy called, opening the gate.

"Hidy," they echoed.

"Anything bitin?" Daddy asked.

The renter shifted his wad of tobacco and slurred, "Few cat and carp." The chickens scurried across the yard when he leaned forward and shot a stream of tobacco juice against the bare earth.

Daddy said, "We thought we'd go down to the trap for the night." The fish trap was about two miles down the river from where we camped, just down the hill from the old house.

"Help yourself," the renter called, and Daddy began to unload the car and hand us as much stuff as we could carry.

"Got to get a hustle on or dark will catch us without firewood," he said. We wound single file down the path through the pear orchard.

Mother took a bite of a green pear and spit it out. "Evelyn, I wish you'd tell me why the Blevinses planted these old Garbers. Little green knots that will be as hard in September as they are right now. If they were Kieffers, I'd make some preserves, but these things aren't worth canning."

Aunt Evelyn laughed. "Why, they didn't know any better. Didn't know their backside from a hole in the ground."

Daddy and Uncle John didn't pay any attention.

Mother yelled at Til. "Pick up that dog and carry him past that barn, and look where you're stepping."

We walked past the cows and piled the stuff together on the river bank. Daddy loaded us women and girls into the flatbottom first. Mother held the sides and sat up rigid as the boat rocked every time Daddy dug his paddle into the dark water. Hollows between the hills became deep, black wrinkles. Birds darted here and there on their way home, and a buzzard circled slowly, high above us. The mist lay white and cold over the shoals where Daddy had to jump out and guide the boat. When goose bumps popped out on my arms, I crossed them and rubbed my shoulders. Daddy threw his lumber jacket around me and eased the flatbottom up against the stone wall that stretched from the bank more than halfway across the river, then lifted us one at a time onto the wall that had been a dam once.

He helped Mother, Maude and Emmy, then swung me to the top with one arm, but he grunted when he grabbed Aunt Evelyn under the arms with both hands.

"Evalina, you're gonna have to leave off some of them vittles," he kidded her. "But then I don't know what I would do for ballast."

"That's enough of your sass, young man," she said, grinning.

He yelled, "If I'm not back in three days, send the posse," and rowed off to get Til and Uncle John and the blankets and food.

"Albert Blevins, I wouldn't have the nerve to joke about a thing like that," Mother yelled after him. Daddy laughed and paddled out of sight, past the corn fields that tilted against the twilight sky.

I followed Maude off the wall into the woods to pick up some firewood. Then, with our arms full, we made our way carefully back to the others on the big wire screen that slanted from the wall into the deep water. It was like a window screen, only lots bigger and stronger, but Mother said she never slept a wink out there with that water lapping at the screen just below her feet. Soon faint stars flickered here and there like fireflies; before long, they would fill the night sky like they did at Aunt Flossie's.

When Daddy returned, he built a fire on top of the wall, then we sat around and talked and waited for the fish to float up on the screen. He knocked them in the head and tossed them into the old zinc tub that had wintered there on the trap. It was half full when we ate. After supper me and Til sat on the wall, still warm from the summer sun, and spit watermelon seeds into the foam below. Daddy handed Aunt Evelyn a cup of black coffee.

She sputtered. "What in the name of tarnation do you call that stuff? Strong enough to float a horseshoe."

"Why, you women don't know the first thing about making good coffee," he told her. "It's simple. Just double the recipe for everything but water." He offered Mother a cup. She shook her head. "I think more of my stomach than to put that stuff in it."

Daddy and Uncle John talked about how the slaves made the bricks for their old homeplace right there on the river bank and how the big iron rings nailed into the timbers in the cellar held the slaves' arms up all night long when they had disobeyed.

"But they was good to em, they tell me," Daddy said. "Worked right alongside em. Why, we don't know the first thing about hard work, and these kids know even less. Eatin their white bread and honey. When we was their age, we walked four mile in the snow to school after milkin half a dozen cows and feedin the stock."

Til pretended to play the violin. Uncle John rubbed his hands together over the fire. "Times ain't like they once was, Albert. I hope they don't ever have to work like we did, but if this Depression keeps up, they may get a taste of how we was raised."

Mother and Aunt Evelyn made pallets on top of the big screen where the water wouldn't lap against our feet. Up in the sky the big dipper's handle looked close enough to touch. In school they would teach me how far away it was and what stars were made of and what held them up and what would happen if Chicken Little was right. What if the sky *did* fall in? As the full moon climbed higher, I scrouged deeper into the scratchy, linsey-woolsey blanket against Til's long, lean body.

Suddenly, Felix let out a yelp, and Daddy jumped up to shine the flashlight on the big rocks in the shallow water below the wall. There Felix was, in the swirling water, whining and struggling to get on a rock. Til started to jump in after him, but Daddy grabbed his arm.

"You couldn't no more jump down there without breakin a leg than you could take wings and fly. Like as not, he'll be right back here in the mornin before breakfast."

Daddy put his lumber jacket around Til's shoulders. Til sobbed. We watched Felix disappear down the river, his head bobbing in and out of the swift water. Daddy said that if he didn't get knocked unconscious on the rocks, he would drift down to calmer waters and swim ashore and find his way back up the bank. Mother said a dog could swim the day he was born and that she'd never heard of a dog getting drowned or lost.

"Why, you can drop a dog across the state line over in Virginia, and he'll find his way back home in a day or two. They tell me it's their second nature," she said.

Til took the flashlight and ran to the end of the dam, still a long way from the bank. In olden days, the dam went all the way across the river, but years ago, Daddy said, when they stopped dredging for sand, they broke off one end so that the little river could go down to the big one and then to the ocean. Slowly, Til laced the water and the bank with the beam. I had never heard him cry like that before. He always told me it was sissy to cry.

I ran to the end of the dam where he was. Daddy walked behind me and stood between Til and me with his arms around our shoulders. I leaned my head against his leg. Hot tears made paths down my cheeks and wet his moleskin pants. Daddy didn't sound angry when he said, "Til, you're callin that dog so loud that you couldn't hear him even if he was to answer you. Now, you might as well quit your snifflin and go to bed."

Til kept throwing the flashlight beam on the bank. I waited for Daddy to tell us that Felix was just a dog, that we could get another one if he didn't come back. How could I tell him that Felix wasn't just a dog? That it was like there were three of us, me and Til and Felix?

Daddy didn't mention Felix again, just turned us toward the pallets and said quietly, "Now, it's time we all went to bed. Tomorrow's gonna be a big day with all that fishin and swimmin and eatin."

Mother called Til to her pallet and held him close. "Why, your teeth are chattering. No need to make yourself sick, son. It's out of our hands until morning." She held up one side of the blanket; he crawled under it and scooted against her and cried himself to sleep.

I crawled under Maude's blanket and wiped my eyes with it.

Emmy slept with Aunt Evelyn, and I don't know whether Daddy and Uncle John ever went to bed or not.

As the fog began to lift early the next morning, we heard whimpers across the river. Daddy and Til jumped into the flatbottom. I stood on the end of the dam and watched Til jump out before Daddy got to the bank. In a minute Til was back in the boat with Felix in his arms. When Daddy eased the boat up against the dam, Til handed Felix to me. Wet and shaking, the dog snuggled against my neck. Dark blotches of blood matted his coat.

As Daddy paddled us back to the campground for breakfast, Til leaned out the back of the boat and scooped the cold water onto Felix with his hands. Weak and hungry, the dog lay in his wet lap, looking at us with tired, but clear eyes. Mother examined the scratches after the blood was washed away and assured us that they were only skin deep, caused by "those old multiflora roses."

"People actually plant those things along their fence rows, and before they know it, they have a jungle," she said, to nobody in particular. "I wouldn't have those things if you dug them up and planted them for me. Would you, Evelyn?"

Aunt Evelyn didn't answer. Either she didn't hear, or she was looking at the white windflowers that carpeted the river bank or the tall, scarlet columbine that clung to the limestone ledges above.

The sun drew the dampness out of our clothes as we rounded "Jumbo Rock," a big hunk of cliff that was the shape of an elephant whose ear had broken off and landed in the water. After we got to the campground, Til and me and Felix went for firewood, while Mother and Aunt Evelyn fixed to cook eggs and grits and bacon and fish for breakfast. Daddy went back to the dam for Uncle John and Maude and Emmy.

Til soon found a grapevine to carry him out over the water for a long drop and a big splash, but Mother made him stay on the bank for an hour after breakfast.

"They tell me there's no pain in the world like those cramps you get from going swimming too soon after a meal," she told him. "Kills a lot of young men."

When he took a run and jump and grabbed the grapevine for a big ride over the water, she wrung her hands and bit her lip. He gave a Tarzan yell as he plunged toward the water and disappeared.

In the middle of the afternoon, she called to Daddy. "I wish you'd make him stop that. He's your only son, Albert, the only one that will carry your name. But he'll never live to be grown."

Daddy laughed softly and said, "Why, Clary, you beat all!"

Aunt Evelyn consoled her. "Quit that worrying, Clara. He's all boy. You wouldn't want him any other way, would you?"

Soon, Mother motioned for us to get out of the water and dry off. "Time to get started home. Dark will catch us," she warned.

It was uphill all the way back to the car. We didn't have as much to carry, but it was heavier. The linsey-woolsey blanket scratched my face and neck as I carried it in my arms, but I finally threw it on the floor of the back seat and crawled in on top, buried my face in the smell of campfire smoke, and slept all the way home.

We bathed and went straight to bed. I wanted Uncle John and Aunt Evelyn to stay forever, but their house was in Washington. Maybe one day, Uncle John said, they would move to Clarksport, but he had business to take care of 3,000 miles away. So, after a hurried trip to the cemetery to put flowers on Granny's grave,

Uncle John and Aunt Evelyn left for Walla Walla. The house seemed empty without them. I thought of Uncle John every time Daddy blew his nose. The strong smell of peppermint oil drifted through the house. Uncle John had brought it from out West and told Daddy that a drop on his handkerchief would keep his head clear.

Eleven

*M*other cleared her throat at the dinner table and told Daddy that Uncle Lee was going to stop by in the afternoon. "If it's all right, I'll tell him his room is ready," she said.

"You know that don't set too well with me, but if he'll hustle and get hisself a job right away, I guess it'll be all right." He cleaned his finger nails with the blade of his pocket knife. "Just don't know where he'll find work in this town, Clary. Tell him to try the mill. They tell me they've took back about half of the men they laid off."

He let me go with him and Til to stock the shelves at the B&B. Til sneaked behind the counter and called a store across town. He put a handkerchief over the telephone and asked, "You all got any loose crackers?" After a pause, he ordered, "Go out and catch me a dozen. I'll be by directly." Then he hung up and opened a box of canned hominy grits with a knife and kicked it over to me and went to call another store.

Mother kept the store at noon so Daddy could take us to the barber shop. She brushed a few strands of hair down on my forehead and suggested bangs.

"We can't let her go to school with a boy's bob and overalls," she said again. I brushed my hair back and dashed around the corner to tell Mr. Matlock, the barber, that I wanted pink hair tonic. It smelled like Mrs. Diggs' strawberries. Pretty soon they'd let my hair grow out, and Maude would curl it on old socks. She put hers up on kid curlers, and Mother put hers up with the curling iron, but they had started out on socks, because that wouldn't split your ends.

When we got back, Til had to leave for his violin lesson with Miss Sophie Artz, who was just one generation removed from the old country where everybody was musical. He never would practice, but Miss Artz convinced Mother that he had talent. Daddy said they might as well strike a match to that dollar every Saturday, but Mother said that exposing that boy to the finer things of life was almost as important as making ends meet.

"There's some music on my side of the house," she said, and Til said if he had one of those Stradivarius fiddles, he might be a famous violinist when he grew up. At recital time he looked just like Little Lord Fauntleroy in his pongee blouse that buttoned onto black velvet kneebritches.

While Til was gone, I waited in the Dodge for Daddy to go on a delivery run. He went in the store to pick up the last order when I heard them coming around the corner. There must have been twenty-five of them, all talking at once, shuffling toward the B&B. I got on my knees and peeked out the car window. If they saw me they would kidnap me for sure. It would be easy for them to shoot Mother and Daddy in the B&B and take me out of the car when they left. The man and woman in front could be the very ones that kidnapped and killed little Charles Lindbergh. Dark-skinned, like Granma, he wore a black shirt open all the way down to his belt buckle and had long black curly hair, even on his chest. He carried an empty burlap bag. She wore a gathered skirt down to her ankles, and her greasy hair hung down over her low-necked blouse. Her big gold earrings sparkled, and gold bracelets clanged on her arms.

Others like them rounded the corner, muttering loudly, carrying empty burlap bags. Two by two, they marched through the double doors that Daddy had propped open to make it easier to load the car with groceries for the Kernses and the Dawsons and the Simpsons. I watched through the big, plate-glass windows as the strangers divided into two rows and walked slowly around the store, scooping cans of everything into the bags. They met in front of the cash register where Mother and Daddy stood. Daddy had got his gun out of the drawer. He yelled, "Put ever last can back where you got it or I'll kill ever last one of you." The women dropped their heavy bags, but the men just swung theirs over their shoulders. Daddy held the gun in front of him. "Now, I mean what I say. Just try to get out of here with as much as a loaf of bread."

They didn't move. Mother covered her face with her hands and leaned against the shelves behind the cash register. Daddy held the gun up so they all could see it. "This ain't no cap buster. I'll kill the whole shootin match."

Mother screamed, "Don't shoot, Albert. For the Lord's sake, don't shoot!"

Daddy didn't pay any attention to her. He tried to speak slowly and clearly, like none of them understood English. "I'm going to count to ten, and if you want tomorrow to come, you had better be out on that sidewalk by then."

I could hear the men grumble as they shoved the cans back onto the shelves and shuffled toward the door. Daddy counted slowly, herding them with the gun. He got to seven before they were all outside, stomping their feet and waving limp burlap bags in the hot, humid air. They shook their fists and shouted. I couldn't understand a word they said.

Daddy yelled, "You varmints! You had better not come back around here." He aimed the gun at them until the last one stomped around the corner.

I bolted out of the car and grabbed Daddy around the legs. His arm fell around my shoulders and we walked back into the B&B. Mother was still sniffling behind the cash register. He laid the gun down and put his arms around her.

"It's all right, Clary. They're gone."

She cried softly. "What would have become of me if they had come five minutes later?"

Daddy handed her his handkerchief. "If that happens and I'm not around, let them take what they want. They won't do you no harm. Just hungry. Good-for-nothin Gypsies. Get Mrs. Simpson to stay with you while Cass and me are gone this afternoon."

At the table that night, Daddy said he was sure they were camping just up the highway. "Another sign of the Depression," he said. "They tell me they's not a mean bone in their body. Why, if they had wanted to, they could have took that gun away from me without a struggle. It woulda been about twenty-five agin one and that kinda fun ain't even been named yet." He laughed.

Mother collapsed into the rocker. "Getting hungry makes a man mean, they tell me. They tell me a man will do anything to get food for his family."

"They steal plenty ever day," Daddy said. "That's their way of life. Foreigners in a way. They tell me they travel in bands all over the South in hard times. Have a real king, they say, drives a big Cadillac."

"Where do they come from?" Mother asked.

"They tell me they headquarter in Birmin'ham and go out in groups like that, movin from one little town to another, helpin theirselves to what they want."

"It comes to a pretty pass when they'll walk right into your place of business and steal you blind right in front of your eyes. It might be time for us to get out of the grocery store, Albert." Mother soaked her hands in a saucer of lemon juice and water to get rid of the blackberry stains. "There's not another woman in this town works like I do. Puts up 35 quarts of blackberries and clerks in a grocery store the same day." Her voice got louder. "And looks after four children. Albert, are you listening to me? I've got to have some relief. You've got to get some help or look into some other kind of work."

Daddy sat in his undershorts and shirt by the open window to read the newspaper. Not a breeze stirred. Mother lowered her voice. "I've got to spend more time with these children, or they'll go straight to the dogs. Can't have Maudie down there at that store with them roughnecks around. Just can't have it. And you've got to spend more time with Tilghman. Lot of boys his age wind up in reform school. Disgrace us all. If I had to do over, we never would have left the farm."

Daddy finally looked up at her. "Been thinkin about sellin the store and gettin on reg'lar at one of the plants. I ought to go into 'lectricity, or start makin toilet paper, as much as these kids use. But this just ain't the time to make a change, Clary. No jobs to be had right now. We're lucky. Eatin while others go hungry."

Mother told us to go to bed. Emmy had gone long ago, and Maude sat in the corner of the room, brushing her hair and reading a new book called "Honeymoon Hotel."

Mother tuned up again. "Surely there's somebody reliable you could get to work a few hours a week down there. Do you reckon Lee knows figures well enough?"

Daddy's voice tightened. "We can't afford it, Clary. You know that as well as I do. It's got to get better one day, and then you won't have to can *nothin*."

"I wouldn't have that old canned fruit at the store. Too much sugar," she complained. "Ruin your kidneys. Weak kidneys run in my family. My daddy's always had weak kidneys." She turned to me and Til. "I'm going to tell you one more time to go to your bed."

After everybody went to bed, the only light in the house streamed through the windows from the stars. Til sat cross-legged on the bed. "Did you say they come down the highway and went back the same way?"

I whispered, "Yeah, where do you reckon they went to?"

"Let's go find out."

I shuddered to think of what would have happened if they had seen me. "Do you reckon they could be the ones that kidnapped little Charles Lindbergh and left his body on that trash pile?"

"If you *aren't* comin, I'll go get Woody. He ain't no scaredy-cat. He'd be better in the dark anyway." Til rolled off the bed and slid into his overalls. He knew that he had said all it would take to get me up and dressed.

He opened the screen door just wide enough for us to squeeze through. We tiptoed down the driveway. The trees cast dim, still shadows under the street lights. I wanted to take his hand, but he ran ahead, and I couldn't catch up with him. He slowed down a little when he got into the dark beyond the street lights in the business district along the highway, but I still couldn't catch up with him. Suddenly, he stopped dead in his tracks. I spotted a wisp of smoke rising beyond the coal yard.

He cupped his hands and whispered loudly, "See? What did I tell you?"

Four old wagons with automobile tires were parked in a circle around a fire. When we got closer, we could see that the wagons had been bright yellow, orange and red, but now they looked like they had been rained on for a long time. Four skinny horses with faces like dried prunes stared at the ground.

We got close enough to hear the Gypsies talking a strange language. I recognized two of the women sitting on a blanket rocking babies. The men leaned against the wagons and talked in low voices. One woman put bread and cheese out of a burlap bag on the tailgate of a wagon.

I whispered, "Are they just now getting supper ready?"

"Looks like it," Til whispered. "No tellin how many places they had to go before they rounded up enough. One thing for certain, they ain't none of that stuff from our store." He checked the tread on a wagon tire with his pocket knife. "Could run over a dime and tell whether it's heads or tails. Wonder where all they been. Like as not Florida and Washington and all over."

"What happens when they get caught?"

"Nothin. Too many of em. Not a jail in the country big enough to hold em all."

"They go to school?"

"What do they need to read and write for?"

I stepped back when one of the men started toward us. He walked between two wagons.

"Just going to get a little dew off his kidneys," Til said.

I shivered. "Where do they go in the winter?"

"Beach in Florida," he answered.

A baby cried. "What if one of them gets bad sick?" I asked.

"Shhh. If they hear you, they'll make you go with them."

I shivered and crossed my arms and pressed my fingers into my shoulders. "I'm cold, Til," I whined. "We'd better go home."

"Shh. I'm thinkin about askin them to take me into their tribe. I'd like to go to Florida for the winter. They do it by scratchin your arm and puttin a drop of your blood in their leader's veins and a drop of his in yours."

I searched his face in the dim light. "You can't go to Florida. We got to go to school."

"Wouldn't if I was with them."

"You might get hungry."

"I'd just walk in a store and get me whatever I wanted to eat."

"You might get shot."

The Gypsies spooned stew into tin cups from a big black pot, then dipped bread into the cups and ate. Til crept behind a wagon and lifted a flap. "Looky here. A whole wagonload of stuff."

I pushed my hair back and blurted out, "We got to go home. Mother will think we've been kidnapped."

"Shh. Mother's asleep."

A wrinkled old man sat cross-legged in front of the fire and strummed a guitar. They all hummed. It sounded like a lullaby.

The babies went to sleep, and the children crawled under ragged blankets spread on the ground. The fire died down and the women got out more tattered covers.

I shivered. "Where do they get their mail?"

Til squatted beside me. "They got mansions in Birmin'ham."

"I heard Daddy say that," I said. My teeth chattered. "We got to go home," I whimpered. "I got to pee."

"You can't pee here," he warned. He unbuttoned his overalls, and aimed his peejabber at a wagon wheel. I cried and wet my overalls when I heard it. He grabbed my hand, and we ran all the way home, and stripped and slipped between the sheets without a stitch on. We played Monopoly, but before we had bought anything much, Til lay down and began to churn himself.

He laughed. "Too bad you ain't got nothin for me to hold onto. Looky how mine's growin."

I thought of Mr. Simpson. Til put my hand on his peejabber and explained again, "Got to exercise it a little ever night, and if you do it instead of me, it'll grow twice as fast."

His peejabber got a little bigger.

"Some of them measure a foot," he said, measuring the air with his hands apart.

"Sounds like one of your fish stories to me," I said. "Mr. Simpson's ain't even but half that big."

"How do *you* know?"

What if he told Daddy? Daddy would shoot Mr. Simpson that very day. What if *I* told Daddy? He would believe me and kill Mr. Simpson even quicker.

I finally answered, "Seen it in his pants leg."

"Don't he wear no BVD's?"

"Must not. It bulged down his leg when he was sitting on the porch." I didn't even tell Til how it felt like Mr. Simpson's peejabber would bust right through his pants when I sat in his lap.

"Why does Mother make Daddy wear BVD's all of the time?" I asked.

"To keep his peejabber from sticking out. Mother says only white trash men go without BVD's, just like only white trash women go without brassieres."

"Jimmie Lou don't wear one, and she ain't white trash."

"Is so. BVD's and brassieres is one thing that separates us from white trash. What do you think Mother makes Maude wear a brassiere for?"

"You white trash?" I asked. "You don't wear BVD's."

"Not big enough yet, just like you're not big enough to wear a brassiere. What would you put in one?" He laughed. "Monkey Ward's won't have BVD's big enough for me. Mine's gonna be twice as big as Daddy's, and he'd bust right out of his pants if she didn't make him wear em. Ain't you noticed?"

I churned and churned, and he squirmed and squirmed, but his peejabber finally fell limp between his legs. He took a deep breath and rolled away from me.

"If you ask me, Fred's wastin his time with Maude. Bet they've never got past holdin hands in the porch swing. She'll never let him in her bloomers."

Relieved, I snuggled up to him with my back against his. "When she got home last night, she looked like she had been crying, and her hair was all messed up. She went straight to her room and closed the door."

"Aw, it wouldn't hurt her none to help Fred out. He's a good ole boy." Til took another deep breath. "She thinks she's got somethin special, and it's just like yours. Nothin to it." He flipped on his back. "Guess I'm too tired. Ever hear Mother say that? Even before it's time to go to bed?"

TWELVE

We could hardly tell when Uncle Lee moved in. He didn't have but one suitcase, and Maude still had to set seven places at table. He didn't talk as much as Granny, but made up for it with his harmonica. We could hear him play it at night after he came back from Laura's. Mother kept after him and Til to play some duets but they never did. Til hardly ever took his violin out of the case unless he was going to have a lesson that day.

At the supper table Daddy said it was rumored that Lee and Laura had better get a preacher right away, that they had got the cart before the horse. Mother said there wasn't a thing to it. Daddy laughed.

"Wait and see. It won't be nothin new. First one always takes just seven months, but ever'one after that takes nine."

"And if you had had your way, we would have had the first one in less time than that," Mother said. "But, for the life of me, I don't see why you want to talk like that in front of the children. They know too much already. Have you noticed Til lately? It's high time you had a good talk with that boy. Should have had his foreskin cut off when he was eight days old, like the Jews do. He'd be cleaner and less prone to abuse himself," she went on. "They tell me if a boy hasn't been operated on, too much blood collects down there all of the time, and he stays on the verge. We need to see about that before school starts. As old as he is, they'll have to give him that old chloroform."

"I never heard of it 'til I was grown and workin," Daddy said. "Don't see a bit of sense in it. Can't afford it."

"We might both be better off if you had, but it's too late for that. I know what I'm talking about," Mother said. "My daddy always said that weak boys make weak men, and he ought to know. He had nine of them. I read in my *Science of Living* book that many men who die young from consumption are victims of self-abuse. Wouldn't hurt you to read that book." She stacked the plates and handed them to Maude. "The Jews knew what they were doing. They are a healthy people. They develop well, love their families and live to be old men."

Til didn't squirm as usual and ask to be excused as soon as he had swallowed the last bite. I knew that what Mother and Daddy were talking about was important, but I'd have to ask him what it was later. When they began talking about Maude, I understood better, because Til and me had talked about her and Fred.

"It's Maude you need to talk to," Daddy said. "Holdin hands with that Fred Gaylor, and if I'm any judge, I can tell you what he'll be up to next, if he hasn't been up to it already."

He said that Maude hadn't acted the same since that day Mother let her get hose and garters. He said it was because that Fred was hanging around her like a sick calf.

"Can't expect that boy to amount to a hill of beans...that triflin bunch has lived hand to mouth all their life. As poor as Job's turkey and as do-less."

Mr. Gaylor went bankrupt a few years ago in the feed business, then took up real estate with his brother-in-law and went bankrupt again. Now he ran the pool hall and sold insurance on the side. Him handling two jobs didn't impress Daddy at all. Daddy said insurance was a fishy business from the day it started. He said, "Why would any self-respectin man pay another man to save his money for him?"

Me and Til didn't have anything against Fred. Every time he came, he flipped us a nickel and told us to go get an ice cream cone. Only thing that bothered me was that he didn't have any chin to speak of and his forehead was all pimply. In fact, I felt sorry for him and Maude both when Daddy came home from the B&B and found them sitting in the swing one day after school. That was the first time Daddy had ever seen Maude in lipstick and earbobs. He didn't waste any time calling her inside, all the way to the kitchen. I followed them, but kept a room between us.

"The very idea! Get that stuff off right now and don't let me catch you with it on again. Your mouth looks like the backside of a possum that's been eatin pokeberries." You could have heard Daddy all the way to the alley. I could hear Maude begin to cry.

"Next thing I know you'll be smokin cigarettes and peroxidin your hair." Still talking, he let the cold water run a minute and got a glass of water. "And another thing. I don't want that boy hangin around here no more. He's doin it for just one thing, and you know what that is as good as I do. Rather bury you as to see you get in a fam'ly way by the likes of him, even if you was married to him."

I stood behind the kitchen door and watched Mother wipe her forehead with her apron and stir the beets she was canning. "Now, Albert, they weren't doing anything wrong. Fred's a good boy, well thought of at school. His folks are church-going. Mrs. Simpson told me his mother went to the tent revival every night."

Daddy acted like he didn't hear her. "This is for your own good, girl. You might as well cut out that bawlin right now."

I went to sit on the back steps where I could hear every word and see through the screen. Daddy got louder. "Clary, I don't want to hear none of that palaver. I know them Gaylors better than you do."

Mother spoke softly. "Now, Albert, you got no right to judge that boy by his daddy. Anyway, as far as I know, his daddy was a victim of circumstances. They tell me his brother cleaned him out." She sounded angry. "And I've never known Mr. Gaylor to look a bit trashier than you do right now. I wish you'd tell me what you get out of wearing your pants that way?"

"My pants. And I'll wear em any way I please." He stuck his thumbs in his belt and pushed his pants down even farther, below the last button on his shirt, then stomped to the back door. "And another thing. If you ever start wearin the pants in this fam'ly, you can wear em any way you want to, cause I won't be here."

"I'd be downright ashamed of myself if I were you," Mother said to him, and put her arm around Maude's shoulders. "I've impressed it upon Maude that a good name is worth more than great riches. I'd rather have them sitting out there on that porch in broad daylight than drinking beer in the back seat of an old car at a road house at midnight." She lowered her voice, "I reckon you never did stop that buggy in the lane after prayer meeting."

He didn't answer her. Just kept talking about Maude. "Just look at her. Them shorts tight as the skin on an onion. Don't have enough clothes on to wad a shotgun."

I moved over to let Daddy down the back steps. He muttered, "Rather raise two boys as one girl any day."

Maude's voice jerked. "Sorry you didn't have two boys instead of me." But he didn't hear her. He was going down the driveway back to the B&B. I went into the kitchen.

"Did he really mean he'd rather have six boys than Maude and me and Emmy?" I asked Mother.

She laughed. "You'll all have to learn to pay no attention to your daddy when he gets upset like that. Granny used to carry on like that when the least little thing didn't go to suit her. Remember? It's a Blevins fit," she laughed again. "You'd better not let me catch *you* having one."

Maude wiped her face with a cold washcloth. "My shorts aren't as tight as Maxine's," she said, "and he's never mentioned how I mop the kitchen floor and wash the dishes and take care of Cass and Emmy."

Mother sat down beside her. "Your daddy is right. He just doesn't say it very well. He's saying that girls have to be much more careful than boys. They have to be cleaner, in their bodies and minds, and they have to make boys behave. I never saw one that wouldn't try a girl every way he could think of. Your daddy was not hard to handle that way, and I suppose that's one reason I married him."

She traced the lines on the oil cloth with her finger as she talked and didn't look at either one of us. "In his own way, he was telling you that a woman chooses her children when she chooses her husband. A child is as affected by its father's ancestors as it is by its mother's. Just because a woman carries a child for nine months, she doesn't have any more to do with its looks or character or personality than its father."

"Who said anything 'bout getting married?" Maude asked. "We study together." She was still snubbing. "Aw, he's held my hand a time or two, and he kissed me on the cheek the other night, but you all think that just because he's a boy and I'm a girl, we pet and love on each other. Well, we don't. And let's not talk about it any more."

"Oh, Maude, we'll have to talk about it. A man has to be careful with his daughter. It's been that way since the beginning of time, and it won't change with you. You're special to him, being the first and all, and he just wants you to be happy. You'll see."

She began dipping the blood-red beets into the hot fruit jars. "Once a woman lets her guard down, a man won't want her any more. Your daddy's right. Have you ever seen a body pull the petals off a rose one at a time? That's the way a man will tug at a woman until he gets her. And once he gets her, he's through with her and goes on to another rosebud. No two ways about it. That's the way it has been since the beginning of time. I believe I'm going to have a dozen quarts of these beets," she said, proudly. "Your daddy wants you to have all your petals when the right one comes along. He doesn't want you to give away your birthright."

"How will I know?"

"You'll know, all right. He'll be on your mind first thing in the morning and last thing at night, and you'll want to spend all of your time with him. You'll know. But you're too young now to have those feelings."

"Fred's smart. He makes good grades. I just want him to help me get through that math."

"And when you get that feeling, watch how he treats his mother. If he's good to his mother, he will be good to his wife. Your daddy was always good to Granny, and, in his own way, he's always been good to me." Mother looked past me out the window.

Maude went back to the porch. I picked up my marble jar and went to the alley where Til was playing with Woody and his little sister Hattie.

"Did you take my steelie?" I asked Til.

"Yeah," he admitted, and dropped the big marble into my jar. "Borrowed it yesterday. Won me thirty aggies with it. Here, I'll give you some." He handed me three peewees. Then he scratched a circle in the black dirt with his big toe and we tossed eight marbles apiece into it.

"No steelies," he announced.

"We ain't playin for keeps, is we?" Hattie asked. "Ma would skin Woody and me alive."

"Any other way's a waste of time," Til answered. "Right, Satch?"

"Right!" I echoed.

When it came Hattie's turn to shoot, she pushed her sheepskin across the line. Before her taw left her thumb, Til yelled, "You fudged! I ain't shootin marbles with nobody that fudges."

"Aw, she's just learnin," Woody said. "She won't do it no more."

Til repeated, "Ain't shootin marbles with nobody that fudges."

Ralph joined us with his jar of marbles, but the game was over. Woody picked up his marbles and told Hattie to get hers.

"Come on," he said, and took her hand. "Momma told us playin with them would end up in a fight." They ran up the alley.

We headed for the loft to play.

Til pulled his peejabber out and asked Ralph if his had grown any.

"Sure thing," Ralph answered, getting his out. "But, man, yours ain't growin much a-tall. What the hell are you doin to help it?"

Til squinted at Ralph's peejabber. "You done had that operation Mother is talkin about gettin me. Did it hurt much?"

"Don't remember," Ralph answered. "I just know all of us boys had it. Mother had it done. Said we'd be cleaner and less prone to play with ourselves, if you know what I mean."

"It's just like you said," Til played up to him. "Ain't nothin but a muscle. You got to exercise it. Want Satch there to help you exercise yours? She's good," he bragged on me. Then he said, "I got a better idea. Take off your overalls, Satch, and lie down there on that bale of hay."

"I don't want no baby seeds in me," I said.

"I told you a hunderd times you ain't gonna have no baby seeds in you. I'll take care of that. Ralph, you got a new rubber?"

Ralph rolled a rubber up his peejabber, but had to hold it to keep it from falling off. He straddled me, and I felt his cold peejabber on my leg.

Til said, "Take hold of it and put it in and let it lay there a minute til she gets used to it."

Ralph's hand was as cold as his peejabber. He tried to put it in, but it hurt, and I squirmed out from under him. He backed off and looked at Til.

"That room just ain't big enough to accommodate me," he said, and buttoned his overalls. "Besides, I don't want to hurt her."

"Shoot, I could show you a thing or two about makin it big enough," Til said, "but that would be incest, and I don't believe in it."

"I know somebody that's got a room just the right size and keeps the door open all the time," Ralph bragged. "And she even furnishes her own vaseline. Only thing is, she makes you wear a rubber."

He was talking about Marcella Higgins, six houses down the street. She was about twenty-one, and since her husband had left her in the spring, sometimes the same big black car parked there three nights in the week. Til said Marcella had a little job on the side. She clerked at the five-and-ten six days a week.

"White trash," Til said. "Just like Jimmie Lou."

"Naw, you can't call Jimmie Lou white trash," Ralph said. "She keeps her door closed except for that feller in that jalopy."

"Bet I could get her to open it for me," Til bragged. "Her and Satch are good friends."

"Hell, that don't make her no friend of yours," Ralph laughed. "Besides, Cass don't go down there to plough. Anyhow, a bird nest in the hand is worth two or three up in the tree. Marcella's good and she don't charge *me* but a nickel. Charges those other dudes a lot more."

"Hell, who's got a nickel?" Til asked.

"Anybody that likes to be ploughed as good as she does oughtn't to charge nothin," Ralph said. "You know that's what fuck really means? Ain't in my dictionary, but I looked it up in the big dictionary at the public library. Means 'to plough' or 'prepare the soil for planting.'"

"Shoot, yeah. Don't need no dictionary to figure that out, do you, Satch? That was one of the first things I told you."

I put on my overalls and went down the ladder. I didn't want Ralph's peejabber that close to me ever again.

When Daddy got home, he didn't even mention Fred. Got straight up from the table and went to the bedroom to hear Lowell Thomas talk about a place near the White House called Anacostia Flats where thousands of soldiers had gathered to ask President Hoover for some money they had been promised for fighting the Germans. Flies swarmed in the tents where babies slept, he said, and the smell of urine was unbearable in the mid-summer heat. But he said Mr. Hoover would not even talk to the soldiers, so they played baseball and dug latrines and said they'd just camp there until 1945. That was when they were supposed to get the money, but because of the Depression, they needed it now.

The day after Lee and Laura got a preacher, Daddy clucked and shook his head at the supper table. He pulled out his pocket watch. "Lee and Laura sure is keepin late hours for newlyweds," he said. "Eight o'clock. They'd better get a move on if they want to see me."

Uncle Lee had got a job at the lumber yard for ten cents an hour. Daddy said he was lucky, with the ranks of the unemployed swelling every day.

Mother put up her sewing basket. "Put your shoes on, Albert. They'll be here any minute. You children can stay up and meet your new aunt, but then go on to your bed. It's high time you started setting good habits for school."

Daddy told Uncle Lee and Aunt Laura they ought to find a little house to start with. "First thing you know," he said to Aunt Laura, "you'll swaller a watermelon seed and have to set back from the table. Next thing you know you'll be feedin three instead of two."

They laughed, all but Mother. She said, "I wish you wouldn't talk like that in front of the children, Albert." She went to make some lemonade and told me and Til to get to bed before she got back.

When the house was dark, Til pulled his overalls on. "Want to go with me?" he asked.

"Where to?"

"Ask me no questions and I'll tell you no lies," he said, and sneaked into the kitchen and got the flashlight. Then we tiptoed out to the garage, and I helped him carry the ladder to the window of Maude's bedroom where Uncle Lee and Aunt Laura were sleeping. He crept up and cupped his face with his hands against the screen.

I called out, "Which way is the big dipper?"

"Shh, dumbbell," Til whispered loudly.

I looked all over the sky. "I don't see it," I whispered. He shone the flashlight on me and I knew to be quiet.

I whimpered, "It's cold. We got to go to bed."

He skittered down the ladder. "Want to see em?" he asked.

I crept up the ladder and looked through the screen. The window was as high up as it would go. I could hear Uncle Lee's deep breathing. In his BVD's, he lay on his back on top of the sheet, and Laura lay on her side under the sheet with her face against his shoulder and one arm across him. He pulled her close and whispered something in her ear without opening his eyes. I almost fell off the ladder getting down.

"You wake them and we'll get our killin for sure," Til whispered. He held out his hands like he was measuring a fish. "His is about the size I want mine to be."

"You couldn't even see it," I whispered.

"Imagination," he whispered. "Look at how big his hands are." He picked up one end of the ladder. "Sometimes I wonder if you're retarded, and in case you don't know it, that's what Si Feathers is. Means you don't have good sense."

We put the ladder away and crept back into the house. Felix was curled up on Til's pillow.

"What did you want to do that for?" I whispered.

"Thought it was high time you learned something from somebody else." He picked up Felix and laid him at the foot of the bed. "I taught you ever'thing you know, and you don't even appreciate it. Should have got Ralph. Me and him could have watched all night."

"Why did Daddy say she'd swallow a watermelon seed?"

"He meant that Uncle Lee would plant a baby seed in her. If he'd said anything else in front of us, Mother would have made *him* wash his mouth out with Octagon soap. Wouldn't *that* be worth seeing?"

"Mother told me not to talk to anybody but her about how babies get born. She called it the birds and the peas."

"Birds and bees, dummy." He laughed. "She's afraid you'll know more about it than she does, and that wouldn't have to be much."

"When a baby grows in your stomach, how does he get out? Looks like he would smother alive under all that cornbread and beans."

"Ask Mother. She'll tell you anything but the truth about it. Probably don't even know the truth. It has somethin to do with her being a preacher's daughter." He shook his head. "I sure don't want my woman to be no preacher's kid."

"How does he get out?" I asked again.

"Nothin much to it," Til answered. "He grows in there for about nine months and then pops out, and they name him and all. Just like a stalk of corn poppin out of the ground."

"Why has the man got all the seeds?"

"Been that way ever since Adam and Eve was in that garden. Women never have known much about plantin."

"Mother said she sure hopes everybody in heaven is neutral. What does that mean?"

Til laughed. "Neuter, dummy. Means ain't got no peejabber at all. Of course, ever'body in heaven is neuter. Has to be. If a man don't have no body, how in the world could he have a peejabber?"

Uncle Lee and Aunt Laura moved out the next day. That was the day the policeman slipped on a board and fell in Washington, and shot and killed a soldier who was waiting for his money. Other policemen fired and another soldier fell down dead. That was when President Hoover called out the tanks and troops and swords and machine guns. Lowell Thomas said that the President took time to meet with a boxing champion, but he didn't have time to talk to the soldiers. When the soldiers wouldn't leave, the troops burned down their shanties and tents and threw tear gas at them. One little boy ran back into a tent to get his pet rabbit, and a policeman stabbed him in the leg. The soldiers, about 15,000 of them by now, and their families vomited and choked and walked quietly into Maryland for safety.

"What's tear gas?" I asked.

"I'll be a suck-egg mule," Daddy muttered. "Shootin would be too good for that dang Hoover. Usin troops against unarmed civilians in the land of the free and the home of the brave." He raised his voice. "You hear that, Clary? 'Lectric chair would be too good for him."

Mother shuffled from the kitchen with her apron still on. "I hear it every night whether I want to or not. Person would be better off not to hear too much of that stuff. Clutter up these children's minds when they need all their wits to start school. I don't worry about Maude, but Til goes into the fifth. You've got to spend more time with him, Albert. You act like you don't notice he's got the things of a man on his mind."

Daddy moved his rocking chair closer to the radio. "Dadgummit, if the voters in this country ain't got their fill of Hoover wagons and Hoover blankets and Hoover flags by now, they'll get exactly what they deserve in November."

"What's a Hoover wagon?" I asked.

"We ain't got one—yet," Daddy answered, laughing. "A Hoover wagon is a broken down jalopy pulled by a mule. And a Hoover blanket is a newspaper, and a Hoover flag is a empty pocket turned inside out. Half the people in this country are flyin Hoover flags right now."

Mother took off her apron. "And from the questions Cass is asking, she's learning stuff that won't be worth a copper to her in school."

Roosevelt's voice came on the air. He didn't mention the soldiers. He talked about the Depression and said the government had robbed millions of their life savings and thrown millions more out of work. Daddy nodded and leaned closer. He made all of us listen.

"History in the making, and you ought to grow up knowin the history of your country. This man is gonna be our President for at least four years. Maudie, as much schoolin as you've had, you ought to be able to name all the presidents in the right order. Can you do that?"

Maude didn't look up from her book.

Roosevelt sounded like Aunt Flossie's preacher again. "…in the hour of our country's need, equal rights to all, special privileges to none."

"Hot dog!" Daddy yelled. "He's just beginnin to light into them. He'll make a humdinger of a President."

Mother interrupted. "Just beginning to sling mud, you mean. Turn it down a little."

Daddy patted his foot to "Happy Days Are Here Again." "About next summer when he's President and the Depression is a thing of the past and the kids is out of school, we'll take us a trip to Warshin'ton. See the big dome of the U.S. Cap'tol and the White House where he'll live and that great marble statue of Abraham Lincoln. Wanted to see that ever since I seen in the paper about it being dedicated. Remember, Clary? It was just a few years after we was married."

He never had talked before about going anywhere, except to the river or somebody's funeral.

"Yessir, we'll climb to the top of President Warshin'ton's Monument and see the whole city at our feet, and maybe go swimmin in the Potomac. They tell me Warshin'ton's homeplace is not far away. We'll go there and sit on the porch and see what him and Martha seen."

Mother interrupted him. "*Saw*. What *he* and Martha *saw*. Now, Albert, don't get the children all wound up about a trip you know we can't take. Roosevelt has not been elected yet, and even if he is, the Depression will not end overnight."

"I mean ever word I say! We'll go even if I have to borrow the money to do it."

"Whose car are you planning to take?"

"Buy a new one when Roosevelt gets 'lected."

"Talk is cheap. And you know as well as I do that things are not going to change that fast."

Daddy hiked up her dress with his foot. "What do you want to bet we'll do it?" he asked.

"If you've got nothing better than that to do, go to your bed," Mother said, laughing.

THIRTEEN

*D*addy read the headlines in the Clarksport paper out loud, "Roosevelt Promises Equal Rights For All," "Six Polio Cases Found in County."

Mrs. Simpson called from the back door. "Have you all heard? They think the little Williams boy has got that old infantile paral-'sis or the spinal men'gitis. You'd ought to keep the chilrun close to home where they won't get no germs. They're both deadly, you know." She shook her head. "To my mind, Mrs. Blevins, that store's as bad a place as a old swimmin hole for them germs."

"I worry about it all the time, Mrs. Simpson," Mother said. "Every Tom, Dick and Harry handling everything."

Mrs. Simpson got a handkerchief out of her bosom and wiped her hands. She held up her right arm. "They tell me that child's done lost use of his arm," she said, and wiped her arm pits, then stuffed the limp handkerchief back in her bossom.

"Joe John said it got up to 96 yesterday."

Joe John was the weather man at the radio station. He insisted that children play in their own yard and drink water from their own faucet. Mrs. Simpson said she was boiling her water and would advise Mother to do the same.

Mother said, "If you know of any way to keep Til and Cass from drinking straight out of the faucet, I wish you'd tell me."

From that day on, we were what Mother called quarantined. Nobody could go swimming or visiting in a house where there was any sickness, even a summer cold. Fred quit coming to see Maude. When she wasn't helping Mother she read *The Way of All Flesh* or brushed her hair or added a teaspoon of ammonia to her "Depression flower." It wasn't a flower at all, just a lump of coal sitting in a mixture of salt, bluing, ammonia and red ink. All of the women on the block who had followed Mrs. Simpson's recipe had red and blue blossoms coming right out of their coal.

And Maude practiced the piano a little every day, but never the music her teacher gave her. She just played whole notes and sang, "Lights Out, Sweetheart" and "Girl of My Dreams."

Til shouted, "Turn it off, turn it off! You sound more like a sick calf than Rudy Vallee."

Maude made sure Mother could hear her. "Look who's talking. You can't even play 'Come to Jesus' in the key of C on that violin."

Me and Til had our regular chores to do, all but milking. Mother and Daddy took turns at that. Mother said those old germs thrive in damp places like the cow bottom. But me and Til did the churning. Til stood up to work the dasher for five minutes, then I knelt on a stool and took my turn. He always took the last turn when yellow specks began to ooze out around the dasher hole. And every afternoon when the paper came I begged him to read me the funnies.

"Shoot," he said, "the ads are better than the funnies." He read like an old lady with a squeaky voice. " 'For five years I couldn't keep anything on my stomach, not even crackers and milk. Then I discovered Scalf's Indian River Tonic, and after seven bottles, I'll put my stomach up against anybody's.' " He showed me her picture.

"You need some of that stuff, Satch, bein as you are a girl."

"Read me the funnies," I begged. "Next year I'll read them to you."

"Shoot, you think you're goin to learn to read in one year?" he asked. "You ain't no genius. You'd already be readin if you was."

"What's a genius?"

"I just told you. A genius is a person can read without goin to school. You ain't one. Do well to read and write by the time you get to the fourth. Spit Ball ain't no genius of a teacher neither."

"What's her real name?

"Spit Ball's only thing I ever heard. All the time wallers a little ball of spit around on the end of her tongue between her lips."

The postman climbed the steps and asked, "Are you Miss Cassandra Blevins?"

I never had got a package in the mail before. It was my old blue dress and two new ones from Aunt Flossie. Mother stood back to look as I tried them on.

"She's got you ready for the first grade," she said. "They both fit perfectly. Your Aunt Flossie was good to do that. I'll have to write her a thank-you note. All of that smocking and embroidery takes a lot of time and patience."

She spread both of the new dresses across the ironing board. "They'll look better on you when you have your shoes on. I just hope and pray that ole infantile paralysis epidemic doesn't delay the opening of school. Which one do you like best?"

I pulled on my overalls and ran out the back door.

That ole infantile paralysis epidemic was on Mother's mind all of the time. "They tell me the air's full of those germs. They tell me they thrive in this heat. Like as not, we'll have them until it comes a killing frost."

"Show me a germ," Til sassed.

"That's enough out of you, Tilghman Blevins." Mother held up her hand, threatening to box his ears. "I never talked to my mother like that in my life. I don't know what you're coming to."

He repeated, "I just said I never saw a germ in my life."

"I hope to your dying day you never do. It worries me half to death to think you could come down with that old disease and get paralyzed from the waist down for the rest of your natural life."

Mother suggested going to the river for the weekend to get away from the germs. She said to her mind the river water was safer than the faucet water. Daddy didn't answer. Barefooted, he slipped out to sit in the swing for a while before bedtime.

I hummed "Life Is Like a Mountain Railroad" through a comb covered with wax paper, and Til harmonized on his Jew's harp. Then we sang our song to the tune of "At the Cross."

At the bar, at the bar where I smoked my first cigar,
And the money from my pockets rolled away.
It was there by chance that I tore my Sunday pants,
And now I get to wear them every day.

Mother interrupted. "I'd be afraid to blaspheme a hymn like that. Let's go out there and sit with your daddy a few minutes. You kids would try the patience of Job."

She turned out the light, and we followed her to the porch. I chased a firefly across Mr. Diggs' yard, and when I got back, I heard Mother whisper, "Of course, I believe you, Albert. What other choice do I have, for crying out loud? You're my husband and the father of my children."

Daddy said it was time to go to bed.

We could hear them better then. Mother said, "Now, all I know is he told me that Laura told him that you flirted with her when you delivered groceries yesterday."

"I told you she invited me in for a cup of coffee, and I went, and that's all there was to it."

"He told me he intends to take you to court."

"He can take me wherever he wants to. I'll put my reputation up against his any day in the week."

"Don't talk about my baby brother that way," Mother begged.

"I knew I shouldn't have let him stay here, but it was Maude I was worried about. He thinks I'm made of money, and he thinks he's figured out a way to get his hands on some of it."

"Ruin our good name if he sues you for alienation of affection, and them just married. Put a blot on this family we'll never get over."

"No such thing," Daddy argued. "He ain't got a leg to stand on."

Mother begged, "Albert, talk to him about settling out of court. He's my baby brother."

"He done talked to me, this afternoon. Nothin would suit him better. He said he'd take fifteen hunderd."

"Fifteen hundred dollars? That would put Maude and Til through college."

"Now, Clary, I ain't gonna talk about it no more. He's just threat'nin me. Talk is cheap."

"Could we scrape a thousand together?" she asked.

"Banks ain't lendin, and you know it."

"Albert, we have to try to settle with him. Can't bear the thought of it going in the paper and having to face my Mother and Daddy. Blood runs thicker than water. And what will the neighbors think?"

"One thing for sure, Clary. If I settle with him, it makes me look guilty. Think about that."

"No, it won't, Albert. It'll just keep peace in the family."

"And another thing for certain. If I do settle with him, I will never darken their door again, not to make a delivery, not for nothin, and I mean it."

"It breaks my heart to think of him doing us like this after all we've done for him." She sighed. "But I do believe you, Albert. You never gave me any reason to doubt you. And Lord knows what I would do without you, with these four children to raise."

They quit talking. In a little while, we heard the bed creaking, and then Daddy moaned. He asked her if she was all right, and whispered that he never felt better.

"We'll weather this storm, Clary. It ain't the first one, and prob'ly won't be the last one."

"That settles it then," she said. "We'll have to figure out a way to scrape a thousand together and get it in writing that he won't breathe a word to a living soul."

Daddy's loud snoring filled the house.

I asked Til, "Just exactly what does flirt mean?"

"Aw, Uncle Lee meant that Daddy tried to hug her or kiss her or somethin."

"Aunt Laura?"

"He probably didn't do no more than hike up her dress tail with his foot."

Til unrolled a rubber up his peejabber and held it on. "Catches all my seeds," he explained, as if he hadn't told me before. "Marcella makes me wear one all the time. Keeps her from having a baby."

"Where'd you get it?"

"They come from the drug store, but I got this one out of a paper poke under Daddy's side of the bed. Mother makes him wear one ever time. Keeps us from having a baby brother."

He put my hand on it. It didn't feel much different from him. Just slicker.

"Want to see how it really works?" he asked.

"No," I answered. "Ralph hurt me."

"I won't hurt you. I promise."

"What if it slips off?"

He laughed. "Your socks ever slip off?" We watched it grow inside the rubber as he churned. "Only thing about it is, you're not supposed to do it with your nearest of kin, like your mother or your sister. They call that incest, and incest is a sin. But with the epidemic on, I can't go to Marcella's and it wouldn't count as a sin. Just circumstances beyond control."

He straddled me and stuck his peejabber between the folds of mine with his fingers. It didn't hurt until he let all his weight down and started jabbing. He couldn't get it in, but all of the air went out of my lungs and I couldn't breathe.

"No, no," I gasped. "Get off me. Leave me alone. Mother and Daddy will hear us."

"It's no use," he finally grunted, and whispered, "You ain't got the hang of it yet. I'd be in there in no time if we had some vaseline and if you'd help a little like Marcella does." He put the rubber in his overalls pocket. "Boy, you ought to see her wiggle and hear her moan! But you'll get the hang of it some day."

Early the next morning, Mrs. Simpson's voice bounced against the walls. "Mrs. Blevins, Mrs. Blevins! I thought you had ought to know they've def'nitely dia'nosed it as that ole infantile paral'sis, but he's holdin his own."

"Poor child," was all Mother had time to say before Mrs. Simpson started talking again. "They tell me that's the way it works. They'll think he's a holdin his own, but all of a sudden, he'll lose the use of ever limb."

"Won't you come in, Mrs. Simpson?"

"No, thank you, Mrs. Blevins. The heat has give me loss of appetite and that ole nervous innergestion. Anyways, home is the safest place a body can be when disease stalks the land."

Still talking, she went down the driveway.

After Daddy closed the B&B, we went to the river and parked at the old bridge that Daddy helped to build.

"Yessir, that was twenty year ago. I worked for 75-cent-a-day carryin water across the falsework, walkin them two-by-eights. Then Mr. Gordon, he was the engineer in charge, he finally put me on reg'lar at $2.75 a day. Want to know how we went about buildin it?"

He didn't wait for an answer. "They was a dozen of us, and the first thing we done was to hold onto a rope stretched across the river and scrub the bottom clean with our feet. Had to wear old shoes to keep our feet from bein eat up by the rocks and gravel. Went all the way to bedrock."

He told about splitting limestone boulders with a wedge and beating them into gravel with a mall. Then they poured concrete into the high wooden cofferdams built around the piers that sat on the bedrock. He said cofferdams were like big wooden boxes.

"On 'lection day we got us a cab and went to town, twelve mile, and drunk beer all night. When we heard Wilson was 'lected, we went back to the river and went to work."

All the way to the cave, high above the water, he talked about how they worked ten hours a day, six days a week from spring to frost. He said he stuck a dime in the last concrete they poured.

"It's bound to be still in there," he said, pointing to the bottom of the pier nearest the bank. "Old man Gordon liked his b-e-e-r, and it had to come in on the train. I used to walk that four miles to the station once a week to pick up his valise. Ever'body thought it was important papers in there." He laughed. "He kept them important papers in the water."

"I don't see a bit of sense in filling these children's heads with all that foolishness," Mother said. "Wish you'd mark a couple of those bubbies so we can transplant them in the fall." The red blossoms smelled like ripe apples.

"Don't have to mark em," he answered. "I can tell em by their bark. Can't you? We went swimmin ever Sunday of the world in the summer. We'd cut old man Kitzmiller's watermelons loose above the sandbar and ride em down the river and bury em in the sand for the next Sunday."

"These children are taking in every word," Mother said. "If you were telling them something worthwhile, they wouldn't hear a single one."

We gathered wood to keep the fire going all night in front of the cave. After supper Mother and Daddy made us pallets inside. I watched the shadows play on the ceiling and scooted a little closer to Til when a bat darted in and out of the firelight, and closer yet when a chipmunk skittered from one crack to another above my head.

After breakfast Daddy unchained the flatbottom and took us into the little cave below the big one. Em stayed on the bank with Mother, who wrung her hands and bit her lip when Daddy sat on his heels and poled us out of sight on the little stream that went through the opening in the rocks. The entrance was as black as a pocket, but the inside was like daylight. The creek trickled across the rock floor. Daddy pointed to a rock that hung like an icicle from the ceiling.

"That's a stalactite," he said. "Water drippin from the ceilin years on end made that.

"They's a lot more rooms beyond this one," he said, "but we'd better get back before your mother has a conniption."

After we got back into real daylight, Til took the flatbottom out in the river while Daddy took a few potshots at buzzards with his sawed-off shotgun. He drew a bead on a buzzard just above Til's head and fired. Til rolled out of the boat. Daddy shucked his shoes and pants and hit the water. Just as he got to the boat, Til bobbed out from under it, grinning.

Daddy laughed. "I ought to bust the rind on you for a trick like that," he said.

Daddy and me and Til fished with cane poles while Mother and Maude and Em looked for wild flowers. Em came back with fringed gentians and turtlehead. Mother held up a purple flower.

"Know what this is? Old jimson weed. Poison. Kills cows."

I recognized the rabbit tobacco and mashed a leaf to smell the lemon odor.

"Show them your snakeroot, Em," Mother said. Em held up a spire of white clusters.

"The Cherokees made medicine out of that when they lived in these hills," Mother said. "And they made tea from the bark of that tree beside your daddy there." Daddy cut off a twig of sassafras for us to smell.

When we gathered to go home, Felix smelled worse than Si Feathers. Mother held her nose and turned away. "Like as not got mixed up with a pole cat," she said.

"No such thing," Daddy said. "Been rollin in kyarn again."

"Carrion, Albert," Mother said. "You've said the word wrong all of your life. It means putrified flesh. I don't know how many times I've told you that."

She handed Til a cake of Octagon soap. "It's good for chiggers and poison ivy. Surely it will get rid of the stink."

Til took Felix to the edge of the water and scrubbed him good, then carried him in a towel to the car.

When we got home Mother made us all bathe in Octagon. Daddy said he was too old to get poison ivy, but he'd use salted grease if any chigger bites showed up, but Mother shooed him into the bathtub after us, and she followed.

The night's paper said two new polio cases had showed up. It was dark when Mrs. Simpson came to tell us that, unlike Mr. Roosevelt, little Robert Williams hadn't conquered polio. He had died that afternoon. She said it was a blessing the Lord took him, because he never would have walked again.

Mother and Mrs. Simpson sat on the porch a few minutes the next day after they came from the funeral. Mrs. Simpson fanned fiercely at the sweat rings in her Sunday voile.

"Never been to a funeral so poorly attended in my life," she said. "Didn't expect no chilrun at them services, but it seems to me the grownups could have showed up out of respect. They tell me a grownup hardly ever gets that ole infantile paral'sis. Anyways, it was distilled in me as a child to pay my respects to the dead and offer my condolences to the family, irregardless."

Mother fidgeted in the swing. "I know exactly what you're talking about, Mrs. Simpson. Guess I'd better get in and start supper." She took a bath and boiled her clothes the minute Mrs. Simpson left.

"How many more days does summer have?" I asked Til.

He placed his hand over his heart. "Today is Tuesday, August 23. Summer dies two weeks from today, but it may live a few days longer if they can't lift this quarantine."

Til sat back on his stool and propped his fork in one hand beside his plate and his spoon in the other hand on the other side. "For dinner they had buzzard gizzards and catfish eyes with cornbread and gravy. Quick, Henry, bring the bucket!" He gagged. "Oops! Too late. Bring the mop!"

Daddy pushed his chair back and unbuckled his belt. "You want me to bust the rind on you, Tilghman?" he asked.

Maude chimed in. "Fred says if you don't make him behave, he'll wind up in the pen for sure."

"Fred, Fred!" Til mocked. "Is he all you can talk about? Ears like pyramids and face like the underside of a nickel watermelon."

"He looks better than you do," Maude said. "You and Cass will have to soak your feet in Clorox for a whole day to get them clean enough for shoes."

"And what kind of skunk water you got on today, Miss Asterbilt? Midnight in Hong Kong? Or is it Afternoon at the Fish Market?"

"For your information, it's from Paris, France, very expensive. You must be smelling your upper lip."

"That's enough out of both of you," Daddy warned them.

"They're both big enough to quit that bickering," Mother added.

"Don't make me have to use this belt on you, big as you are," Daddy threatened.

Mother said quietly, "I wish you'd tell me why they bicker at the table all the time. Bad for the digestive system they always told me. My daddy would have slapped me away from the table for that."

"They'll change their tune in a few days, to my way of thinkin." Daddy buckled his belt.

"None too soon," Mother said. "They're going to be the death of me if this epidemic isn't over in a few days, but, like I said, it may take a hard freeze to get rid of those old germs. Cass, why don't you play school with Em this afternoon? Show her how to take giant steps?"

I didn't look up.

"You could teach her her letters, smart as you are. She's just one year behind you, you know. And it's high time you quit shooting marbles in the alley with those colored children. Bad enough for Til to be out there with them so much. And I don't want you up in that barn loft with Til and Ralph no more."

I pushed my hair back and blinked the tears out of my eyes. I had the same feeling that I had when we went down Unc's driveway that day to come home because Granny was bad sick. I knew that things would never be the same again. I felt like I was all by myself. Why did Mother want to keep me away from my friends? Not so much Ralph. But Woody and Hattie. And I liked the smell of the hay in the loft. Sometimes I went up there all by myself and put a little hay in my overalls pocket and listened to the birds.

I didn't really know Emmy like I did Til and Woody and Sadie and Jimmie Lou. We never had been together by ourselves much. Granny was her best friend, and now that Granny wasn't around any more, she talked to her doll. And I couldn't even understand her. What did she mean when she said, "Bored-eye, bored-eye, bored-eye," over and over again when we were at the table talking? And why did she yell it out loud when Daddy was reading somebody's title clear? Why did she cry so much? Was it just to get Mother to rock her like Granny used to?

Maude was old and not at all interested in the stars and the birds as far as I could tell, and she didn't want Felix in the house at all. She was always brushing her hair or putting it up or taking it down. I liked her, but she didn't like me and Emmy, because she had to look after us so much. Thank goodness Mother hadn't mentioned Jimmie Lou's name. But she kept on talking.

"And we won't go to the barber shop for a while, and pretty soon your hair will be long enough for Maude to put up."

That meant that Mr. Matlock wouldn't put any more strawberry tonic on my hair on Saturday morning. Did it mean that I couldn't even go to the barber shop with Daddy any more?

I slid off the stool and ran out the back door. Felix sat beside me on the step. I pulled him against me and left hot tears on his neck.

The sidewalks filled with children a few days later when Joe John and the newspaper announced that the infantile paralysis scare was over.

"Wouldn't you know it?" Til moaned. "Just in time for school to start."

Polly fought flies frantically with her tail, but Til said he couldn't spray her before we milked, because the poison might get into the milk.

"Might be what gives people infantile paral'sis," he said. "Poison milk. I wonder if they ever thought of that?" Polly gulped down the dry chop and licked the empty pan.

"Wanta milk?" he asked. I rubbed my hands down my overalls and sat on my heels just like Til. I pulled and pulled but the milk didn't come.

Til yelled at me. "You'll pull her titty plum off that way. Have you already forgot how?"

He showed me again, but I was out of practice and couldn't get more than a thin stream. He milked with both hands at once. Then we went over to the tent to watch the Holy Rollers a few minutes. We stood at the door. They shook and yelled and rolled in the aisles, but I didn't get religion. I couldn't even sing "Standing in the Need of Prayer." On the way home I just kept thinking of all the things I stood in the need of prayer for.

How could I keep from going to the first grade and still learn how to read and write? How could I keep from getting married to the likes of Til and having a baby? And what would I do if Mr. Simpson ever tried to put his big peejabber in mine?

Fourteen

Granma's was the last place we went every summer, when the arbor in the back yard was bent to breaking with grapes. She was the only grandmother I had since Granny died.

Granma said that fall was already in the air that Sunday when Daddy clipped two bushel baskets to heaping with full bunches of dark blue Concords.

"I've never seen nothin like it," he said. "Big as damson plums and twice as juicy. They'll make a batch of wine to beat all."

Mother warned him, "Don't you say anything about making wine in front of them. You know what the mere mention of strong drink does to my daddy."

"You ought to give him a bottle for Chirstmas. Would do him good to have a little snort now and then," Daddy said, laughing.

"How do you know that?" Mother asked. "The Bible tells us that it causes all men to err who drink it."

"Yeah, and the Bible says not to drink water no longer, but to take a little wine for the stomach's sake."

" 'The drunkard shall come to poverty,' " Mother said.

"You Methodists are all alike," Daddy said, cocking his head. "You know more about the Bible than anybody else – or anything else."

Til began eating grapes, skin and all, and then started shooting the juicy insides into his mouth and tossing the skins on the grass. When he had had his fill, he took off down the hill.

"Race you to the spring," he said.

"Now, don't you kids go off anywhere. We're about ready to go home," Mother called as I ran behind him. My feet were so tough that the gravel didn't hurt. But suddenly, I felt sick in my stomach, and a sweet, sticky taste filled my mouth. The coolness of the grassy bank at the spring swept across my mind, and I saw the cherry tree's branches sway in the soft breeze, and heard Til's voice, "Hurry. They'll be wonderin what's happened to us."

I looked up the hill behind me and started back toward the arbor.

"What's the matter?" Til called. "I'm not gonna push you in, scaredy cat."

I didn't answer him. I ran to the car and opened the door as Daddy struggled across the yard with a basketful of grapes.

After we got home, I watched Daddy knead the grapes in the big crock and strain the dark juice through a cheese cloth. He set aside a skimpy bushel for jelly. Although Mother had already canned two crops of tomatoes and beans, four gallons each of blackberries and cherries, and two bushels each of apples and peaches, she declared every day that if it didn't come a good rain, there'd be nothin fit for the table come winter.

Clarksport shriveled under a merciless sun as the thermometer jumped to 95 before noon every day. Mother had to iron as well as wash on Mondays to keep the clothes from mildewing, and she put rice in the salt shaker to keep the salt from turning into a sticky gob. She wore an apron around the house instead of a petticoat, and sighed every night when Joe John reported that thundershowers had circled the town again, and that streets in communities across the state line were flooded. She wondered out loud what we had done to deserve such heat and humidity. The grass around the house crumpled under foot, and where there was no grass, the ground cracked and gaped. Birds quit chirping at sunup and settled on shady limbs until sun down. Women felt safe from neighbors' criticism when they sat barefooted in the porch swing after dark. Mother made us take two baths a week.

Rain clouds gathered again, and thunder rolled beyond the mountain. After we had stocked the shelves at the B&B, Mother gave Til and me a dime apiece and told us to go home and put the windows down, and then we could go to the picture show.

After we got the windows closed, Til decided there'd never be a better chance to sample Daddy's wine. He siphoned two little jelly glasses full out of the big glass jug in the basement. I took a gulp.

"Vinegar!" I gasped, and spit it on the concrete floor. "Tastes worse than that pop you made me out of vinegar and baking soda."

Til gulped down both glasses. When he turned around to run up the stairs, he stepped on the blade of the garden hoe standing against the wall, and the handle fell across the jug. Wine streamed toward the drain in the floor.

We sopped up as much as we could with grass sacks, wrung them out in the back yard, and spread them across the dark stains. As we raced toward town, the thunder rumbled closer, but the sun still poked hot rays through the black clouds.

Sure enough, the Chinaman was sitting in front of his little laundry in a straight-back chair. Til ran across the street before we got close to him, and I followed. Til told me a long time ago that Mr. Soong hadn't been gone from China long enough to be civilized. He couldn't even speak English, just said "ello" in a high voice when you asked him how he was. The Soongs brought three children with them – all boys. Til wondered out loud every time we walked by there if they had any girl babies before they left China.

"You'd better thank your lucky stars you weren't born in China," he told me. "Them Chinks don't give girl babies a chance. They just cut em up and throw em in the river. And the ones they let live, they bandage their feet so tight they can't walk."

"What's wrong with their feet?" I asked.

"Nothin," he answered. "It's just an old custom. Keeps their feet from growin big and ugly. Anyhow, they don't have nowhere to go, don't have nothin to do but have babies and perpetuate the race."

"What does that mean?" I gasped, running back across the street behind Til.

"Perpetuate the race? Means keep it goin. The ones they let live are the prettiest and healthiest, and they don't do nothin but have babies." He slowed to a walk after we got half a block beyond the laundry. "Just think. If you had been born in China, you wouldn't be runnin down the street. More than likely, you couldn't even *walk* down the street, *if* they let you live. And considerin your looks, your chances would be slim."

I didn't even cry any more when he talked to me like that. I just got an empty feeling inside like the feeling I got when I thought of how far away Aunt Flossie and Unc were.

We dashed into the Strand Palace just as the show began. Laurel and Hardy weren't as funny as they had been the other time we saw them.

Daddy no more than got home from the B&B when he smelled the wine.

"Sure hope the preacher don't come callin tonight," he yelled to Mother and headed straight for the basement stairs. "That wine is sure workin."

"Tilgh-MAN!" You could have heard him clear to the cow bottom. "Cass-an-DRA!"

I whispered, "We're in for it now. He *will* skin us alive this time!"

Til whispered back, "Might as well go down there and face the music. The longer we put it off, the louder it will get."

We crept half-way down the steps, with me in front. Daddy stood in the middle of the grass sacks with his arms crossed.

"You kids know anything about this?" he asked. I looked at Til. Til looked at me. Daddy said, "I guess it just fell apart of its own accord."

"That's right," Til volunteered. "When we come home to put the windows down, I smelled it upstairs, and when I got down here, there it was. Exploded! We tried to clean it up."

Daddy took off his belt. "That was a four-gallon jug! Dadgummit! I'll clean you up if you don't learn to leave things alone that don't concern you."

He took Til to the bathroom and closed the door and told him to take off his overalls. I heard the belt hit Til over and over again. He sobbed and screamed. When he walked by me in the hall, he hid his face in his hands.

Daddy called after him, "Quit that snifflin or I'll whip you again."

Mother put her arm around Til and held him close to her. He shook with sobs as he tried to stop crying.

Daddy called for me, and I began to cry before he closed the door. Then I noticed that he had already put his belt back on. But I cried anyway, because I didn't understand.

He looked at me hard, and said, "Now, I'm tellin you for the last time. If you want to stay out of trouble, stay away from Til. It's in a boy's nature to learn things the hard way, but not in a girl's. Let this be a lesson to you." He motioned me out the door.

Supper was quiet. Daddy read a post card from Uncle Jesse. "I've joined in a movement not to let any produce go to market. We ain't even gatherin in the corn, just turnt the cows and hogs into the fields. Nobody will sell their milk for two-cent a quart no more. If a body tries to take their milk to town, farmers along the road take and rip open the cans and pour it out on the road."

Mother lowered her voice. "Albert, you are going to have to spend more time with your son. Never thought it would be up to me to tell you that the sap's rising. He's getting too big for his britches, if you know what I mean. I didn't look for it to happen this soon, but it *is* happening. I'm just sure it would help to get him circumcised. Seems to me you could look at that boy or take him to Dr. Shaw. You need to put some BVD's on him, too, and explain a few things to him before he hears them all wrong from Ralph. He's entirely too thick with that boy. Why, Ralph looked like he would bust right out of his pants when he came by here yesterday. And he's gotten so he can't look a person in the eye when you're talking to him. That's a bad sign, according to my *Science of Living* book. It most likely means that he is abusing himself. And I'd be willing to bet that he's never been circumcised."

She sighed. "Albert, are you listening to me? Surely you don't expect me to talk to him. Surely, you know it's a father's place to talk to his son about those things. Am I going to have to make an appointment with the doctor and take him to get that little job tended to before school starts?"

Daddy yawned and got up to go sit in the porch swing a few minutes before going to bed. "Almost time to hit the hay. Tomorrow's gonna be another long day."

He called from the front door. "Somebody's gettin a good rain. Can smell it in the air. But the stars is all out again. Almost time for em to start fallin."

Mother sighed again. "We must not be living right. Seems like it will never rain again."

"Always has," Daddy said, and sat down in the swing.

Me and Til went to lie in the yard and watch for shooting stars. One made a white scratch on the black sky, and we wondered where it would land. He told me that if we dug straight down through the front yard for a month of Sundays we'd get to China.

"Is China about as far as Walla Walla?" I asked.

"Shoot, no, by comparison Walla Walla's not even as far as the B&B," he answered.

"I don't want to go," I said, grabbing both feet.

"See that little cluster of stars over there—six of them? That's the Pleiades. Seven Sisters."

"Just six," I counted.

"Granpa told me one is lost to our eyes, because she hid before she was a star."

"Why?"

"Ashamed of herself, Granpa said, because she was a goddess that fell in love with a man. Probably got herself knocked up.

"And I'll tell you somethin else most people don't know. The moon goes round the earth, and the earth goes round the sun and spins like a top while it goes round. The earth goin round the sun is what causes winter and summer, and it spinnin like that is what causes day and night."

I sat up. "I'll learn all about it when I go to school, like you did."

"Shoot, if you'd listen to me, you'd learn a lot more than you ever will at school. Spit-Ball don't know as much about the stars as Granpa does, and Granpa told me ever'thing he knows. Miss Byers probably don't know nothin about it, cause she just teaches first. Want to know how long it takes the earth to go round the sun? About 365 days, and that's what makes a year. We're about as close to the sun tonight as we'll ever get. If you could stop the earth from turnin and spinnin right now forever, it would be summer and dark here all of the time."

"How many more days does summer have?"

"Get yourself a calendar. This is Thursday, September 1. I told you a hunderd times summer dies on Tuesday, September 6."

"How many hours left?"

"Five times twenty-four is…five four's is twenty, and five two's is ten and carry two…a hunderd and twenty. We had almost that many *days* when it was early June. But we have to sleep about eight hours out of ever day, and that means about eight times five…is forty in bed out of that hunderd and twenty. So, forty from a hunderd and twenty leaves…eighty. Shoot, we ain't actually got but about eighty hours left."

He rolled over on his stomach and leaned on his elbows with his head in his hands. "But you got to get vaccinated first. And if it don't take the first time, they won't let you go to school until you get vaccinated again."

"Does it hurt?"

"Shoot, what do you think? When Dr. Shaw sticks that needle in your arm, it feels like it's comin out the other side."

Mother came to the door, but she didn't sit down in the swing with Daddy. She called for us to come in and take some medicine before bedtime.

"Castor oil?" Til yelled. "What for? I ain't sick."

Daddy called from the porch. "Do what your mother tells you to."

Mother had the medicine in little jelly glasses lined up on the sink. "It's Dr. Jayne's Vermifuge. Tastes just like licorice."

I smelled mine. "Yeah, and pawpaws taste just like bananas." I gulped it down, but Til pretended to drink his, then poured it down the sink when Mother wasn't looking.

"What's vermifuge?" I asked.

Maude was cleaning up the kitchen. "You'll find out soon enough," she said. "It's a long time before you have to take Latin in high school." She was the only one who didn't have to take the medicine.

"But I'm not sick," I said, "and Til's not sick, and Em's not sick. At least, I wasn't sick before I swallowed that stuff."

Maude rinsed out the glasses. "If you must know, Em passed a pinworm today."

Til looked at Emmy. "Is that why you've been scratchin your butt all the time?"

Then he looked at me. "That means you'll be passin em tomorrow."

Mother turned off the kitchen light. "Tilghman, I never wanted you to be a smart aleck. Go on to your bed before I call your daddy." She shuffled back to the porch to sit with Daddy a few minutes.

"What's a pinworm?" I asked Til.

"Looks like an earthworm, only it's white and littler," he answered.

He really did know just about everything. I wondered if he ever had to say, "I don't know," to anybody.

When the shelves at the B&B were filled for Saturday, and new flypapers hung from the ceiling, Daddy swept the floor from the meat counter to the front door.

"Think I'll go to the Moody sale for a couple of hours in the morning if it's all right," he told Mother.

She flipped through the charge slips in the cash register. "What do you want to go to those old auction sales for? Not a copper in them for us. And when do you intend to collect from the Kernses? They owe us $18."

"She'll pay it, somehow, but I don't know what she's livin on. He couldn't have left her much after the way those kids run through with his money."

"I always did envy her that pretty complexion. It's a pity that not a single one of those three girls took after her."

"In more ways than one," Daddy said. "I'd rather bury one of mine as to go through what they went through with that baby girl. Broke Landon's heart."

Daddy locked the front door. "I'll take Cassandry with me," he said. "Tilghman can stay at the store with you 'til time for his violin lesson. I'll be back before then if nothin happens. I still say that's one expense we could do without. Won't amount to a pinch of snuff."

When we got back to the B&B, I couldn't wait to show Til the dollar bill that man gave me for drawing a number out of a hat. I took it out of my overalls bib and dangled it in front of him. He grabbed it and pulled a magnifying glass out of his pocket and focused on George Washington.

"Just look at all them dots in his coat and hair, and look at his eyes, half closed. If I had me a pinpoint fine enough and some of this paper, I could make me a dozen dollar bills a day."

Mother sent us home from the B&B together. Jimmie Lou called as we passed, and I skipped to the porch.

Til yelled, "First thing Maude will do is ask where you are. What would it be worth to you if I told her a lie?"

I climbed into the swing with Jimmie Lou. "Daddy and me been to the Widow Moody's auction sale and I almost won me a calf. See what I got for drawing the number that won?" I waved my dollar bill and asked, "Want a sno-jo?"

Jimmie Lou pointed to George Washington's face. "Mr. War-shin'ton, Father of Our Country, First President. He used to be my boy friend, Cassie." She laughed and held me close. "Want to know who my boy friend is now? Ulysses S. Grant. He's on a thousand-dollar bill."

"This'll buy us a lot of sno-jos," I said.

"You'd better hang onto it, honey. You'll need it for pencils and a tablet in a few days. And when you learn to write, you can mail me a letter."

"Why? When I can stop by to see you every afternoon on my way home from school?"

"Honey, I won't be here. Me and Joe is going to Dee-troit right away. That old lady jumped on me one time too many. Last night when she got after me for not wearin a petticoat around the house, I just went to the phone and asked Joe did he have anywheres near that hunerd. He said he did, so he's comin after me in a few days."

"Where is it?"

"Dee-troit? Up in Michigan, about four days from here. That's where they make all them big cars. Joe's gonna get him a job puttin them together. Only place in the country that's hirin right now."

"They speak the same language?"

Jimmie Lou laughed. "Sure they do, honey. It's still the U.S. of A. Course, me and Joe has got to get married before we leave. Daddy would kill me if I was to go off with him and us not married."

"When will you be back?"

"When we swap that jalopy for one of them fine cars. Want to go with us? We could adopt you and then your last name would be the same as ourn."

"Parris?"

"Pertier than Blevins, ain't it? Or McCormick? Anyhow, if your name began with P instead of B, you'd get to set in the back of the room at school."

"But I am a *Blevins.*"

"Aw, honey, I was just teasin." She hugged me again. "They wouldn't let me take you off. Maybe you can spend your vacation with us next summer."

"Are you going to have a baby?"

Jimmie Lou laughed. "Not no time soon, Lord forbid."

"Could I have a baby?"

She laughed again and held me so close I could feel her heart beat. "What has your momma told you about that?" she asked.

"She just said I grew in her stomach. Til told me how I got there to begin with. Do babies ever drown in there?"

She squeezed me again. "Honey, I ain't the proper one to talk to you about this, but ain't they told you you have to be grown to have a baby?"

"No, but Til told me how baby seeds get planted."

"He ain't the proper one either. Your momma's the one. I bet he don't know near as much about it as he lets on like."

"Daddy and Til know just about everything."

Jimmie Lou took my hand. "Well, honey, you can't have no baby 'til after you menstr'ate."

"Menstr'ate? That the same as bleed?"

"That's right. See, you know more about it than you thought you did, honey. Women call it the curse, and men call it a gift of God, and some people call it the pip."

"Is that what chickens get when they yawn and die?"

"Naw, honey. What your chickens get is a disease. The curse ain't no disease. Just a nuisance. You bleed a few days a month, but not before you are twelve or thirteen. Why don't you ask Maude about it?"

"Does it hurt?"

"Naw, nothin to it. Just messy, sometimes ruins your best dress when you get caught out somewheres without no Kotex."

"Do men bleed, too?"

Jimmie Lou laughed. "Naw, honey. They got a good deal, and we got a raw deal, and it won't change none when we all get that new deal Mr. Roosevelt keeps talking about. It got started when Eve ate that apple."

"Ladies don't climb trees," I said. "I bet it was Adam that climbed that tree and gave it to her. I heard about that at Sunday School. I don't believe it, do you?"

Jimmie Lou laughed again. "It's fixed that way so the sperm, that's the seed, can fertilize the egg in the right place. Just like hens and roosters. Did you know a hen can't lay no eggs 'til she's been with a rooster?"

I held my arms out in a big circle in front of me. "How does the skin on your stomach keep from busting when it gets that big? I saw a woman at the Widow Moody's auction sale that big."

"Lordamercy, Cassie, you don't need to worry your perty head about all that stuff yet. Plenty of time. But it's not your stomach he grows in. He's got a special place in there." She held me closer to her. "You don't want a baby, do you?"

"No," I answered. "No, not ever."

"Aw, you'll change your mind when the time comes, and you meet the right feller. You'll want to have his son for him. But for now, just be careful about settin down on a toilet away from home. They tell me them sperm live on and on in a place like that."

"Is that why Mother makes us put toilet paper on the seat even at church?"

"That's a smart thing to do, honey. Why, a friend of mine down home got in a family way from settin in the bathtub."

"When are you going away?"

Jimmie Lou pushed the swing gently with her foot and held me close. "Joe's comin for me as soon as he can. I'm all packed. And I don't intend to leave no forwardin address, except for you and my folks."

I buried my face in her lap. "Don't go away. Please don't go away."

"Why, Cassie, me and you will never really part. We'll always be friends."

"Promise?"

"Cross my heart and hope to die! Now, you'd better run along home. We'll talk some more tomorrow."

I squirmed off the swing. Jimmie Lou called after me, "Just keep them galluses up, honey. Perty as you are, little boys will be after you ever recess."

"They're going to make me wear a dress," I said.

"Why, of course, you won't be wearin them overalls to school. Boys don't like girls in em. I don't even wear overalls to do the milkin down home."

When I got home Til was in the back yard with a newspaper under his magnifying glass. "You going blind?" I asked.

He held the glass over my arm. "Want me to burn the hair off for you? Ladies ain't s'posed to have hair on their arms."

I jerked my arm away.

Daddy reminded us again at the table that it was a good thing he was in the grocery business. I belched like Til.

Mother said, "If you get any more like a boy, Cassandra, nobody will like you. People just naturally expect a little girl to have more manners than a little boy. How many times do I have to tell you that?" She lowered her voice. "Albert, if you don't listen to me and talk to that boy, the first thing you know it will be more than a belch that gets him into trouble, and it will take more than a beg-your-pardon to get him out of it."

After supper, Mother sent me though the house with a fly swatter. "They're easy to kill this time of year," she said. "They'll be on the walls and window panes. Don't kill any on the table. Don't know why in the world we have to put up with the nasty things." She cleared the table while Maude washed the dishes. "Dispose of their bodies properly," she called to me. That meant flushing them down the toilet.

When the house got dark, except for our room, Til owned Boardwalk and Park Place, and I was in jail. But my mind was not on Monopoly.

He said, "You're gonna have to concentrate better than that, or you'll never make it to second," and shoved the Monopoly set under the bed. I crept down the dark hall and crawled into bed with Emmy. I was afraid to go to Maude's room, because I'd have to go through Mother's and Daddy's room to get there.

Mother made me wear a dress and shoes to get vaccinated the next day. "And put on clean bloomers. Always put on clean underwear before you leave the house. You never know when you might end up in the hospital from being hit by an old car," she warned.

Before we sat down in the waiting room, she asked the nurse if Dr. Shaw had begun vaccinating girls in the leg.

"I hear some doctors are doing that now, because that old scar lasts a lifetime. It's so ugly with short-sleeved dresses," she said.

The nurse nodded and Dr. Shaw came in and rubbed some cold wet cotton on my leg and counted out loud as he jabbed the same little spot over and over again, 25 times.

Mother said, "She's the third Blevins you've vaccinated for that old smallpox. I'll bring her back in a few weeks for her typhoid and diptheria shots. She'll want to be in the blue-ribbon parade with our other two."

School children who had been to the dentist and the doctor during the summer paraded down Broadway behind the high school band every fall just before school started. They were all dressed in white and had little blue-ribbon pins on.

Mother handed Dr. Shaw a dollar, and we walked home. The red spot on my leg stung and burned all the way. She took a good look at it when I changed clothes. "Don't want you wearing those old overalls for a while. Overalls rubbing against it might get it infected and keep it from scabbing over. And you have to be careful when it scabs over. Don't pick at it. It has to come off of its own accord." She put some Cloverine salve on it. "I wish they had been vaccinating in the leg when Maude got hers. That old scar will be ugly for years."

Wearing a dress didn't keep me from shooting marbles in the alley with Til and Ralph. But it wasn't comfortable kneeling down on one knee and pulling my dress down over the other one when I aimed my steelie toward the marbles in the middle of the ring. And baseball was even worse. It was hard to slide into a base and keep my dress where it ought to be at the same time. And I always ended up with questions that I couldn't ask anybody. Did I have to quit playing marbles forever? Forever was a long time. What about baseball? Til and Ralph both had bragged on how good I could catch. We used to play until dark, but now almost every time we were together, we went up to the loft to talk after a few innings.

"Hear the one about the two priests goin to the dirty movie?" Til asked. "After it was over, they was walkin down the street, and one said he had to go back, that he had forgot his hat. And the other one said, 'No, you didn't! It's hangin in your lap.' "

They guffawed. Then Ralph asked. "Hear the one about the travelin salesman?"

"Which one?" Til asked. "Heard a hunderd."

"You ain't heard this one Marcella told me about the salesman goin to Mexico on a business trip, and when he got home his wife found these rubbers in his suitcase. He told her they were souvenirs for her, Mexican money bags. The next week he was in Salt Lake City and wired his boss, 'Finished in Salt Lake City. Shall I proceed to San Francisco?' The boss wired him back, 'Proceed to San Francisco, and take a slow boat to China. Your Mexican money bags are on display at the church bazaar.' "

I guffawed with them.

"Getting any lately?" Ralph asked Til.

"Little, here and there," Til bragged. "Bet Marcella missed me."

"Her business didn't fall off none. Infantile paralysis don't strike grownups."

"Been busy gettin Satch ready for the first grade," Til said. "Tell him your ABC's."

My face got hot. "He probably taught em to you in the first place," I said.

"No, he didn't. I made em up," Til bragged.

I started. "A is for ass. B is for balls. C is for cock. D is for dick. E is for...can't say that word."

Til said, "Ejaculation."

"F is for fuck."

Ralph interrupted. "She had any yet?"

"No," Til said. "She's too little. You want to try again to help her grow?"

"Don't want to hurt her."

"It won't hurt her none. If it does, she can tell you and you can stop."

"I don't like to start nothin I can't finish," Ralph said.

Til turned to me. "Sometimes you have to do this a little bit at a time to make you grow." And he told me to take off my dress and bloomers and lie down on the bale of hay. He asked Ralph, "You got a new rubber?"

"I told you, you don't need no rubber with her. She ain't even bled yet. It don't matter how many seeds you plant if they ain't bled."

"I thought Marcella makes you wear one."

"That's different. She's already bled. What's the use of goin to bed with your shoes on if you don't have to?"

Ralph let his overalls slide to the floor, and looked between my legs. "Might hurt a little. Might not be able to get in there. I don't want to make her bleed."

I closed my eyes and put my hands over my face. Ralph straddled me, and I felt his clammy peejabber against my leg. It was hot and hard. He raised up on his elbow and put his cold finger in me.

"Got any vaseline around here?" he asked Til. "She's dry as a gourd."

"Nope," Til answered. "You'll just have to make out, and be careful and don't knock the scab off her vaccination. Mother'll whip her."

Ralph fell full length on top of me, rocking and grunting. All of me was under him. As he rose and fell against me, his peejabber felt like a big, hot needle. It punched and jabbed between my legs.

legs. I could feel his hot breath on my hands and face. His body arched, and his face came down against mine. I bit his ear lobe, hard, and slid out from under him, and knelt against a bale of hay, crying and pounding it with my fists.

Ralph jumped up and hovered over me. He grabbed my hands and pulled me up to face him. I tried to talk, but only sobs came. I pounded his chest with my fists.

"Aw, come on Cass, quit actin like a baby," Til said. "It couldn't hurt that bad. It's like a vaccination, somethin you have to get to grow up, and the sooner you get it over with, the better off you'll be. It don't hurt but once."

Ralph's angry eyes wouldn't let me look at Til. He backed me onto the bale of hay and fell heavy on top of me again, and rocked and grunted, rising and falling against me, faster and faster. My insides burned and stung, and hot tears filled my ears and dripped down my neck into the hay. Suddenly, he groaned, and his whole body fell on me and stayed, his wet face buried in the hay above my head. I turned my head to breathe. I thought he never would move. Til finally pushed him off me, and he rolled over on the floor, his dark, curly hair plastered against his forehead.

My legs felt like they would never go together again for walking. I never had hurt like that before, not even when I hit the side of Unc's barn.

"I knew you could do it," Til said to Ralph.

Ralph bragged. "Never seen one yet I couldn't do when I really put my mind to it."

Til turned to me. "Did you feel anything?"

Whimpering, I crawled over to put my dress and bloomers on, and crept down the ladder.

As the screen door slammed behind me, I could hear Lowell Thomas and Roosevelt. They said the same thing night after night, and Daddy thought he had to hear it every time. "Happy Days Are Here Again" rang out as I ran into the bathroom and closed the door behind me. I got a drink of cold water and held the cold wash rag to my face. That didn't stop the tears. When I rinsed out the wash rag, I couldn't take my eyes off the blurred face in the mirror.

"I hate you, Cassandra Blevins," I whimpered. "Ugly thing you. I wish you were dead." I rubbed my eyes with the cold wash rag and then rubbed it between my legs. It was streaked with blood.

"I wish you were dead," I whimpered again, and wondered how long the hurting would last. And the blood. The vaccination scab still clung to my leg. I washed out my bloomers and crept into the bedroom to get a clean pair. When I opened the dresser drawer, I heard Til laugh. They were looking in the window.

"Don't worry," he said to Ralph. "She ain't gonna tell. She's all right. She's tough."

And they ran. I put my wet bloomers on a coat hanger in the back of the closet.

Nobody noticed that I didn't talk any more that day. I crawled into Maude's bed early. I don't know why I moved even farther away from her when she got in.

The next day me and Til didn't talk when we took turns cranking the ice cream freezer. Mother asked where Ralph was.

"He has a way of turning up every time we make ice cream, especially when it's fresh peach," she said.

"He's probably gone to prayer meetin with his mother," Til said, and licked the paddle clean.

Maude ate a bowl of ice cream and said something about getting too fat, and Mother made Emmy stop after two bowls. Daddy said that only folks with their own cow could afford ice cream twice a week, and Mother said that old stuff you get at the drug store was not worth carrying home, was more like flavored ice water pumped up with air.

My stomach hurt so bad I cried, even though I didn't finish one bowl. Mother put me in her bed after giving me a dose of paregoric. She closed the door, and they all went out on the porch.

"Cass might be a little nervous about starting to school," she said.

Pretty soon, I saw the dim outline of a man and two women in the bedroom. They all wore white. He looked familiar. Sure enough, it was Dr. Shaw and his two nurses. They were whispering to each other. "Poor little girl...would have started first grade next week...can't save her...but I don't believe it's infantile paralysis...we've done all we can do." Dr. Shaw shook his head. "Her vaccination looks good...scab's still there...what in the world can be the matter with her?"

I screamed for Daddy. He ran into the room and picked me up without turning on the light. I beat on his chest with my fists as hard as I could, and cried until I lost my breath. He held me close and rocked back and forth on the bed.

"You were just havin a bad dream, Cassandry," he whispered. "That's what comes of havin eyes bigger than your stomach."

I put my hands over my face and sobbed against him. He rocked and sang softly, "Bye baby buntin, Daddy's gone a huntin, gone to get a rabbit skin to wrap the baby buntin in."

Mother came in to see if I was all right. "Too much ice cream," she said.

Daddy said, "She can sleep in here with you tonight, and I'll sleep with Til."

He teased me the next day. "The very idea! What in the world was after you, Cassandra?"

Some nights in my sleep the Chinaman at the laundry chased me down the street with a big butcher knife. But this time it wasn't the Chinaman. I don't know what it was.

FIFTEEN

*E*verybody but Em took turns stirring the apple butter in the big iron kettle in the driveway. Me and Til kept the fire going under it while Maude scalded jars. When nobody was looking, I ambled down the driveway, and ran down the sidewalk to McCormicks. I had to see Jimmie Lou before school started the next morning. But when I saw Mrs. McCormick sitting in the porch swing, chewing on her snuff stick, I ran right on by.

She called out, "You lookin for Jimmie Lou? She ain't here. She up and left yesterday afternoon. That boy picked her up right after dinner."

Jimmie Lou had gone off to Detroit with Junior, and I didn't even get to tell her good-bye. I didn't want Mrs. McCormick to know I was crying, so I looked across the street and started running home.

She called after me, "Her daddy taken sick of a Saturday evenin, and they takin him to the clinic down home. He's had that ole spastic cola for years. She 'llowed she'd be back 'bout Thursday."

I skipped up the street without stepping on a single crack in the sidewalk. Mr. Simpson was on the porch reading the newspaper. When I heard him call my name, I skipped faster and pretended not to hear. I never did answer him. I had to take my turn with the big paddle in the apple butter. Daddy helped me.

After supper, Mother sounded tireder than usual. "You kids take a bath and get to your bed, and I don't want to hear a word out of you about it being Monday instead of Saturday."

I slipped out the back door into the cool night. Til followed. "Want to go to the Holy Roller meetin with Woody and me?" he asked. "Your last chance to get saved before school starts."

"I have to take a bath," I answered, "and so do you."

Mother called through the screen door. "Tilghman, Maude's out of the tub. You're next, and the water is running."

"Keep your shirt on," Til muttered under his breath.

Mother called, "What was that, Tilghman?"

"I said I'd be there in a minute," Til answered, and sauntered down the path to the barn.

I picked Felix up and went into the house. Mother was scrubbing the sink. "Tilghman, keep an eye on that tub, and don't let the water run over."

I put down Felix. "It ain't Tilghman," I said. "He told me I could take my bath first, and he'll be here in a minute."

"It *isn't* Tilghman," she corrected me. "How many times do I have to tell you there is no such word as *ain't*? Where *did* he go now?"

I stepped out of my overalls. "He's out in the yard with Woody, studying the stars. He told me all about the Pleiades."

Mother folded the dishrag across the spigot. "Go on and get in the tub," she said, "and start scrubbing. You may have to get Maude to help you a little with those feet. They may take a little Clorox," she laughed. "Now tell me the honest truth, Cassie. Would you put those dirty feet into your new shoes?" She took hold of my shoulders and aimed me toward the bathroom. "And be careful with that smallpox scab," she reminded me. "It will take at least another week for it to fall off."

I never knew when Til came in. I slept with Maude.

In the middle of the morning, Mother buttoned up the back of my new dress and gave Til his instructions. "Now, remember, take her to Miss Byers' room and introduce her. You're big enough to do that. Can I depend on you?"

Til buttoned the cuffs of his new shirt. "Want to go to the picture show, Satch?" he asked, grinning.

"That's enough out of you, Tilghman. You're supposed to be at school by 10:30, so you'd better get a move on." Mother looked him in the eye. "Are you listening to me, Tilghman Blevins?"

"How could I help it?" he answered.

"And don't make her cry. If you do, she will tell me just as sure as you were born. And your daddy will take care of you when he gets home tonight."

Mother tied my sash in a big bow and fluffed it out in the back. "Tilghman, have you combed your hair?"

She hadn't even noticed the high roach he had slicked back with water. He grabbed my hand.

"Come on, Satch. We got to go. Old Lady Byers is waitin for you."

I pulled my hand away from his and followed him out the front door.

Mother called after us. "And don't you call her Satch. You hear me? Tell Miss Byers her real name." She called louder when we started down the sidewalk. "Don't run and get all sweaty. And don't jump across that creek. Go around the sidewalk. And Til, don't you run off and leave her after school."

I hadn't ever jumped the creek before with all those clothes on. That's why I landed a little shy of the dry part of the bank and got my new shoes muddy. I lagged behind Til to wipe them off, then rubbed my hands in the grass.

We crossed the street to the school yard where six-year-olds clung to a mother or father or big brother or sister. Til took my hand, but I pulled away and put both hands behind my back.

The odor in the long hall behind the double doors reminded me of Si Feathers. I pinched my nose. But Miss Byers' room smelled clean, like Aunt Flossie, like Ivory Soap. I kept my hands behind my back, because grownups always wanted to shake hands when they met you. Sure enough, when Til blurted out, "This is my little sister, Cassandra Blevins," Miss Byers held out her hand and asked, "Another Blevins? Why, Til, you didn't tell me you had a little sister."

I kept my hands behind my back. He answered, "Yes ma'am, I've got two. The other one will be here next year." He turned around and was gone. His homeroom was upstairs.

I expected Miss Byers to look like Aunt Flossie, but she didn't. Til had told me she was so thin that she had to stand twice to make a shadow, but he hadn't told me about her pretty face. He hadn't told me that when she laughed, her blue eyes laughed as much as her mouth. He hadn't told me that her black hair, which tumbled in loose waves to a low knot on the back of her head, looked just like Jimmie Lou's, or that her soft, low voice made you want to be quiet so you wouldn't miss a word she said. Her Old Lady Comforts cupped at her ankles as she walked, and the knots in her garters showed just below her knees when she crossed her legs, but her flowered dress had a short jacket with big white buttons just like Maude's Sunday suit.

I sat on my hands in a little chair between a pale-faced girl who wouldn't take off her shiny, red raincoat, and a fat boy who couldn't take off his wet overalls. The legs of his cane-bottom chair straddled a thin puddle of pee.

Smiling, Miss Byers leaned over and asked, "Cassandra, do you want to go to the bathroom?"

"No ma'am, but he might," I answered, pointing to the fat boy. Miss Byers ignored him.

After she had called out our names and written down our addresses and asked if anybody in our family had been in her room before, she held up some books.

"Which one would you like to hear, *Goldilocks* or *Epaminondas* or *The Three Little Pigs?*" she asked.

When we all answered at once, she held her hands over her ears and decided that we would vote on one story at a time. *The Three Little Pigs* won, and after she had read about huffing and puffing and blowing your house in, she pulled the white cloth off some paper cups on the table.

"Line up nicely, children, and take one apiece," she instructed.

Everybody but the fat boy in the wet overalls got up and took a cup of lemonade. After she whispered in his ear, he got in line, too, while she wiped under his chair.

"Drop your cups in the wastebasket when you're through," she said, "and we'll have our art lesson. Pull your chairs over to the table, and take a pencil from the can and draw me a picture of your family."

She went from one to the other as we drew, asking who the stick figures in our pictures were and bragging on our smudgy skies and trees. Some of the boys stood in their chair and held their paper against the wall to draw, and others crawled up on the table and chewed their pencils. Mother had warned me a long time ago about wetting the end of the pencil to make it blacker. Pencil lead is poison, she said.

Miss Byers leaned over a little girl who cried quietly, "What's the matter, honey?" she asked.

The only answer was a loud sob. She asked again, but still got only sniffles, and finally lifted the little girl onto her lap. Between gasps and sniffles, the little girl told her that she couldn't draw her family, because she didn't have one. She lived with her aunt who wasn't married and clerked at the ten-cent store. Miss Byers told her to draw her aunt, but the little girl just hovered over the paper and cried softly.

When she got to me, Miss Byers bragged on the house I had drawn. The big woman at the front door was Mother, smiling and beautiful, and the small man going down the porch steps was Daddy, curly-haired and laughing, on his way to the B&B. Maude and Til and Emmy sat in the swing, all smiling. Maude was reading a book, and Emmy held a doll. Felix curled up in Til's lap.

"Where would you sit if there were room in the swing?" Miss Byers asked.

"Between Til and Em," I answered, "but there ain't room. If I had my color crayons, I would color everybody's eyes. All of us but Em have blue eyes, and hers are brown."

"You mustn't leave yourself out," Miss Byers said. "Put yourself there on the porch somewhere. You can be standing there beside your father."

When she came back in a few minutes, I had drawn myself. I barely came to Daddy's knees.

"Why, Cassandra, you're much taller than that," Miss Byers said. "And give yourself some eyes and a nose and a mouth."

She didn't seem to hear me when I said, "It's through."

"What are you wearing there in the picture, Cassandra? Overalls?"

"Yes ma'am."

"Why don't you have on this pretty little dress?" She put her hand on my shoulder.

"It's just for school and Sunday," I answered. "I always wear overalls at home."

She walked away. "Children, you may take your pictures home with you. We'll meet here again at 8:45 in the morning to hear another story and draw some more. Bring a tablet and your color crayons. And we'll sing some, too."

Til stuck his head in the door, and I grabbed my picture and followed him. When he looked at the picture, he mumbled, "Why didn't you make Daddy bigger? He's the boss. And why did you make me so little? I'm as big as Maude. And what happened to you?"

I didn't answer him. He broke into a run and yelled. "That's first grade for you! Draw pictures all day and listen to silly stories. We spent the day on higher math, and Old Hatchet-Face Horn gave us homework!"

When we got home, Mother pinned my picture over the one on the calendar above the sink.

"Goodness gracious!" she said. "We've been hoeing two rows at a time around here. I plain forgot to tear August off." She ripped the page off the calendar and counted the days she had X'ed. "Eight," she said. "Eight mornings with heavy fog in August. That means we'll have at least eight snows this winter. And watch for the wooly worms! I'll bet they have wide, black bands. Sign of cold weather."

Daddy came in the back door and went to the kitchen sink to wash his hands for dinner.

Mother said, "Albert, why can't you do that in the bathroom. It's nasty to wash dirty hands over the dishes."

"Ain't they dirty, too?" he asked, and turned to me. "How did you get along today, Cassandry?"

Mother pointed to the picture on the calendar. "You'd never guess we have an artist in the family," she said. "But now that I think about it, I'm not surprised. There *is* some art on *my* side of the house."

Daddy walked over to take a closer look. "I got a idea, Cassandry," he said. "You make me a dozen pictures like that, one for every month, and I'll get us a calendar made up with B&B GROCERY STORE printed across the bottom, there where it says SLOAT INSURANCE COMPANY. We'll give em to our favorite customers with their Christmas order."

For October, I would draw me stacking oatmeal and Daddy behind the cash register, waving his gun at a Gypsy. For November, I would draw me and Til feeding the chickens and Mother pointing to one for Thanksgiving dinner. For December...

Til went back to school after dinner, but I couldn't go. It would be next year before I could go all day. I spent the afternoon working on October.

As usual, Daddy went in to hear Lowell Thomas and Amos and Andy after supper. Lowell Thomas said that Roosevelt was on a tour through the West, waving his battered felt hat at every train stop between Kansas and California, looking into the eyes of thousands of Americans who wondered if he could possibly be the Messiah. Daddy told me that Messiah was just another word for God, and Mother corrected him.

"It really means the Anointed One, Jesus," she explained, reminding us that her daddy was a Methodist minister.

"FDR's got about six weeks," Daddy said, "before he swaps the Governor's mansion in Albany for the White House in Warshin'ton. He'll be the first President we ever had that talked plain enough for us to understand."

"I wouldn't be too sure of that," Mother said. "Lots of men change as soon as they take the oath of office or vows of marriage.

"Albert, Dr. Shaw will circumcise your son in the morning at 10," Mother announced. "I think it's your place to go with him. It won't take over an hour."

"I'll take him," Daddy said, "but it means you'll have to go to the store when I go. I still don't like to leave you there alone. And Saturday's the busiest day of the week. Cassandry or Maude can stay with you."

Til was quiet the next morning when he put on his knickers. We didn't talk much as we ran down the street to meet Daddy. I helped Mother clean the shelves while they were gone. She let me use the feather duster.

He was quiet when he came back to take me home. He walked up the street with his legs far apart, like he was on stilts.

"Did it hurt much?" I asked.

"Nothin to it," he answered. "He just took a pair of scissors and clipped it off. Didn't even bleed. Just stung a little bit when the feelin came back."

"Clipped it off?" I asked, picturing Til without a peejabber.

"The extra skin at the end, dummy," he said.

Til was in bed before Daddy came home from the B&B that night. I crawled in beside him, glad that he wouldn't want his peejabber churned.

One afternoon the next week I was skipping home from school when I saw Jimmie Lou in the porch swing.

"When did you get back?" My heart was beating as fast as I talked.

"Last night," she answered. "I been settin here waitin for you. I know you'd have to come up that street sometime this afternoon."

"How's your daddy?" I asked.

"Daddy was real bad sick. I was beginnin to wonder if I'd ever get back up here to get my things. But he's home from the clinic now, and he's so grouchy that we know he's gettin well."

I jumped on her lap and put my arms around her neck. She hugged me tight.

"I was afraid you were gone to Detroit," I said. "Had left without telling me goodbye."

"You know I wouldn't do nothin like that, Cassie. Like I told you, we'll never part," she said. "How's school goin?"

"We learned two new songs today, 'My Bonnie Lies Over the Ocean' and 'Sweet and Low.' Do you know them?"

"Sure do. Reckon they've been singin those in the first grade ever since Noah sent that dove out."

"Which one do you want to sing?" I asked.

"Let's swing to 'My Bonnie,' " she answered, and began pushing her feet against the porch floor. She knew all of the words, too.

"Who's your teacher?" she asked.

"Miss Byers. Same one that Maude and Til had," I answered.

"Who's in your room? Anybody you know?"

"Know them all now, but didn't know a one before school started."

"Hon, one of the first rules is that you don't talk to nobody 'bout nobody, cause you might be talkin 'bout some of their kin," Jimmie Lou said, laughing.

"We don't talk about people," I said. "Just draw birds and trees and houses and sing. And Miss Byers reads us stories like *Goody Two-Shoes* and *Dame Wiggins of Lee*." Her black eyes looked happier than they did before she left. "When are you going away?" I asked.

"Tomorrow mornin, hon. Joe's comin early."

"You won't be here ever again when I walk home from school?" I asked.

"That's right, Cassie, but like I said, you can come a visitin."

"When? I have to go to school until Christmas and then I have to stay home so Santy will come." I moved closer to her as she pushed the swing slowly with one foot. "When will you come back?"

"I'll write you, hon. We'll be back to visit the folks in a year or so if Daddy don't get no worse. Next summer maybe. Promise me that the first letter you write will be to me."

"Cross my heart and hope to die," I said. "I promise," I said. "How long will it take me to learn to write?"

"Not long, honey, as quick as you are to catch onto things."

"There's lots of things I need to talk to you about, Jimmie Lou."

"It can wait," she said. "I have to pack tonight, and the old lady has a couple a jobs she wants me to do 'fore I leave. I reckon I'll oblige her and do em."

"I'd better go. They'll wonder where I am."

Jimmie Lou saw the tears cut a path down each cheek. "Ah, Cassie, now don't go and make me cry. We got nothin to cry about. We both got work to do, and love don't die with distance. Just remember that. I do hate to miss any of your growin-up time, cause I love you, but we'll have lots more chances to talk and touch hands. And remember, honey, it's just like some poet said, 'Lovin comes easy, but hatin takes too much heart.' "

"I love you, too," I said, staring at the porch floor. "I love you more than anybody." I took off my shoes and socks and started down the porch steps. When I turned around to wave, she leaned over and kissed me on the forehead. My arms went all the way around her waist.

I didn't know what she meant when she yelled after me, "Don't you take no wooden nickels from nobody, hon, not even Til, not *nobody.*"

Sure enough, Mr. Simpson was sitting on the porch. I heard him call my name and broke into a run toward home. Already I was sorry I hadn't told Jimmie Lou about Mr. Simpson. She would believe me. But it was too late. And I couldn't ask Maude to write her a letter about him. I'd just have to wait until I could write it myself. Daddy might believe me, but I knew that he would shoot Mr. Simpson dead.

SIXTEEN

Going to school didn't keep Til from "engineering trouble," as Aunt Flossie called it. I never did know where he got that spool of fine copper wire that looked like a strand of henna-rinsed hair. Saturday night when we sat in the car on Main Street waiting for Maude to quit clerking at the Kress Five-and-Ten-Cent Store, he got the wire out of his overalls pocket and handed me the end. Mother and Daddy had taken Em with them when they went to meet Maude in front of the store. Til knew we had a little more than ten minutes, because the big clock at Baylor Hardware said ten minutes before nine, and Kress's closed at nine.

Til ordered, "Tie it to Dr. Shaw's door knob across the sidewalk there. He's done gone home."

"What do you want me to do that for?" I asked.

"Ask me no questions, and I'll tell you no lies," he answered. "Hurry up, and don't let nobody see you."

I wrapped my end of the wire around the door knob several times while he wrapped his end around the radiator cap.

"That ought to be about the right height," he said, as we crawled back into the car.

"For what?" I said, and suddenly realized that nobody would be able to see that wire. "Somebody's going to get hurt."

"Just shut up and watch," he ordered.

Pretty soon two women came up the street, their hands full of packages. The wire hit one across her neck, and the other, across the chest. Packages went flying in all directions, and the women fought like they were all wrapped up in cobwebs. We got down in the car, and Til roared with laughter and pounded his fists on the floorboard.

I asked him, "What if that wire cut somebody's throat?"

"Shoot, it won't hurt nobody," he answered. "Ain't strong enough to cut their throat. You ain't no fun no more, Cass. Don't you never get bored? I was just passin the time of day."

The telephones were more fun. Til strung the copper wire between the two Calumet Baking Powder cans. I took one over to Mr. Diggs' house and sat by the window so I could see Til in Mother's and Daddy's bedroom. When I held the can to my ear, I heard lots of noises, like the wind in trees, and the ocean in Aunt Flossie's conch shell, and then Til's voice sounded like a toy that had been wound up. It was so high-pitched that he sounded like the woman that played "central" down at the telephone company. When you picked up the telephone at the B&B, she would come on the line. "Number please," she would say, like she was about to sing a song.

"What are you doin, Cass?" Til asked.

"Listening to you," I answered.

It worked! I tossed the can out the window and bounded across the yard between the two houses to tell Til.

"But what good is it?" I asked. "The wire's not long enough for you to talk to me from school in the afternoon. And we don't need it here at the house. I don't need to go to Mr. Diggs' house to talk to you."

"Knothead, I was just tryin to show you how the real ones work," he said.

Mother overheard him from the porch. "Where did you hear that, Tilghman? Don't let me hear you call your little sister that ever again."

"But you can call all over town on the real ones," I said.

"That's because they got wires strung all over town, dummy," he said. "Why don't you do me a favor? Drop dead."

Mother sounded mad. "Tilghman, I mean what I say. I'll ask you one more time not to call her 'dummy.' Neither one of you is dumb, but they tell me you can make anybody dumb by calling them that often enough."

"Shoot, she don't listen," he answered. "It won't hurt her none."

"*Any*, won't hurt her *any*. Will you ever learn not to use a double negative? Sometimes I think it's pure stubbornness," Mother said.

He ambled up the street with the phones to show Ralph his latest invention. I didn't care if he left me at home, because I wanted to work on my calendar and study the Pledge of Allegiance.

I knew the Lord's Prayer which Miss Byers led us in every morning, but I had trouble remembering all of the words to the Pledge of Allegiance. We never did say that at home or at church, just like we never did sing "I'll be a Sunbeam" at school, or "Sweet and Low" at church.

I didn't know whether I liked school or church songs better, but I really wanted to be a sunbeam.

Jesus wants me for a sunbeam, to shine for Him every day,
In ev'ry way try to please Him, at home, at school, at play.
A sunbeam, a sunbeam, I'll be a sunbeam for Him.

But every time I sang it when we were shooting marbles, Til yelled, "Turn it off, turn it off! Worse than Maude dronin 'Tea for Two.' I'd rather hear a heifer bawl any day as to hear either one of you try to sing."

So, when I was with him, I stopped, but sometimes when I was with Mother and Maude, we sang together. Mother always wanted to sing a sad hymn like "In the Garden" or "Uncloudy Day." I liked the tunes, but the words made me lonesome and reminded me that I was not saved. From what the Reverend Carmack had said, I wasn't even a virgin like Mary any more, not since Ralph put his peejabber inside me in the hay loft. I couldn't think about that very long without wanting to go hide somewhere all by myself. Sometimes I did that, and Til would yell for me and find me in Polly's manger or under the big blue hydrangea bush in Mr. Diggs' front yard.

Everybody said Maude had a good voice. Mother's was too high when she tried to sing that old sacred-harp harmony. Mine was too low for a girl. It was even lower than Til's or Ralph's or any of the boys' in the first grade, but it got a little higher when Miss Byers called on me for my ABC's. It took me a long time to remember her way, but it didn't take me long to figure out that

Til's way was all wrong. His way *did* help me to remember the order, but I had to say it the wrong way to myself first, then say it the right way out loud: "A is for apple...B is for baby...C is for cow."

When I got home from school, Mother told me I could have a birthday party Friday afternoon, and I could invite my whole room to play games in the front yard and eat ice cream and cake.

Of course, Maude helped her serve, and Til and Em were there, too, but they weren't guests and didn't give me anything. Guests were Gerald and Jenelle, Lovely and Minnie Jo and Otho and Elsie...thirteen in all besides me. After we played "Go In and Out the Window" and "Drop the Handkerchief," Mother and Maude led us into the dining room for big slices of angel food cake covered with vanilla ice cream. Mother read the words that Maude had printed on top of the cake in blue, my favorite color. "Happy Birthday, Cassandra." I wanted to save it until Daddy got home, but Mother cut the cake so that everybody got a letter or two. I felt funny eating part of "Cassandra."

Gerald brought me a handkerchief that his mother had embroidered my initials on. He was so poor that he never wore anything but overalls to school, and his mother worked so hard doing other people's washing that he had to make a pair last two weeks instead of one. His daddy had been laid off from the cotton mill for six months.

Otho brought me a little draw-string bag full of aggies. Mother said later that she was surprised at him because marbles was a boys' game. She said he probably wanted them himself and I should give them back to him, but I never had seen him shoot marbles at school. He had seen me do it at recess, but I didn't tell her. Otho was so clean every day that his face looked like a pair of white patent leather shoes.

Mother and Daddy gave me a pair of black patent leather shoes with two buttons for my birthday. I had never had more than one button before. Jenelle gave me a little bottle of Radio Girl perfume. She had the prettiest clothes in the first grade. She was the one that wouldn't take off the shiny, red raincoat the first day. And I got three new books with lots of printing in them. My old books had mostly pictures.

After September, the days raced by, and the leaves turned gold and red and orange, then brown, and fell, one at a time, as we walked and raced to school. During the long and lonely afternoons, I walked on the stilts that Til had made with two-by-four's and tin cans, or memorized new songs, or rolled my hoop on the sidewalk. Going *up* the sidewalk kept me from going by the Simpsons' house. A lot of the time I just lay on my stomach on the porch and worked on the B&B calendar.

When Til got home, we played catch with a paper poke full of fallen leaves until it broke, and filled our lungs with the cool air and wondered how the moon and stars could be so close. Sometimes, cold rain beat on the tin roof all night long, and Mother said that soon it would freeze to a bare earth, and that soon the sun's yellow blaze would dim to white. She reminded us every little bit that winter was not her favorite time of year.

Of course, summer was my favorite time, but in lots of ways I liked winter, too. We would be in the house together by the cookstove a lot more, and Mother would have time to read to me and Em. I would be able to study without wanting to be on the sidewalk with my hoop or in the barnyard with my rubber gun. One of the best things about winter was that I wouldn't have to take tomatoes or beans to the Simpsons, and Ralph wouldn't come by as often. Maybe I wouldn't miss Jimmie Lou so much, and we wouldn't have to swat flies every day. Til didn't expect me to help him grow more every night because I was sleeping with Maude most of the time. Anyhow, I didn't have time for Monopoly any more, what with having to learn how to read and write and all.

At nights while I worked on the calendar pictures, Daddy listened to Lowell Thomas.

Mother listened more than she let on. "I believe this is the first time a woman has had anything to do with a national campaign," she said. Mother liked Mrs. Roosevelt. She had been a schoolteacher, too. And she stuck by her husband through thick and thin, helping him to learn to walk again after he got that old infantile paralysis.

Mother said, "She must have the patience of Job. They tell me that he's always been a momma's boy, that his mother tells them where to live and how to raise those five children."

"She's ugly as a mud fence," Daddy said.

"Pretty is as pretty does," Mother reminded him. "Actions speak louder than looks. She doesn't sit at home and wait for him to come back from a trip; she goes with him and does some of the talking herself. She might make a good president herself some day."

"For cryin out loud, Clary, what are you talkin about?" Daddy asked, hiking up her dress tail with his foot. "It'll be a cold day below when the country elects a woman to guide the ship of state."

"What makes you so sure?" Mother asked, narrowing her eyes at him.

"Man's place," he muttered. "Why them other world leaders wouldn't give her the time of day, much less *do* what she says. You know that as well as I do."

"I don't know any such thing," she said, quietly. "Just what do you think would become of him without her? That woman has been his eyes and his ears since he got all crippled up. You heard Lowell Thomas say just now that FDR sent her out to watch the people's faces. 'Look at their clothes on the wash line,' he told her, 'and find out what kind of car they drive.' That's a lot to ask of a woman who's raising five children. Besides, they tell me she runs an antique furniture factory and teaches at a girls' school in New York two days a week, drives down from Albany."

"Well, to my way of thinkin, she oughta be home raisin those children," Daddy said.

"Why, they're practically grown, Albert," Mother said. "That girl is twenty-six years old, and the youngest boy is about sixteen."

"How come you know so much about it?" Daddy asked.

"Mrs. Simpson's 'Woman's Home Companion' had quite a story about the family last month, with lots of pictures. Good-looking family, but she had her head down in every photograph, looking at a baby. Why, that man kept her pregnant the better part of ten years. And he had his mother in every family portrait."

"They couldn't be anything but good lookin with him for their father."

"They can thank their lucky stars those chidren are all normal. My *Science of Living* book says that when cousins marry, their children are apt to be either retarded or deformed."

"Not likely, as smart as they are, both college graduates and him a lawyer," Daddy said.

"Well, I wish I were more like her," Mother said. "Wish I could go to a League of Women Voters meeting once in a while instead of two PTA meetings a month."

"He sure didn't marry her for her looks," Daddy said.

"You're out of something to say now," Mother said and began singing "Blessed Assurance," putting the chorus in front of the verses as usual. "This is my story, this is my song, praising my Savior all the day long."

Em sat in her little red rocking chair and rocked Betty Boop to sleep. The big-eyed little doll with the spit curls and high heels was an early birthday gift to take Emmy's mind off Granny's death. She still cried in the middle of the night once in a while, and walked in her sleep looking for Granny, but the doll seemed to comfort her. She hummed what now and then sounded like "I Want to Be Loved by You."

Til stalled every night about going to bed. "Ralph showed me how to hypmotize somebody today. Wanta see me do it?" He turned to me. "Stand up there on the bed, Cass, and I'll show you."

Daddy went to the bathroom as Til jumped up behind me and locked his arms around my chest and began squeezing, easy at first, and counting slowly. By the time he got to ten, I was numb and sleepy, and when he got to fourteen, I slid out of his arms and slumped to the bed just as Daddy came out of the bathroom. He unbuckled his belt. "Til, I oughta bust the rind on you. You can call that hypmotizin if you want to, but you have just squeezed all of the air outa her lungs," he said quietly. "I'll take you down a notch or two with the razor strop if I ever catch you doin that again." He took off his belt and tossed it on the bed.

His voice was far away, and, although sweat had popped out on my forehead, I felt cold and clammy all over. Daddy kept talking. "Get to your bed right now. And I don't want to hear another word out of you tonight."

Til went to his room. I lay in Mother's and Daddy's bed and stared at the ceiling. I expected Daddy to follow Til and whip him, but he didn't. He walked to the bed and leaned over me.

"You're gonna be all right in a few minutes," he said, gently. "Just lie still and breathe deep. And I'm not gonna tell you but one more time that you can't do everything that boy tells you to. What if he told you to go jump off of the river bridge?"

Mother answered, "Why, she'd do it as fast as she could. I hope to my Lord we live to see all four of them grown. What really happened to Cass?"

"She fainted," Daddy answered. "It's bedtime."

I never had fainted before. It didn't feel good at all. But I felt all right the next night when we went to Bristol to hear the Carter Family sing.

That night Jack Frost painted the ground white just as Mother predicted he would. Then she predicted the first snow would fall Thanksgiving week, and Daddy talked about cleaning off the garden and getting Polly's stall ready for winter.

Mother put on her shimmy shirt and switched us to long underwear and long stockings. I wore my brown velvet bonnet with the ruffled brim to school every day, whether we were having a birthday party or just a regular day. And I always carried pumpkin seeds in my pocket whether I had on my overalls or a dress. Mother dried them on the sink drain every time she made a pumpkin pie.

I liked to lag behind Til on the way home from school, unless it was raining. Then we ran all the way. But I was happiest at school. We sang and laughed a lot more than we did at home. I could go inside myself and draw and sing and forget how much Mother worried about Til and her bad teeth and how much Daddy worried about the Depression and the election. What if FDR didn't get elected? How soon would we be eating violet tops and dandelion greens? And what would we eat winter after next? The shiny jars of fruit and vegetables lining the shelves in the basement would be plenty for the winter a few weeks ahead, but what about the next one? And when was the Rev. Carmack coming back to the cow bottom so I could get saved? I had to be very careful crossing the street, because eternity meant forever and hell was the hottest place in the world. Everybody knew that.

Sometimes when I was thinking about all the questions I had and couldn't ask, I'd catch Mother looking at me out of the corner of her eye. "Why are you so different from the others, Cass? I don't want you to be different," she would say.

I didn't understand what she meant, but it made me want to be at school. Miss Byers bragged on us every day, about how we had learned our ABC's faster than last year's first grade did, and about how we were beginning to recognize words. Sometimes she sat in our reading circle in a little chair just like ours. We heard *Epaminondas* every few days, about how the butter melted when the little Negro boy ran from the tiger, and we heard how Mother

Goose rode a slick gander and how Little Miss Muffet sat on a tuffet, eating her curds and whey.

Sometimes Miss Byers read about "our hero of the day." Once it was Colonel Charles A. Lindbergh, nicknamed "Lindy," the first man to fly alone across the ocean to Paris, France. He was also called "The Flying Eagle." I wondered if he was little Charles' daddy, but I was afraid to ask Miss Byers. I was pretty sure he was, because I remembered that little Charles was called "the little eaglet." When I got home, Mother said I was right, and all of the fame in the world was probably meaningless to him and his wife after that child's tragic death.

"Election day will be here before we know it," Mother said, ripping October off the calendar. "And the snow will be blowing before November ends."

"The ground will catch it, Clary," Daddy said, hiking up her dress tail with his foot.

On election eve we gathered around the radio and listened to FDR tell his neighbors in Poughkeepsie about the great crowd under the capitol lights in Jefferson City, Missouri, and about the people in Wyoming who had come hundreds of miles to see him, and the children in wheel chairs in Warm Springs, Georgia.

"His voice *does* smile," Mother said. "All of those years of debate are paying off. He was a good student, Til, a scholar. Have you ever thought of taking up debate? Two of your uncles on my side of the house studied rhetoric at Hiwasee College."

Til didn't answer. He was trying to keep his top spinning on a particular faded flower on the linoleum.

Daddy warned him, "You're gonna be in real trouble, son, if that thing gets away from you and flies through the window."

Til kept on singing. "Oh, the monkey wrapped his tail around the flag pole and skinned his ummm hole."

"I'll ask you one more time to quit singing that nasty song," Mother said. "Where in the world do you learn all of that foolishness?"

Roosevelt went on. "A man comes to wisdom in many years of public life. He knows well that when the light of favor shines upon him, it comes not of necessity, that he himself is important. Favor comes because for a brief moment in the great space of human change and progress some general human purpose finds in him a satisfactory embodiment."

Roosevelt spoke of "the great understanding and tolerance of America" which "came out to meet me everywhere; for all this you have my heartfelt gratitude." He added, "Out of this unity that I have seen, we may build the strongest strand to lift ourselves out of this Depression."

Daddy clapped. "That man can talk to any of em, them world leaders," he said. "And he can talk to them Kansas farmers just as good. Never heard nor seen nothin like him before in my life."

Mother said, "He could be over-confident, because people like you are beginning to think he is the Messiah. Hope to goodness you don't get disappointed. She's the one that has to keep his feet on the ground. Wonder how she feels after listening to a lifetime of that political bunk."

That same evening Lowell Thomas said that an exhausted Hoover, pale and red-eyed, warned America again about "false gods arrayed in the rainbow colors of promises" as he spoke from the presidential train in the Nevada desert. He was going home to California to cast his vote.

Election day dawned cold and damp after three days of rain, but by the middle of the morning the sun began to push the fog away and dry the earth.

Daddy closed the B&B while him and Mother went to vote. He laughed when he handed her two dollars and tried to get her to promise him she'd vote for FDR.

She told him he'd have to pay her poll tax, no matter who she voted for, because she never had more than a few pennies in her pocketbook. She even had to ask him for change for the Sunday School collection every week.

"Why do they want an arm and a leg for what is rightfully yours to begin with?" she asked. "Nobody in this country ought to have to pay a penny to vote, and women should have had suffrage as soon as the popular vote counted."

"That's a woman's opinion," Daddy said.

"What's suffering got to do with it?" I asked.

"That just means the right to vote, Cass," Mother explained. "Doesn't have a thing to do with suffering. Comes from Latin, I think."

The day was just like any other Tuesday until Daddy got home that night, except there was nothing on the radio but news. FDR's family and friends sat with him in a little room off Democratic

Headquarters in the Biltmore Hotel in New York. The newscaster said that FDR's steady voice remained calm, and his smile remained constant as returns began to pour in. Before long we knew that three million more people had gone to the polls that day than in 1928, and that state after state went Democratic. Daddy told me how it worked.

"Electric college?" I asked.

"Electoral college," he answered. "That's when a state has so many votes reckoned by its pop'lation and the pop'lar vote, the number of people who voted for a person. Like Tennessee has eleven 'lectoral votes, and more people voted for FDR than they did for Hoover, so FDR gets all eleven 'lectoral votes."

Mother called us to the table three times for supper. Daddy would have sat right there by the radio and let her bring it to him. But she said that being at the table at night was the only time we were all together and she wasn't about to break that habit.

"Let's go to town and see what's goin on," Daddy suggested after supper. We piled into the car and parked in front of the Strand Theater.

"You all can go to the picture show while I visit a while with the boys up the street," he said. "I'll be up at Starnses' Fruit Stand."

"Why do you want to go up there?" Mother asked. "You'll just load up on that old beer and have to be up all night. Nothing in the world but an old beer hall. Don't see for the life of me why they call it a fruit stand. And I'm not sure we ought to spend that eighty cents on a picture show," Mother said.

By the time she stopped talking, Daddy had bought the tickets. "It's a celebration, Clary," he said. "Time we celebrated the end of the Depression and the beginnin of prosperity, don't you reckon? What's this picture show about? I could count on the fingers of one hand the number I've saw."

"In my opinion, you'd be better off in there with us than you will be where you're going," Mother answered. "Maude, you've read *Ramona*, haven't you? A love story about an Indian girl giving up everything for Alessandro, an Indian boy she loves, and how they fought the greed of the pioneers going west."

"Yes," Maude answered, eager go to inside. "It's a love story by Helen Hunt Jackson."

Mother and Maude sniffled now and then, and Em went sound asleep. Til whispered the big words to me as they flashed across the bottom of the screen. More and more states wanted FDR to be the President.

I heard the song that Aunt Flossie had played on the Victrola 'bout "Ramona, the mission bells are calling." At least, I heard part of it. The people were clapping so loud about FDR winning the South that they drowned out most of the words.

We all cried when Alessandro got shot for something he didn't do, about the same time they had a baby girl. They named her Ramona, too. Even Til cried.

Before the picture show ended, we knew that FDR had won, but they didn't announce it. The words that ran across the bottom said that he had seven million more votes than Hoover and carried forty-two of the forty-eight states.

When the lights came on, Mother carried Em up the street to Starnses, and Maude held my hand while Til ran ahead. The streets were bare, except for a couple of policemen with their night sticks, but as we got close to the newsstand, we heard the rowdy sounds that men make when they drink beer. They were trying to sing "Happy Days Are Here Again." Mother sent Til in to get Daddy. I wanted to go, too, but she said it was not a fit place for a little girl.

"I hope you are ready to go home," Mother said. "We've got to get these children to bed. School tomorrow."

He took Em and laid her head on his shoulder.

"And I've got to be in the store all day tomorrow. Meat man comin from way up in Virginny at daybreak," he answered as we started to the car. The street lights were dim, but the stars were bright. Dampness floated in the night air, and the moon sat in a circle of rain, Mother said.

Daddy hummed "How You Gonna Wet Your Whistle" as we walked to the car. "Things is gonna be better, Clary," he said, opening the car door for her.

"For goodness sakes, you *are* feeling good to do that," Mother said, laughing. It's been a coon's age since you opened a car door for me. Come to think of it, I believe it was a buggy door you opened."

"Never felt better," he said. "Never won a suit from a Republican before neither. Hate to take that suit off of ole Henry, but he shoulda knowed better than to bet with me on FDR. I'd sure like to see him 'bout now. Betcha he's one sick man. That Kuppenheimer suit will cost him 'bout seventy-five dollars."

They let us stay up another half an hour to hear the newscaster finally say that Roosevelt had become President by a landslide and would move into the White House in March. I didn't know what a landslide had to do with an election, and it sounded like somebody could have gotten hurt, but I didn't have a chance to ask. Daddy clapped and grabbed Mother to do a jig around the room. I never had seen him do that before. Every little bit, he would yell out, "Promenade" or Dos-a-dos." Mother said that was French for "back-to-back."

The newscaster said that while all of the rejoicing was going on in the Biltmore, FDR walked away from the crowd and went over to his wife and said, "I wish I knew what you are really thinking and feeling."

Mother said, "Now, isn't that just like a man? He expects her to be overjoyed. And all he's done is to imprison her feelings and thoughts. Surely, she never wanted him to be President, the shape he's in and her with all of those chidren."

Daddy reminded her, "They're almost grown, Clary. You said so yourself. And he was just tryin to tell her that he really cares about her feelins."

"No doubt, he is the lesser of two evils," Mother said, "but, for crying out loud, don't get it in your head that he's perfect. He puts his pants on the same way you do, one leg at a time."

Daddy took off his shoes and socks and hiked Mother's dress tail up with his bare foot. "Happy days *are* here again, Clary," he assured her. "He'll make jobs for lots of men that have been idle. Did you know that farm income in Georgey has dropped from $206 to $83 in the past three year?"

I had never seen him that happy. Maude and me could hear them still talking, and pretty soon, we could hear Daddy snoring.

After school the next day, I worked on the March picture on the floor of Til's bedroom while he was making a kite out of wallpaper big enough for me to lie on spread-eagle. He promised to tie my hands and feet to the cross bars if I couldn't hold on when the wind got up in the spring.

In my picture, *he* was stretched out on the kite, spread-eagle, with *his* hands and feet tied down. The long, white-sheet tail stretched straight behind. I was holding the string, ready to run across the potatoe patch to get Til up. Felix watched.

I still had to draw pictures for April, May, June, July and August, but I already had the picture for every month in my head. Daddy had already talked to the printer downtown and let me pick the print for "B&B GROCERY STORE, 1933." Every picture would have my name, Cassandra Blevins, in the corner, just like Maude's sampler had hers.

I hadn't shown any of my calendar pictures to Mr. Simpson. In fact, I wasn't going to show him anything, ever again.

Photo: David Rees

Born in Iron Mountain, Michigan, in 1925, Liz (Elizabeth Anne) Barnes spent her growing-up years in Kingsport, an industrial town in the mountains of East Tennessee. She studied English literature, journalism and creative writing at Virginia Intermont College, East Tennessee University, and The University of North Carolina, Chapel Hill. After several years as a reporter on the Kingsport Times-News and the Richmond (Virginia) News Leader, she taught journalism, English and women's studies at Stephens College, Columbia, Missouri, from 1957 until her retirement last year. In 1980–81, she was on leave from Stephens to teach at the College of Santa Fe in New Mexico and at three nearby pueblos. This is her first novel. Her home is in Columbia, Missouri.

SPINSTERS INK
SAN FRANCISCO

Change The Future With Books That Change Women's Lives

Spinsters Ink, a women's independent publishing house, has been producing quality, innovative books of women's art, literature and non-fiction since 1978. Our commitment is to publishing works that are beyond the scope of mainstream commercial publishers: books that not only name crucial issues in women's lives, but also demonstrate healing and change.

Spinsters publishes books that flourish between the cracks of what will be accepted – and what can be imagined.

Your support, through buying our books or investing in other ways in the company, enables us to bring out new books, books that keep helping women envision and create the kinds of worlds in which we all can live.

For a complete list of our titles, or a brochure explaining our investment plans, please write to us.

SPINSTERS INK
803 De Haro Street
San Francisco, CA 94107